Daring embrace...

"Is this really necessary?" she asked faintly.

"It's only necessary," he growled, "if you wish to have a fifty-fifty chance of getting to Moreau's island alive. If you wish to lower the chances, skip the wedding. And the honeymoon."

Sarah glared at him. "There's no need to be nasty, Mr. Sutter," she snapped. "I have no problem marrying the devil himself if it'll get my sister out of that man's clutches."

"Why thank you, Ms. Dunning," Sutter told her with a sarcastic look and a bow. He turned toward Raymond. "I have a couple of things to take care of before I leave town. If you need to reach me, call me at Sarah's tonight."

Sarah's eyebrows lifted. "You're coming to my house tonight?" she asked, taken completely by surprise.

He grinned like the devil she'd sworn she'd willingly marry. "Of course. Where else would a groom stay on his wedding night?"

Dear Reader:

As usual, we've gathered the cream of the crop for you this month in Silhouette Intimate Moments. Start off with Beverly Sommers and the first book in a terrific new trilogy, "Friends for Life." In *Accused* she tells the story of Jack Quintana, a man accused of a murder he didn't commit. His defender is Anne Larkin, a woman whose memories of Jack are less than fond. As they work together to clear his name, however, they discover that love isn't necessarily the most logical of emotions. In the next two months, look for *Betrayed* and *Corrupted*, the stories of Anne's friends Bolivia and Sandy. These three really are *friends for life*.

Also this month, Heather Graham Pozzessere returns with *A Perilous Eden*, a story of terror on the high seas and passion under the hot Caribbean sun. It's an adventure not to be missed. Lee Magner brings you *Sutter's Wife*, the story of a make-believe marriage that quickly becomes the real thing. Finish the month with new author Dee Holmes and *Black Horse Island*, a stunning debut performance from a writer to watch.

In coming months, look for new books by Emilie Richards, Barbara Faith, Marilyn Pappano and Jennifer Greene, not to mention fall treats from, among others, Linda Howard, Kathleen Korbel and Patricia Gardner Evans. Something great is always happening at Silhouette Intimate Moments.

Leslie J. Wainger
Senior Editor

Sutter's Wife

LEE MAGNER

Silhouette Intimate Moments

Published by Silhouette Books New York

America's Publisher of Contemporary Romance

SILHOUETTE BOOKS
300 East 42nd St., New York, N.Y. 10017

ISBN: 0-373-07326-7

First Silhouette Books printing March 1990

Printed in the U.S.A.

Books by Lee Magner

Silhouette Intimate Moments

Mustang Man #246
Master of the Hunt #274
Mistress of Foxgrove #312
Sutter's Wife #326

LEE MAGNER

is a versatile woman whose talents include speaking several foreign languages, raising a family—and writing. After stints as a social worker, an English teacher and a regional planner in the human services area, she found herself at home with a small child and decided to start working on a romance. She has always been an avid reader of all kinds of novels, but especially love stories. Since beginning her career, she has become an award-winning author and has published numerous contemporary romances.

To Mom, with love
and thanks for our Cayman Christmas

Chapter 1

The champagne cork's loud pop ricocheted through the room like a bullet. Alexander Sutter's entire body tensed for a split second. His mind knew there was no danger. Instinct wasn't so easily convinced, however. It's just a damned champagne bottle, he told himself. It's all right. Relax. Sutter's shoulder and thigh muscles eased and he restlessly prowled across the room. A thirty-six-year-old man ought to be able to stroll through his own jewelry salon's office without making an ass of himself, he thought in disgust. It was a time to party, not panic. His mouth twisted in wry amusement at his own inability to shake free of his past. Maybe now was as good a time as any to show them the coral he'd found.

"In honor of our yearly celebration, I've brought a new piece back from George Town," Alex announced, having fully regained his usual calm. He pulled out a small object from the inside pocket of his suit jacket. "What do you think of this, Blake?" Sutter dropped the little thing into his partner's hands.

A black coral turtle gleamed in the man's outstretched palm. He turned it, examining the figurine carefully while its almond-shaped emerald eyes glittered back at him seductively. There was a soft sheen on the watery dark surface broken here and there by the brilliant white sparkle of diamonds criss-crossing its back in the pattern of a shell.

Blake Malone, the man examining the elegantly carved piece, lifted a brow approvingly and smiled. Their jewelry salon, Malone's, was well-known for its unique—and expensive—items. Pieces such as this little turtle were one of the reasons why. Malone returned the miniature sea turtle to his business partner. Emerald eyes winked as it changed hands.

"Very nice. Elegant. Original. And it has a lot of character," Blake commented. "Nice way to celebrate, Alex," Blake added in amusement. He paused for a moment, his face creasing thoughtfully. "Why don't you see if you can get the artist to make twenty-five. Each one a little different."

Sutter gave his partner a wry look. "Twenty-five? Are you kidding?" He fondled the little black turtle affectionately and sighed as he recalled the persuasion it had required to get just this one. "You have no idea what I had to do to get this little fellow."

Blake laughed and reached for the bottle of champagne that had been chilling in the silver ice bucket next to him. "I can just imagine," he said, grinning even more as he poured the pale liquid into three crystal flutes. "And don't tell me you didn't enjoy it, Alex. We wouldn't believe you. Would we, Grant?"

Their third partner, Grant Macklin, shook his head and settled himself comfortably on the corner of Blake's antique desk. "Alex Sutter has never sacrificed himself to a woman," he agreed with a chuckle.

Blake, one of the finest gemologists in Washington, contemplated the black coral-and-diamond turtle now in Alex Sutter's palm. "You didn't have to wait until we'd been in business for five years to bring us something like this," Blake joked. "Look, why don't we try for thirty? That's one of the most intriguing pieces you've brought back from the Caymans. That artist is going to be famous someday." Blake picked up one of the glasses of champagne and handed it to Sutter. Grinning, Blake added, "She'll be famous faster if she sells to us. Persuade her, Alex. Like you usually do."

Sutter took the flute. "You've just asked me to do the impossible," Alex pointed out dryly. "Twenty-five turtles and sea denizens? Thirty?" Sutter asked in doubtful amusement.

"Anna Jenet takes her sweet time, Blake. You'd be lucky to get nine pieces from her in eighteen months. She's a perfectionist. She'll never release a piece she's not satisfied with. And she's emphatic about not working more than twelve hours a week. She says it interferes with other important things in her life. Fishing, for example. Or spending a long weekend with her friends on one of the other islands. Or thinking about the pieces she's working on. Or swimming off the beach with her grand-children."

Or her recently separated, blatantly man-hungry daughter, Alex thought with very mixed feelings. The daughter had been happy enough for his company and he'd kept the daughter en-tertained so Anna Jenet could carve. Not exactly an unpleas-ant way for a man to occupy his time for a month, but hardly what he wanted to do on a steady basis. Alex shook his head.

"Think small, Blake," he advised him. "I'm getting too old to keep up with Anna Jenet's daughter."

Blake appeared unimpressed with the problem and merely shrugged it all off. "I'm sure you can handle the details. Espe-cially with women." Blake sighed in mock envy and shook his head. "One of these days I want you to explain to me exactly how you do it. Were you born persuasive or is it something you could teach, do you think?"

Alex laughed. "You don't need any teaching and you damn well know it," he retorted. "I'm just a butt of all your feeble jokes around here. My reputation appears to be getting quite inflated."

Sutter walked across the plushly carpeted office and handed the turtle to Macklin, who had been observing the exchange in amused silence. Macklin took the figurine in his big hand and held it up for closer scrutiny.

Sutter remembered the first time he'd met Macklin. It had been four years ago. He'd known then that Macklin was a man he could trust. That was rare. Rare for Macklin, too, he knew. Macklin's head had jerked ever so slightly when that cork had burst into the air. Sutter wondered if Macklin was getting tired of it, too—tired of the feeling that you always had to be alert, that you could never completely relax your guard.

Macklin was impressed with the coral-and-diamond piece. His eyes were steady as he said, with a remarkably straight face,

"I think Alex can find a way to get as many as we can sell. He *hasn't* met the woman who can turn him down." Macklin chuckled as Sutter speared him with an annoyed look. "Sorry, Alex. Your reputation precedes you." He laughed more, in a throaty, male way, and gave Sutter a calculating stare. "You've got enough stamina to entertain half a dozen of Anna Jenet's daughters." Macklin handed the piece back to Sutter. "Go turtle fishing, pal. And be sure and take a big enough net for your haul."

Alex ran his fingers over the turtle's polished back. He wasn't pleased but he couldn't think of a way out of it on the spur of the moment. He'd tired of being seen as a ladies' man. He'd tired of a lot of things lately, as a matter of fact. Well, that was no reason to hold back a good business deal, he supposed. He resigned himself to wining and dining Anna Jenet's daughter, her whole damn family, if necessary.

"I'll see what I can do," Sutter conceded reluctantly. "But don't be surprised if my powers of persuasion aren't completely successful this time, gentlemen." He glanced from one straight-faced partner to the other. "What I do for the business..." he said on a mildly self-sacrificing note.

His partners laughed.

Grant leaned forward with an affectionate gleam in his eyes. "Alex, you know, personally, I wouldn't mind seeing some of your charm dented a little one of these days. I have the feeling that's exactly what's going to happen to you, too. Yes, buddy, you're going to meet your match. I can feel it in my bones. And when that woman lays you low, I'm going to take great pleasure in reminding you of what an arrogant stud you were for all these years and how hard you finally fell when you met her."

Sutter shrugged and dropped the figurine back into the inside pocket of the jacket of his suit. "Don't hold your breath, Grant," he advised good-naturedly. "That feeling in your bones is probably just the beginning of rheumatism." Alex ignored the outraged snort of laughter erupting from his friend. "I like being alone. And I like to travel. Can you see any woman being happy with a man who spends half of his life in airplanes?" He shook his head. "No thanks. Dinner, a week in the sun, a weekend in bed—that's my limit."

"You're young, Alex. You've got plenty of time," Macklin pointed out, obviously relishing the thought of some pretty young thing leading his untamed friend around by the hand. "And I don't think you're as happy with all that as you used to be." He ignored Sutter's sarcastic look of denial and shifted the subject slightly. "By the way, Alex, whatever happened to that leggy model you were sharing quarters with a year or so ago?"

"Last I heard she was living with a movie producer and hoping to start on an acting career."

Blake wandered over to them and handed Macklin his champagne.

"I agree with Grant, Alex. I think you're the kind of man who takes to a wife like a duck takes to water."

Sutter nearly choked. "How poetic."

Blake shrugged and gave Macklin a deadpan look. "What shall we call this woman who's going to tie Sutter in knots and lead him around like a domesticated barracuda?"

Grant laughed. "Why, 'Sutter's Wife,' of course."

Sutter didn't think it was nearly as amusing as they did. "If you two don't mind a change of topic, I'd like to remind you we're here to celebrate our business success, not your predictions of my matrimonial prospects," Sutter growled.

Blake and Grant turned their attention toward him.

Blake regained control of himself and nodded. "Sorry, Alex. To another successful year's partnership," Blake proposed, lifting his glass. "And to Alex's success in persuading Anna Jenet to work a little more, a little faster," he added irreverently, a grin breaking across his face at the last.

Sutter swallowed his exasperation and took the ribbing in good humor. Three heads tilted in agreement. Three glasses were raised in toast.

"To another year," they echoed.

"And to Anna Jenet," chorused Blake and Grant.

"You guys never give up, do you?" muttered Alex.

"No," they replied, grinning.

In unison they drank.

The intercom buzzed discreetly. Blake crossed to his mahogany desk and depressed a button on the telephone console.

"Yes," he said.

"Excuse me, Mr. Malone," his secretary apologized. "But there's a gentleman here who says he would like to speak with Mr. Sutter."

Blake looked at Sutter questioningly. Sutter shook his head, indicating that he had told no one that he was back in the country yet. "What's the man's name?" Blake asked.

His secretary hesitated fractionally, then said, "Mr. Jones." Her hesitation clearly communicated her doubt that the man's name was really Jones. "Mr. *Raymond* Jones," she added at the visitor's murmured insistence.

Blake and Grant both looked skeptical and turned their eyes toward Sutter, waiting for him to indicate what he wanted to do.

Sutter narrowed his gaze. "His name is Jones, all right. I know him," he told them. "We had some . . . mutual interests a few years ago."

He smiled ever so slightly at his partners' expressions. They were simultaneously amused and exasperated that his colorful past had interrupted their annual celebration. Especially since they'd each made it a point that no one should know they were here today. Sutter shrugged regretfully.

"He wouldn't be out there asking for me if he wasn't absolutely certain that I'm here. You might as well let him in. He can be a nuisance when he wants to be." Sutter frowned slightly. "And he wouldn't have gone to the trouble of locating me unless something serious has happened."

Macklin snorted. "Something serious is *always* happening." He met Sutter's gaze levelly. The two men understood each other. They had both spent many years picking their way through the mine fields of intelligence activity, although in different hemispheres. There was a weariness in the look they shared, but beneath the weariness lay a core of steel. When they came looking for you, it always meant serious business of the kind you couldn't easily walk away from. "I think I'd better leave. Mr. Jones and I may have met . . . by some other set of names," Grant added with a wry grin.

He took his champagne with him as he headed toward the far wall. He reached up and pressed his fingertips against the outline of a small crane delicately depicted in the hand-painted wallpaper. A narrow bookcase to his right silently opened like a door. Macklin nodded to his partners. "Keep in touch," he murmured, disappearing into the hidden room. The bookcase quietly slid shut after him. He was a silent partner. He preferred it that way. His comings and goings were as invisible as possible.

Blake turned to the intercom.

"Send Mr. Jones in, please, Janet," he told his secretary.

A moment later the door to Blake's expensively chic office opened and his secretary led in a middle-aged man in a black raincoat.

"Mr. Raymond Jones," she announced. Quietly she withdrew, shutting the door after her.

The newcomer looked more like an aging bureaucrat than a spy master. He was graying at the temples, balding at the pate like a monk. Beneath his worn raincoat swelled an unmistakable midriff paunch. He wore a sheepish smile on his plumpish face, but there was an alertness in his nondescript eyes that belied everything else. There was nothing stupid or unplanned about Mr. Raymond Jones.

Sutter put down his glass and held out his hand.

"Hello, Raymond," he said casually. "You're looking for me?"

The man shook hands with Sutter and glanced curiously at Blake. Sutter read the question and made the introduction without further prompting.

"This is Blake Malone, the owner of the establishment you're in." Sutter lifted a dark eyebrow. "And when you're through shaking his hand, I'm sure we'd both appreciate knowing why you've come."

Blake was the model of courtesy as he shook Jones's outstretched hand. Jones blinked and cleared his throat uncomfortably.

"It's an honor to meet you, Mr. Malone," Jones said, a slight touch of awe in his voice. "I couldn't help admiring your jewelry when I was waiting in the showroom. I've never been in your store before. Store—it's hardly the word for it, is it? It's more like an art museum or a gem display or a modern wonder of the world." Realizing he was rambling on too enthusiastically, Jones forced himself to stop. He cleared his throat again. "Your jewelry is as beautiful as they say it is."

"Thank you," Blake told him. He smiled courteously. "I'll be happy to show you around sometime, if you like."

Jones chuckled and shook his head.

"I'm afraid you're way out of my price range, Mr. Malone."

Blake smiled amiably. "No problem. I enjoy looking at the pieces. You're welcome to join me." Blake glanced at Sutter and, understanding the slight movement of Alex's head, moved to leave them. "I assume that you'd prefer to talk with Alex alone. Why don't you use my office? If you'll excuse me?"

Jones brightened. "Thank you."

Blake inclined his head as he left. The door closed after him, sealing the room. It was soundproof.

Sutter sat on the corner of a twelfth-century Chinese chest and looked at Jones. "What is it?" Sutter asked. "And how in the hell did you find me?"

Jones chuckled and strolled around the room. "Nice place," he murmured sincerely. "Thick gold carpeting. Chinese wallpaper—silk, perhaps? Antique Oriental chest. Antique European desk. All the elegant trappings of success. Geez! This is the life."

Sutter's black eyes were unmoved. "You went to the not inconsiderable trouble of tracing me in order to tell me that?" he asked dubiously. "Get to the point, Raymond. I'm not being paid to listen to you anymore. You're wasting my time."

Raymond grimaced and rubbed his short, stubby fingers together nervously. "Sorry. I haven't been out of the little gray offices in quite a few weeks. This is like going to another planet." He sighed. "A very nice planet."

Sutter's expression relented slightly. He knew Raymond Jones very well, and he had no doubt that the man was speaking the absolute truth. It was just that he had no interest in renewing his relationship with Jones and the many networks that Jones represented. Being approached made him angry. He'd quit, damn it all. Whatever they wanted with him, he didn't want to hear it. He wanted to be left alone.

"Sorry, Raymond," Sutter told him. "I'd managed to forget how bleak working for the government could be." He sounded cynically amused. "And I'd like to remind you that I have no intention of having my memory refreshed. I'm through. Does that help shorten this visit?"

Jones no longer looked quite so abashed. He dragged his eyes away from a small Japanese *netsuke* on the mahogany desk and turned to stare somberly at his old friend. "I came because I thought you would want to know about this." Jones looked sorry that he was having to bring the news.

Alex frowned. He couldn't think of a single thing that he'd be interested in hearing from Raymond Jones. Only an extremely long list of past activities he'd specifically *not* wish to hear about again. "What are you talking about?" Alex asked bluntly.

Jones glanced around suspiciously. "I'd rather tell you someplace where I'm sure it's safe."

Alex's expression hardened. "No place is safe, and you know it." He reined in his annoyance, adding, "The room is used for the most private of business discussions. It won't leak secrets. You have my word."

Jones nodded. Sutter's word was good enough for him.

"A plane went down in the Caribbean two months ago. Our people just got word to us. Apparently the pilot and copilot bailed out but no one picked them up and they're presumed drowned." Jones paced over to a locked display case with worn silver pieces of eight and burnished gold doubloons on one shelf. "There were some items on that plane that several governments would very much like to retrieve."

Sutter shrugged disinterestedly. "They have my permission to retrieve them," he said, raising his brows. "I wish them good luck."

Jones looked a little chagrined. "They've left the retrieval plan in my hands. Three governments that are barely on speaking terms have agreed to let me coordinate the search."

"Congratulations." Sutter stood up. "You're going to be a busy boy, Raymond. But I repeat: I'm retired. Don't even think of asking me to get involved, Raymond. *I quit.* I didn't like the work anymore. Remember?"

Raymond lowered his eyes and nodded. He prowled the room, admiring the wallpaper, and the bookcase with rare editions of eighteenth-century political treatises. He eyed them closely. "Would you be interested if I were to name a price?" he murmured gently, fingering the edge of the case.

Sutter laughed. "Do I look like a whore to you?" he demanded in amusement.

Jones turned and looked directly at Sutter. "Say...a million dollars?"

Alex stopped laughing and his face darkened in anger. "Not for one million. Not for ten." Sutter declined bitingly. "I'm hardly the only person you could ask to do this, Raymond. For instance, how about trying the navy? I hear they still involve themselves in underwater searches." He hoped the sarcasm would make his position crystal clear.

Jones merely grinned sheepishly. "I told them you wouldn't like being bought." He shrugged. "They insisted I start with that."

Sutter's eyes gleamed dangerously. "Who are *they*? And why did you drag my name into this?" Anonymity had been his trademark. No one but Jones had known his real identity when he'd been working for intelligence.

Jones waved a hand reassuringly. "I didn't mention your name," he hurried to explain. "And actually, they think you're two men and a woman."

Sutter rolled his eyes heavenward. "You still have your imagination, I see," he said dryly.

Jones chuckled. "It's the only way to keep my sanity in that gray metal office they make me slave in." He returned to the main point. "Back to the reason I'm here. There is a little more to it than locating the plane. And the navy *is* looking, as discreetly as it can from a very great distance."

Sutter knew he wouldn't get rid of Jones until he'd heard the whole pitch, so he resigned himself to listening. "Go on."

"The man who owned the plane lives on an island within a hundred miles or so of where the plane is believed to have crashed. Some of his hired help were out searching the area with sonar when they came across a couple of divemasters in their own boat. The hirelings went over to talk to them and noticed a piece of the airplane control panel in the boat. They took the two divers and, in the struggle, apparently killed one of them. They sank the boat to make it look like an accident, and took the other divemaster back to their boss's private island to report what they'd found."

Sutter nodded perfunctorily. He'd heard worse stories over the years. "I don't see what this has to do with me," he reiterated.

Jones became almost solemn. "The man who owned the plane, the man who owns the island, the man whose men killed that divemaster, sank the boat and kidnapped the second diver—he's someone you once had a reason to dislike quite violently."

Sutter stared at Jones for a long, tense moment. His eyes narrowed and his jaw became hard with anger. "Antonio Moreau." Sutter said the name in a chillingly hard voice barely above a whisper.

Jones nodded. "Yes. Antonio Moreau."

Sutter looked down at his hands. There had been a time when he would have given anything he possessed to have been able to wrap his hands around Moreau's neck. That hot lust for vengeance had grown cold over the years. Especially when he'd realized how endless the cesspools of the world were, how hard it was to find one despicable character among so many. Yes, the sharp taste for vengeance might have cooled, but it was still there. Bitterly, harshly, profoundly there.

"I thought that you might be interested in knowing where he is," Jones said quietly. "We can tell you that. We can even help you get to him. But in exchange, we need your help. We want you to help us get that divemaster off the island and safely into our hands before they can make her tell them exactly where that plane is."

Sutter laughed derisively. "What makes you think that they don't already know where it is? What makes you believe that your precious divemaster isn't already shark bait?"

Jones explained. "The divemaster that was taken to Moreau's island is a woman. A very attractive woman..."

Sutter's face hardened. "Moreau likes women, but why would he keep her alive if he wanted what she'd found?"

"Apparently he's smitten by her. He's keeping her locked up, but not brutalizing her, not torturing her..." Jones's voice drifted off apologetically.

"How do you know that?" Sutter demanded.

Jones shrugged. "We have a contact in Jamaica who knows one of the people who live on Moreau's island. When they came in for supplies, our contact had a little conversation over the vegetable stall."

Sutter paced across the room. "If Moreau hasn't tortured her, then he's certainly turning over a new leaf in his old age," Alex observed harshly. Moreau had overseen the torture and slow murder of a village full of Central American peons whose only crime had been that they had sheltered Alex and refused to give him up when Moreau and his fellow drug runners had been pursuing him. "I swore I'd avenge them," Sutter murmured, remembering.

Jones nodded. "I figured you had." He sighed. "That's why I came to you first, Alex. You were right to begin with. I could have asked one or two other people to help me with this. But I thought of you first. This is something you would do for nothing. That kind of commitment is something I rarely see." He frowned. "And in this case, I feel especially in need of that kind of commitment."

Sutter heard the undercurrent in Jones's voice. His black eyes bore into Jones's. "What haven't you told me?" Sutter demanded suspiciously.

"There is a plan for getting to the divemaster, for getting her out alive, but it involves having a civilian go in with the professional. You being the professional, of course."

Sutter looked at Jones as if he were completely mad. "Forget it!" he snapped. "I'll consider helping you, but not with some amateur hanging around to add to my troubles."

Jones shook his head. "There are several problems in getting the diver off the island. One of the biggest involves the guard dogs on the place. One of them is even stationed in the room where the woman is locked up. And he's trained to kill if she tries to leave."

"So?" Alex retorted. "Drug them. Kill them. Big deal."

Jones shook his head. "The dogs are wearing electronic collars that monitor their vital signs. If anything happens to them, it will be known immediately. In order to keep Moreau ignorant of the escape as it occurs, the dogs must be kept conscious and functioning."

Alex gave Jones a penetrating stare. "And the amateur you want me to take along is going to magically entertain the dogs?" he asked sarcastically.

Jones braced himself. He was sure that Sutter wasn't going to like his next revelation. "Basically, yes."

"How in the hell is he going to do that?"

"She trained three of them to start with. We're expecting that they'll remember that and obey her commands and not kill any of you."

Sutter looked as if he didn't believe he could have heard correctly. "Did you say *she*?"

Jones nodded. "Yes."

Sutter walked around the room to keep from doing something he would regret. "You want me to take a female dog trainer onto Antonio Moreau's island to free a female divemaster who may have the coordinates to an airplane that went down with items dear to the heart of several as yet unnamed governments?" Sutter demanded incredulously.

Jones exhaled as though a great weight had lifted from his chest. "That's about it, Alex," he agreed.

"Why in the holy hell would I want to agree to this?" Sutter exploded.

"Aside from your interest in seeing Moreau meet an unfortunate end at the earliest opportunity?" Jones asked hastily.

"That aside. Yes." Sutter growled.

"The dog trainer is the divemaster's sister. And if we don't use her, we may not be able to get the divemaster off. And we've got to get her off, Alex. We've got to get the plates or Moreau will be able to engineer the biggest economic disaster the western hemisphere has ever seen. Do you want that, Alex? Think of this as a chance to protect your wallet, if you don't want to admit you care about anything else."

Sutter stood in the middle of the room, shaking his head. "I used to think that I'd heard it all, Raymond," Sutter told him. "But that was before I'd heard *this*."

Raymond was ushering him toward the door. "I hate to be pushy, Alex," he said ingratiatingly. "But time is working against us. We've got to get this plan in action quickly. Who knows how long Moreau will keep up this cat-and-mouse game he's been playing with that diver."

Sutter irritably opened the door and indicated for Raymond to precede him. As they passed Blake in the elegantly discreet display area, Sutter murmured, "I'll be gone for a while. There's some old business I need to attend to."

Blake kept an admirably straight face and accompanied them to the door. He said quietly, "Take care of yourself. If you need anything, we're here."

Alex gave him a brief nod. "Thanks, Blake."

Jones reached for the keys to his battered old car. "The hard part," he was muttering anxiously, "is going to be explaining this to the woman who trained the dogs."

Sutter was having a tough time comprehending how that could be any more difficult than convincing him to take her with him, but he let that comment pass for the moment. "What's her name?" he asked as they got into the car.

"Sarah Dunning."

Chapter 2

Sarah Dunning watched the black Labrador lying absolutely still in the grass across the field from her. A breeze rustled the long green blades and rippled the black hair on his shoulders, but the dog did not flinch. His narrowed gaze was fixed intently on her. Good boy, she thought. The sudden shriek of a man behind him did not seem to register with the dog at all. Nor the sound of a target pistol being fired somewhere off to one side. Nor the sound of a heavy man's tread approaching.

He watched Sarah as if his eyes were glued to her. She brought her hand up and across her chest, silently ordering him to come to her, and the sixty-pound male leaped to his feet and bounded forward, a blur of curling legs and rippling coat eager to reach her. Good work, boy, Sarah thought, willing him to give his best performance. She always rooted for the underdog, and, boy, was this one in that category.

She held her arm straight up, then quickly lowered it into the hand signal meaning "lie down." The big black animal twisted in midstride and dropped instantly to the ground, eyes still trained on her. Only on her.

Sarah grinned and called to the two uniformed lawmen who'd been shrieking, trampling the ground and shooting the gun.

"I hate to say I told you so," she said, much pleased, putting her hands on her hips, "but . . ."

The two men grinned.

"But you told us so," the older of the two wryly conceded. "I wouldn't have believed you could get him to do that in a year, much less a week." He just shook his head at the wonder of it.

Sarah signaled the Labrador to come. His tongue lolled in a grin and his brown eyes shone as he sat proudly at her feet. She gave his head an affectionate pat.

"He'll be fine," she assured them. She snapped a leather leash on his collar and handed it to the older man, accepting his check in return.

He, in turn, patted the dog, who had started to rub his nose affectionately against the man's pant leg.

"It was getting embarrassing to be the sheriff and not even have my dog do what I told him to!" The man laughed, still a little chagrined at that old problem. He turned to his young deputy. "Sarah's dogs are as well trained as the police's and the military's. You oughta see some of her attack and guard dogs." He turned toward Sarah questioningly. "Do you have any with you now?"

Sarah shook her head. "No. The last three went to their owners last week." She grinned at him. "I was even thinking of taking a vacation."

The sheriff laughed. "Getting tired of being around dogs all the time, Sarah? Finally getting a little hankering for men again?"

Sarah laughed, but gave him a dangerous look.

The deputy was a little confused and the sheriff nodded for him to head toward the car. "Sarah says she'd rather spend her time working with her dogs. She says they're more honest and loyal than any man she ever dated," the sheriff explained with a very male grin. "Sometimes I can't say I blame her. Course anytime you want to change your mind, just let me know, Sarah." He said it teasingly, but it was obvious that he meant it deep down. "And in the meantime, you could quit calling me Sheriff all the time and call me Aldo."

The sheriff noticed that two men were standing a few yards away. His grin shifted into a mild frown. "They weren't here when we started working my dog," he muttered. "I didn't hear them drive up, either. They prowl pretty quietly." The sheriff clearly didn't like quiet prowling.

The strangers' car was partially obscured behind a tree on the far side of the bare dirt ground that Sarah used for parking. The men were close enough to have heard what was being said, but their faces were both bland. Sarah took a closer look and reconsidered that. The black-eyed man, the taller of the two, had a definite glint in his eyes, as if he had found the remark about Sarah's preference for dogs and the sheriff's indirect, low-key pass mildly amusing. She frowned. What business was it of his?

The two newcomers nodded and the sheriff, who'd intended to leave, hesitated. "Maybe I should stick around for a while, Sarah," he offered.

Sarah lived out in the middle of nowhere in a small, tumbling-down old house with nothing but a telephone and three dogs to keep her company. She knew the sheriff and everyone else thought she was crazy to do it, even if she did have the dogs for protection.

Sarah laid a reassuring hand on his arm. She sensed from his stiffening posture that he was serious about not wanting to leave her alone with the two men. She didn't know who they were, but she wasn't afraid. And she didn't want Sheriff Aldo Barns hovering over her as if he had the right to, even if he was a sheriff and she generally found him a nice guy to deal with.

It had been Sarah's experience that males whose protective instincts got the better of them could be very difficult. She'd certainly found that out often enough. Her father, her brother, her boyfriends—they were all worse than ill-tempered dogs standing over a favorite old bone. She made a small motion with her left hand and something black rustled slightly next to the front porch.

"Don't worry, Sheriff," she said. "I've got my troops in position. Besides, they might be bringing me a lot of business. I wouldn't want you to frighten them off."

The sheriff relaxed a little. "In my line of work, I guess you start seeing trouble everywhere, even where there isn't any," he admitted. He headed on toward the marked car, put the dog in the back, nodded curtly toward the silent newcomers and turned to wave goodbye to Sarah. "Thanks, Sarah. See you for coffee next time you're in town."

She grinned and waved as the sheriff and his deputy pulled away and disappeared down the winding dirt road. Then she turned her attention to the strangers, who'd begun approaching her the minute the others had driven away. Her grin faded into a suitably courteous smile of welcome. She wondered why they'd been so reticent, why they'd hung back, as if reluctant to speak in front of the sheriff. She noted the semihidden position of their car and wondered who or what they were trying to conceal.

Men in business suits and raincoats didn't really alarm her, but she prepared herself to hear something unexpected. Usually unannounced visitors were lost; these two didn't look the slightest bit lost to her. As a matter of fact, they looked as if they'd never been lost in their entire lives.

At times like this, she was very glad that she had well-trained dogs with her. She held out her hand and said forthrightly, "Hello. I'm Sarah Dunning. What can I do for you?"

The shorter one, a plumpish man with a slightly embarrassed smile, shook her hand briefly. "Hello, Miss Dunning. I'm Raymond Jones." He glanced at the tall, dark-haired man standing beside him. "And this is Alexander Sutter."

Sarah automatically nodded an acknowledgment, then released Raymond's hand to clasp Sutter's. The difference between the two was unbelievable. Raymond's hand had been softly warm and politely distant. Sutter's hand was hard and firm and vibrant. She looked into his eyes and felt the unexpected impact of his black-eyed stare. How did he do that? she wondered faintly. Was he hooked up to an electrical circuit?

"How do you do, Mr. Sutter?" she said, marveling how years of practice could make the words come even though her mind had temporarily ceased to give the necessary orders.

"I do well, Ms. Dunning," he replied, the slightest ring of amusement sounding in his voice.

She loosened her fingers and forced herself not to take a small step back. Mr. Sutter had a peculiar way of acknowledging an introduction, she thought. She turned her attention back to Jones, definitely the easier of the two to talk to.

"Are you here to discuss having some dogs trained to protect your business?" she asked, taking a wild shot in the dark. Maybe not *too* wild, she amended. They were in business suits and she did train dogs.

Raymond looked apologetically toward her ramshackle, clapboard house. "Would you mind if we talked with you inside?" He looked embarrassed to ask and was clearing his throat. "I know it must seem odd to you, having us drop in like this, but we have some bad news for you. And we didn't want to tell you over the phone."

Sarah immediately felt great concern. She was about to ask Raymond what was going on, but she saw the implacable look in his eyes and realized he wouldn't relent on the issue of the quiet room. "All right," she agreed. "This way."

She led them into the house, opening the door for them and insisting that they precede her. She flicked her fingers and the black shadow emerged stealthily from beneath the rotting porch to follow at her heels.

"Please go into the kitchen," she told them. "It's straight ahead."

The kitchen was quite large, especially considering how square and small the rest of the one-story home was. There was a large white-painted metal table in the center with half a dozen chairs around it, none of which were hewn from the same pattern. Like the rest of the place, it looked as if it had been furnished from a series of yard sales and sheriff's auctions.

Raymond and Alex were standing as she joined them. Their eyes shifted to the silent black dog that had accompanied her. The animal was utterly expressionless, and his brown gaze was fixed on them.

"Nice dog," Raymond said lamely, running a finger around his collar. He murmured to Alex, "This is why I never do fieldwork. No guts." He sighed. "Would you tell your dog not to eat us for dinner, please, Miss Dunning? I swear we're good guys."

Very carefully, Raymond lifted his identification from inside his jacket. The dog seemed much more intently interested in it than Sarah. She had turned on the gas under the kettle on the stove and was rummaging in a wall cabinet in search of three mugs.

She put the mugs, none of which bore the same pattern and all of which looked as if they'd served through a war, down on the table and smiled a little.

"My dog will be much more comfortable when *I'm* much more comfortable," she told them. "So the sooner you tell me what brought you here, the better." She nodded toward the chairs, which neither man had shown any interest in pulling out. "Sit down." When they didn't make any move to do so, she added coaxingly, "You'll be much less likely to be eaten for dinner if you're sitting at my table."

The men sat down. So did the dog.

She had the feeling this wasn't going to be a quick conversation, so she put out some instant coffee, half-and-half, sugar, spoons and napkins. She poured boiling water into their cups and joined them. As she stirred her drink, she looked at Jones and said, "You said something about bad news...."

Raymond was studying her in the soft-eyed, unobtrusive way that he'd perfected over the years. The look was intended to convey empathy and kindly concern. It usually relaxed the person on the other end of it. He hadn't noticed it having that effect on Sarah Dunning yet, but he kept using it anyway.

"It's about your sister..." he began.

"Gabrielle?" Sarah asked in surprise, still not convinced she should believe them. It was true that her sister frequently dangled from one difficulty or another, but Gabrielle would have called her if she'd been in trouble. Unless Gabrielle couldn't for some reason... Sarah tensed and leaned forward as dreadful possibilities began to buffet her imagination. "Has she been in a diving accident? Is she hurt?"

"We think she's all right at the moment. No, there wasn't a diving accident," Jones said soothingly.

"What, then?" Sarah demanded crossly. "Stop dragging this out. Tell me!" The dog rose into a crouch behind her. Sarah made a quick motion with one hand and the dog lay down.

Sutter, tiring of Jones's reluctance to be blunt, interrupted. "Your sister's been kidnapped and is being held on an island in the Caribbean," he said succinctly. If she couldn't take bad news straight up, he'd just as soon know it right now. Especially considering Jones's asinine plan to involve her in the rescue effort.

Sarah's shocked gaze flew to his. Sutter's callous words felt like a blow to her. She searched his face, hoping that he'd not meant what he'd said, but there was only tough, unvarnished truth staring back at her. Her heart sank precipitously. Sarah had always thought of herself as a reasonably courageous person, but the threat of physical danger and death had never come so near to her or to anyone she loved before. She hung on to her nerve with gritty effort.

"Kidnapped?" Sarah repeated in a shocked voice. Sutter nodded. His black eyes were hard and unwavering. He was offering no sympathy, no soothing words, no balm to take the edge off the message. He was giving her the news like a hunter hitting a rabbit between the eyes with a slingshot. Oddly, after her initial shock faded, Sarah found her strength coming back faster because of the ruthless way he'd told her. He thinks I can't take it, she realized. She swallowed her fears out of pride and gathered her strength. You'd be surprised, Mr. Sutter, she thought. Her protective instincts began to rise.

As their gazes held, something began to sizzle between them. Sarah had the strangest feeling she was touching a hot electrical wire and the current was zigzagging through her body. She shook off the sensation and focused on the unbelievable claim that Sutter had so abruptly made.

"Don't be ridiculous," she challenged. Her brown eyes darkened as anxiety warred with distrust. "Why would someone do that? Not for a ransom; we're not rich. And Gabrielle certainly doesn't get involved with anything that would make her a threat to anyone." Sarah looked from Raymond to Alex. "Maybe it's some other woman who's been kidnapped. Who on earth would do that to Gabrielle?"

"A very nasty man, Ms. Dunning," Alex said with biting sarcasm.

He'd felt the strange current between them and didn't like it at all. It was a relief to say something cutting to her, to punish her for the peculiar effect she'd had on him. He tried to repress the urge to get up from the table and go back to the car. He wanted to tell Jones that he'd heard more than enough, that this woman was too green and too young to drag into this. She didn't even seem to have the good sense to be horrified at the news they'd given her. To hell with it. He'd leave them to discuss it. He'd formed his opinion. Sutter shoved back the chair and began rising to his feet.

Jones put out a restraining hand. "Don't throw in the towel yet, Alex," he implored him. "We haven't had a chance to explain to her."

Alex, half out of his chair, put his palms on the table and turned his blistering attention on Raymond.

"I don't need to watch you explain *anything* to her. She'd be nothing but a hindrance down there. Look at her." He sent a critical look at Sarah. "She's just a young woman from the boonies. What good would she be?" He shook his head. "Forget it."

He straightened and walked around the table. The dog's eyes bore into him, but he displayed no concern and coldly strode out of the room with only the curtest of nods as a farewell to Sarah.

Sarah watched Sutter's exit with indignation. A woman from the boonies? Lacking the sense to be horrified? *Nothing but a hindrance?* Her indignation blossomed into rich, ripe anger.

"He's got a lot of nerve!" she said angrily.

"Yes." Raymond sighed, running a chubby hand through his thin, graying hair. "That's why I'm trying to convince him to help us get your sister out."

Sarah had barely glanced at the ID he'd shown her earlier. Now she could hardly remember what it said. He had left it on the table and she reached for it, taking a very close look this time.

"I think you'd better explain the whole situation." She gave him a steady look. "And this time quickly, Mr. Jones. Don't waltz around the details to spare my—" she glared in the direction Alex had taken "—girlish feelings!"

Half an hour later, Sarah sat staring blankly into space, trying to absorb the impact of Raymond Jones's story. She handed him back his identification and let her hand fall limply to the table.

They were right. It *was* Gabrielle. And the man who had her was worse than words could describe as Sutter had so sarcastically pointed out. Sarah closed her eyes and prayed for strength as a tremor shook her hands and shoulders. Tears stung the backs of her eyes. She refused to let them fall. There wasn't time for that. Later, she promised herself; you can cry later, Sarah. She just wished she weren't so alone right now. How she longed for the comfort of her family, their warm and robust good humor, their pragmatic approach to every difficulty, their comforting presence. If she could talk to them, she'd be more certain about what to do, and she desperately wanted to do the right thing. There wasn't going to be room for second thoughts. Doing the right thing was going to be a matter of life and death. Gabrielle's. And perhaps other people's.

"I'd like to call my brother," Sarah murmured, rising to go to the telephone. "And my parents."

Raymond put up his hand. "No."

She frowned at him, surprised and suspicious. "Why not?"

Jones rose gingerly from the table, keeping one eye on the black Labrador who'd become even more alert looking now that he was on his feet.

"In order to protect your sister, we need to make Moreau believe that no one thinks she's missing. She and the diver who was killed apparently weren't expected to be in contact with anyone specific for another two or three weeks. He was staying with your sister, on a diving vacation. And your sister was expected to be gone for a couple of weeks. She'd told her friends that she was taking this guy out on a series of dives, and they were planning on taking the boat to several different islands during the course of his visit. She has connections with all the diving facilities down there, so she'd be able to resupply at any number of places. Unfortunately, the moment a public search for your sister begins, Moreau may be tempted to... do something rash..." Raymond's voice trailed off and he looked deeply sorry for having to be the bearer of such grim tidings. "We don't want to stir things up with a lot of obvious investigation."

Sarah leaned back against the counter and put her face in her hands. "Oh, Gabrielle," she murmured weakly. She drew in a deep breath and forced her head up. She gripped the counter edge with her hands. She had to be strong. This was not the time to get weak and weepy.

"All right," Sarah said stoically, swallowing hard. "I'm willing to assume—for the sake of argument at least—that you're who you say you are, that Gabrielle is where you claim she is and that your desire not to tell the rest of the family about the rescue attempt is based on your wanting to have the element of surprise on your side." She looked at Raymond. "But why are you telling *me* all this?"

Raymond was encouraged by her attitude. "Do you remember training three Doberman pinschers last year for a lawyer in Key Biscayne?" he asked her.

Sarah wrinkled her brow. Dobermans? She'd trained nearly a dozen last year. After a little thought, she recalled the lawyer who'd called her from the Keys and the nervous little man who'd brought the dogs to train for surveillance. They'd paid in cash, which had seemed odd at the time. That had to be what he meant. "Yes. What about them?"

"The lawyer was procuring them for the man who kidnapped your sister. One of those dogs is guarding her in her cell. He'll attack her if she leaves without permission from his handler."

Sarah paled, but she was still perplexed.

"Surely someone could tranquilize him? Put something in his food or drink?" she suggested. Surely they could figure that out themselves if they had any intelligence, not to mention training, she thought, beginning to feel a little exasperated. "Are you asking me for technical advice on how to call him off?" she asked in amazement.

"Not exactly." Raymond explained about the electronic monitoring.

Sarah bit her lip. "That's difficult," she murmured. "Still, there's got to be a way around it."

Raymond took that as a perfect lead and said, "I had hoped you would consider going onto the island with our agent, posing as innocent—" there was a slight hesitation "—tourists whose boat had some trouble. You would then be able to ex-

ercise control over the dogs, permitting our agent to execute the
rest of the rescue effort and get all three of you off the island
before anyone was hurt. We figured that you were the one person who could countermand an order by the dogs' handlers.''

Sarah gaped at him. "You're kidding!" she exclaimed.

Raymond sighed. "That's more or less what Alex said," he
admitted regretfully. He rubbed his neck. "I must be losing my
touch. I never used to have people laugh in my face at my
plans.''

Sarah wasn't laughing, however. She was positively beside
herself.

"You mean, if I don't come along, you may not be able to
neutralize the dogs without raising an alarm and that will mean
that Gabrielle could be..." She couldn't bring herself to say it.

Raymond wasn't so kindhearted now. He knew she was on
the edge of seriously accepting the whole scenario. He had
many years of experience in judging people and he knew when
to push a little, just enough to get them over the edge, to get
them to do what he wished.

"Yes," he said, nodding solemnly. "In that case, I think she
would face immediate execution."

Sarah looked at him bleakly, her face colorless from the
shock of visualizing what he'd just told her. She swallowed and
pushed herself away from the counter. She reached for the
phone and dialed her sister's number on Grand Cayman. There
was no answer. Very slowly she hung up and turned to face the
portly little man. Her sister could just be out, of course, but if
he were telling her the truth, time was of the essence. She
needed to find out how he'd come up with the information he
claimed to have. She needed to know if he was lying to her, for
some bizarre reason.

"I want to see your office," she told him grimly.

"No one goes there but me," he protested in surprise. He had
to hurry around the table to keep up with her, however, for she
was leaving and her dog was trotting along at her heels. "I can't
take you there. It's against the regulations."

"Too bad," Sarah declared. She pulled out a silent dog
whistle and blew on it. Within twenty seconds a huge German
shepherd had bounded to her side as she crossed the unsur-
faced parking lot. Sarah opened her car door and the two dogs

happily jumped onto the back seat. She'd buttoned her plain blue wool jacket on her way to the car and stood there, fingering her car keys. She stared at Raymond Jones and told him, quite calmly, "If I see your office, and if your evidence to support this story is convincing, I'll do whatever you want. If you won't agree to show me your office or don't have convincing proof, and if I can't get Gabrielle on the phone, I'm going down there myself on the next plane."

Sutter had toured Sarah's aged property, examining with mild interest the clean kennels and runs, the neatly kept grounds laid out for various types of dog training. He hadn't seen any other dogs around. From the information that Jones had managed to compile on Sarah, he knew she took on assignments regularly, however. This apparently was a small lull between jobs. He wondered what kind of a young woman would bury herself in the marshy farmland along the Chesapeake, training dogs. And guard dogs and attack dogs, at that. She was well respected. A number of security firms referred their clients to her regularly. The girl had made a terrific name for herself in the past three years. Her own three dogs had won every obedience trial worth winning in the country.

He amended his thoughts. She wasn't exactly a girl, he had to admit. She was lithe and girlish in figure, but she was twenty-eight years old and clearly a young woman in every physical sense. He'd heard the comment the sheriff had made about her preferring dogs over men and recalled what Raymond had told him about the one boyfriend they'd unearthed in her past. Two years ago, right when she began to make her mark in the obedience-training world, her live-in beau had tired of it all and pleaded with her to forget the dogs and marry him.

She apparently hadn't had to think too long. The beau moved out shortly thereafter and no other men had been observed by any of her curious neighbors since. The neighbors were unanimously delighted, too, it appeared. No man was good enough for her, if their raving testimony could be believed. A local vestal virgin, he thought cynically. Well, perhaps slightly tarnished.

Sutter's attention was drawn abruptly to the slight sound a few feet to his left. There, crouched, snarling and—fortunately for Sutter—chained, was a huge black-and-brown male rottweiler.

Obviously he'd found one of her other three dogs, he thought wryly. Carefully he backed away. The dog eased up out of his crouch and the snarling subsided.

She trained her dogs well, he thought begrudgingly. They were unseen until it was too late to escape from them. And she used her own dogs for the very same purpose she trained others. To attack, defend and guard.

He wondered grimly whether even Sarah could call them off once they'd been ordered by their handler to guard something. Or someone.

A black-and-white streak of canine fur passed him at a dead run and he followed it visually to its destination in the parking area. The girl had her coat on and Raymond looked like he was almost pleased. That meant she was considering doing what Raymond wanted, Alex realized.

"The fool," he muttered. He was sorely tempted to tell Raymond to get himself another "professional." He didn't like having Sarah Dunning participate in this.

She trotted in his direction, giving him a sweetly acid smile as she passed by.

"I think you'll be more comfortable in the car," she told him. "I'm going to release my dog now. He's trained to guard the property against all strangers as soon as he's unchained and free to roam." She hesitated. "Mr. Jones is taking me to see his evidence for Gabrielle's kidnapping. He wasn't sure whether you were coming along or not. He said you hadn't decided to accept the assignment."

Sutter stared at her enigmatically, his implacable black eyes steady and unrevealing.

"That's right," he said evenly. He watched her unchain the dog. "Nice-looking animal," he said. "What's his name?"

"Sweet Pea," she said.

Sutter was surprised; then, in spite of himself, he laughed. "You sure know how to hurt the dog's pride, don't you?" he said, looking sympathetically at the burly animal.

The huge rottweiler leaped free and licked Sarah's hand, then turned to stalk around Sutter suspiciously, hackles raised warningly. Sutter stared down at the dog, not moving, not looking particularly concerned. Slowly the dog walked away.

Sarah looked at Sutter curiously and a soft smile came to her eyes. She let the crack about naming her guard dog Sweet Pea pass. "You're not afraid of him, are you?"

Sutter shook his head. "That could be fatal," he observed dryly. "Dogs are more likely to attack people who are afraid of them."

Sarah nodded. "You're right." Under other circumstances, she thought she almost might enjoy Alex Sutter's company. It was really too bad he was so annoying. She smiled at him, not a tremendous smile exactly, but a peace offering of sorts. "We'd better get going," she said softly, and walked back to her car.

Sutter shook off the peculiar feeling that her softening look had engendered in him. He wondered what it would be like to hear her laugh in pleasure, smile in happiness. There was something fresh and uncomplicated about Sarah Dunning. Something innate to her that appealed to something deep within himself. He doubted it would be wise to dwell on that, so he didn't. He pushed the impression aside and silently joined the others.

Sutter got into Jones's car. They led the way. Sarah and her dogs followed in her car.

"I think she can do it, Alex," Raymond said with quiet conviction.

Sutter made an impolite sound of disgust. "You know, I used to think you were one of the few sane people I worked with."

Raymond's face was positively cherubic. "Thanks, Alex."

"I said *used to*, Raymond. *Used to.*"

Jones laughed and glanced in his rearview mirror. She was following nicely. Nicely indeed.

In her car, Sarah was muttering under her breath. "Mr. Jones, this had better be good."

She tried not to think about Alex Sutter at all.

Chapter 3

Jones pulled over to the side of the road when they reached a small town just outside the Washington beltway. Sarah pulled in behind him and killed her engine just as a tanker barreled by well over the speed limit. As Raymond hastily walked along the shoulder to get to her car, a black stretch limousine with unusually dark windows did a fast U-turn in the road and slid quietly up behind her. It obviously had something to do with their stopping.

Sarah rolled down her window, curious to hear what Jones had to say. In the back seat, the dogs growled softly as he leaned down.

"Uh," he began apologetically, "I called and asked for the agency to send me a car. Remember, I told you it's against regulations for me to take you to my office? Well, technically I just can't let you see where it is or how to get into it." He drew in a long breath. "However, if you get into our car—" he nodded in the direction of the limousine "—we can drive you in."

Sarah thought he looked rather strained, and she decided that he'd probably had to do some very fancy talking to get his higher-ups to agree to her request. His explanation made the whole thing seem even more cloak-and-daggerish. That was both encouraging, in that it meant he might be telling the truth, and frightening because it meant she really would be getting involved in something deadly if she agreed to their plan. She swallowed and forced away the sliver of fear. Gabrielle's life might be hanging in the balance. Sarah forced herself to remain strong.

"Okay. Let's go," she said, wondering if they intended to blindfold her. She let the dogs out of the car and locked it with cool fingers.

Raymond had been staring oddly at the dogs. "Uh . . . they can't come."

"Where I go, they go," Sarah told him firmly. "Don't worry. They won't wet on the carpet." She walked over to the limousine; her two four-legged shadows trotted silently at her left side.

"But we've never had dogs in the place," Raymond was saying anxiously. "And dogs trained like yours, well, if my bosses knew, they'd—"

"They'd have a cat," Sarah supplied cheerfully. "Too bad. They'll get over it. They'll just have to consider my point of view. I'd be completely alone and at your mercy without my dogs. Would you want your daughter to do something like that? After all, I only have your word that you are who you say you are." She could see that Raymond understood her plight. "Now, we can either go to your office with my dogs or I can drive over to BWI to see how quickly I can get on a flight going down to Grand Cayman. Which do you prefer?"

Sutter was standing by the limousine watching in amusement as Raymond sweated over the institutional repercussions he was going to have to face.

"You might as well let her and the dogs in, Raymond," Sutter advised him. "We're wasting time arguing the point. And losing time is going to bother them even more than having attack-trained dogs on the premises."

Jones swallowed and, with a very pained expression on his pudgy face, opened the back door. The dogs bounded in and Sarah followed.

She sat in the middle seat, while the dogs rustled around on the seat behind her, searching for the most comfortable position. Jones, instead of sitting next to her as she'd expected, closed and locked her door and went around to the front to sit next to the driver. There was a dark charcoal-colored glass between the passenger seats and the driver's seat, however, and she could only make out shadowy images of the two men. She'd never seen any car windows so difficult to see through. As Alex slid into the seat beside her, she peered frowningly through each of the other windows in the car. They were all made of the same nearly impenetrable material.

Sutter noticed her expression and offered an explanation. "It's almost opaque. People outside can't see you, only a smoky shadow of you if they're very close and the sun is in the right position. Passengers inside can see only the shadows of objects less than a foot away from the glass. Everything farther away is blocked from your view. You won't know where you're going. You won't be able to see a thing."

He fastened his seat belt and stretched out his long legs.

"Oh," Sarah murmured, impressed. "Thanks for explaining."

She'd been looking at him as he spoke, and she wondered how the fairly attractive, remarkably normal-looking man such as Alex Sutter had gotten into this line of work. There was probably something perverted or bizarre about his personality, she thought. What normal person would want a life of lies and hiding? She felt a twinge of regret at that. He projected a rather solid and comforting strength that might have been appealing. Well, to some women anyway. Not to her, of course. Sarah turned her head, somewhat embarrassed at the drift of her thoughts.

The limousine pulled away, and in a little while Sarah felt almost ill. Without being able to see outside, the car's motion was faintly nauseating to her. She'd never realized how accustomed she was to seeing the world pass by her, how she'd clung to that reality when she'd driven. Riding in the car like this was making her feel claustrophobic.

"Do you get used to this?" she asked faintly. "Or should I ask for the airsick bags?"

Alex grinned. "We could talk. That might take your mind off of it." Besides, they were boxed in together and he might as well learn something about her while they were here, he told himself reasonably.

She gave him a grateful smile. "Okay," she agreed. "What shall we talk about?"

He was a striking man, she thought. His six-foot frame was elegantly stretched out in the spacious seating. The neatly pressed dark trousers and raincoat bespoke a man who spent his time in the upper circles of business and society. His hair was dark . . . a very dark shade of brown, she decided. Almost black. It was neatly cut and styled, barely touching the tops of his ears, brushing the collar of his coat. It had been trimmed by a very expensive barber, she thought.

She decided that his eyes made her feel uneasy at times. He could stare with a fathomless black gaze that made her feel stripped naked. Sometimes there was an icy hardness in their depths that nearly made her shiver, and she felt a curl of fear twist inside her as she met his gaze now. He was a dangerous man, in spite of the smooth and sophisticated facade he projected. Sarah knew she had excellent instincts when it came to judging things like that. She didn't question her intuition where Alexander Sutter was concerned.

"Have you memorized what I look like?" he asked, obviously amused at her completely open study of him.

"Yes," she replied. She lifted her chin slightly, refusing to look away. His amusement annoyed her. Her cheeks rosied. "You look like James Bond," she told him coolly. She hoped he'd loathe the comparison. "Do you like the work?"

His amusement chilled. He didn't want to discuss his "work" much less his attitude toward it. "I don't work for Jones," he told her bluntly. "You've seen too many movies."

Sarah looked skeptical. "That wasn't the impression I got from him." She tilted her head to one side. "If you don't work for him, why are you here with me?"

"I'm still wondering that myself," he murmured, letting his gaze travel over her in a desultory fashion. "I work for myself, Ms. Dunning," he added, speaking quite softly and very distinctly.

He let his attention linger appreciatively as his gaze reached her thighs. In blue jeans, the shape of her legs was attractively clear. Regrettably, her bulky wool jacket had swallowed the shape of the upper half of her body. He'd seen enough of her in her kitchen to know she was physically attractive. He'd just not bothered to let her see that he'd noticed that at the time. Now he let her see what he thought. When his gaze wandered back to her face, she was almost laughing, which surprised him. He hadn't expected her to have that much confidence.

"Are you trying to intimidate me, Mr. Sutter?" she demanded.

He raised a dark brow. "Now why would I want to intimidate you, Ms. Dunning?" he asked.

"Habit?" she suggested. "Perversity?"

Sutter laughed. "Perhaps you just plain bother me, Sarah Dunning," he said. He watched the frown gather on her brow. She wasn't used to being played with, he thought.

"Sorry," she said, not a whit of apology in her voice. Sarah shifted uncomfortably and pursued a different line of conversation. "You don't want me to go along. Why not?" she asked.

Sutter was surprised she'd ask, especially after what he'd said in her kitchen. "You've never done anything like this before. You're an unknown quantity, a potential loose cannon, to use a popular Washington term. I wouldn't want you rolling around on a ship deck of mine, especially when my life would be at stake along with everything else that's hanging in the balance."

Sarah thought that was quite reasonable and smiled ruefully.

"I can't blame you at all," she told him. "But if they can't think of a way to neutralize the electronic monitoring, it looks as though I'm everyone's best shot at slipping Gabrielle past the dogs." She frowned. "I don't understand why they can't just lay siege to the place, though. Surely he wouldn't kill her if he were surrounded and knew that people were aware she was there."

Sutter shook his head. "He'd kill her and cremate her on the spot, if necessary. Besides, the island is his. The country that technically has jurisdiction over it has looked the other way for years, thanks to his hefty financial contributions to the pockets of a few key political leaders there. They certainly aren't going to bite the hand that feeds them. No one wants to be accused of assaulting a neutral country, and that's exactly what it would take, so other nations sit and gnash their teeth. It would require launching a military assault on him to shake him loose. He's outfitted the damn place to withstand a military attack, so it couldn't be done quietly or easily. The diplomatic community . . . prefers not to use force.''

Sutter's expression was neutral, but Sarah sensed his deep, long-standing dislike for this man and his arsenal,

"Do you think someone *should* attack him?" she asked in surprise.

"No. That would cause needless bloodshed." But that wasn't the reason that an overt assault wasn't being pursued and Sutter knew it. It was the public embarrassment that the diplomatic community wished to avoid. If they could have figured out a way to militarily attack Moreau without drawing international cries of protest, they would have done it in a minute, no matter whose blood was spilled.

Sarah wondered why Alex suddenly looked so fiercely annoyed. "You look awfully angry," she observed cautiously.

Sutter straightened his face, a little surprised he'd let his feelings show like that. "Indigestion," he muttered curtly.

From having to swallow things he didn't like, Sarah decided. She hadn't expected that he might have a sense of morality about this, and she was surprised. She trusted her feelings though. Alex Sutter was more than just a gun for hire. "How could he afford to fight back on such a big scale?"

Alex began to wish he hadn't started explaining to her. Carrying on this conversation was revealing more about him than about her, he realized with disgust. He tried to estimate how much longer it would be before they reached Jones's building. Absently he answered, "Moreau trades in drugs and arms. He keeps a top line of military samples for his own use."

Sarah swallowed her distaste. The information was obviously common knowledge as far as Sutter was concerned. It sounded more like things Sarah read about in the newspaper. The world he knew was a very different one from hers obviously. "I see," she said quietly.

"Do you?" he asked, turning to stare at her, unconvinced. "Do you know what they'll do to you if they have the slightest suspicion that you're lying to them, that you're not who you say you are, that you're there to wrest your sister from their grasp?"

The image of this innocent young woman being tortured by Moreau and his men had suddenly become painfully clear in Alex's mind and he wanted to scare her with it, chase her away before it was too late, before she was too involved to escape.

Sarah looked straight at him then, and anger began to simmer within her.

"Do you know anything about the Dunning family, Mr. Sutter?" she demanded tightly. "Have they got a thick enough file there at Mr. Jones's office to convey to you how much we mean to one another? Or didn't they bother with such unquantifiable things as love? Does it tell you that we can do anything we have to when one of us is threatened with harm? If it didn't, the analysts had better get out from behind their little desks and ask a bunch more questions." She looked away from him, seeing her sister as she stared ahead of her. "If Gabrielle's there, I'll do anything necessary to save her. No matter what the risk." She gave him a hard look. "And I won't be doing it for money, Mr. Sutter. I'll be doing it because I love her. Because I don't want anyone to hurt her."

He sensed the fierce determination in her and wondered if perhaps she could pull it off in spite of her inexperience. She had a valid point. Motivation was definitely an important variable in operations like this. He'd seen amateurs do horrendous things when their loved ones were at stake. However, although it was conceivable that Sarah could come through like a pro, he wasn't sure there would be enough time before the operation had to start to know that for certain. Time. There was never enough time.

"We'll see, Ms. Dunning," he said evenly. "We'll see."

Sarah stared at him, biting back the impulse to tell him that he most certainly would see. She thought she saw a glimmer of annoyance in his eyes, as if he knew what she wasn't saying and found it aggravating.

They were poised to fight and Sutter was damned if he knew exactly why. Usually he didn't react like this. Maybe it was too much jet lag. Sutter decided to redirect the conversation slightly.

"Tell me about your family," Alex suggested. "Jones's people sometimes do miss things when they have to compile a dossier in a hurry," he conceded. "And I would imagine they'd have to dig a long time to unearth much dirt in your past."

Sarah shot him a startled glance. "You make that sound like a criticism," she exclaimed indignantly.

He shrugged. "We're not used to clean-living people, Ms. Dunning," he reminded her. "You'll have to excuse us."

A wet nose shoved the back of her shoulder sympathetically.

"Thanks," she told her loyal dog, scratching his black forehead. Her eyes narrowed as she looked at Sutter. "I suppose that means you're not particularly clean living yourself?"

His slow grin and staring eyes answered the question.

Sarah felt her cheeks warm and she looked away. She wondered what kind of life he had led that would make him look at her like that. Probably full of fast, beautiful women, flashy cars, jets and one dramatic climax after another. Right on the edge of the law. Maybe on the wrong side, too, once in a while, she thought uneasily. Alex Sutter was as smooth as glass, as handsome as a leading man and as ruthless as a pirate. It was all there in his grin and his bold, uncaring eyes.

Sarah lifted her chin and looked back at him, her eyes clear and determined. "I'm glad at least one of us won't be accused of rank ignorance," she said calmly. "I trust that you've had enough unclean living for both of us, Mr. Sutter?"

Sutter rapped the back of his knuckles slowly against the window next to him. "I probably have, Ms. Dunning," he assured her dryly. "Why don't you tell me about your family. Start with your brother, Christopher, the Canadian ice-hockey pro. Go on to your parents, Anson and Lois, who retired and left for Alaska to get a little elbow room a year ago. And fill me in on the details about your widowed sister, Gabrielle Lorenzo, who's been struggling for two years to keep her late husband's diving business alive."

Sarah was impressed and she didn't mind showing it. "They did a very good job on short notice. Is all that in the file Jones has on us?" she asked.

Sutter nodded. "Those are a few of the highlights. They sometimes miss the most important things about a person, though. It's easy to overlook small, apparently insignificant details. Tell me about your family." He glanced at his watch.

"You've got about thirty minutes before we arrive at Jones's office, so you'll have to boil it down to the most important essentials. Can you do that?"

Sarah wasn't too happy. "It's strange, thinking that your life, personal facts about you, are written down in a file sitting in a cabinet and studied by total strangers somewhere." She stared blindly at her shadowy reflection in the smoked-glass window behind Sutter. She shifted her gaze back to him. He was watching her steadily. "It's like being watched secretly by someone while you're undressing and don't know they're looking."

Alex's jaw tightened slightly. She'd have to get used to worse than that before it was over. "Don't think about it," he suggested evenly. "Whether or not I accept this assignment, it might help for you to tell me about your family and their habits. I might pick out something that could help. You never know when something can foul up plans like this. You need to know as much as possible about each person's background and—" he paused "—their *significant others*."

Sarah wondered why he held significant others in such low regard. From the slightly amused cynicism, it was clear that he did. He probably was a love-'em-and-leave-'em type, she decided. Maybe he'd only been involved with women willing to tolerate that kind of a relationship. She shook her head slightly, trying to stop her drifting thoughts. It didn't matter what kind of man Alex Sutter was. It certainly didn't matter what his relationships with other women were like. She forced her wandering mind back to the business at hand.

"If you're asking if Gabrielle is involved with another man or men, the answer is no," Sarah replied rather tartly. "I don't think so. If she is, none of us have heard about it, and that wouldn't be like Gabrielle. When she fell in love with Bernardo Lorenzo, we all knew it immediately. She called me after their first date to talk about him. She mentioned him in a birthday card she sent to Christopher. She told Mom about him after he'd started taking her diving with him. Besides—" a shadow crossed Sarah's face "—Gabrielle loved him very, very much. His death has been a terrible tragedy for her. Keeping and building his business is the only thing that has kept her from going nearly insane with grief. She's done it for him. As a personal homage and act of love."

Alex had been watching her face as she'd talked and wondered if Sarah felt things as deeply as her sister. From what he'd read in the few lines about her live-in boyfriend, he doubted it. She'd been relieved to see him go, according to the neighbors. Funny, he wouldn't have thought that. There was something about Sarah Dunning that felt so straight-arrow honest and stubbornly loyal. Well, it wouldn't have been the first time he'd guessed wrong about a woman. It didn't happen too often, but it did happen.

"She sounds neurotic," Sutter observed, trying to draw Sarah out by baiting her a little. He watched her angry reaction show in her flashing eyes. She was pretty, he thought vaguely. And easy to tease.

"She's a completely normal, wonderfully loyal, magnificently strong woman!" Sarah snapped at him. Behind her, two dogs growled and their snarling jaws poked over the seat. She patted their cold black noses and ordered them to sit. "Sorry," she muttered. "But you shouldn't have said that about her. You don't even know her." Her eyes burned with outrage. "Who are you to sit in judgment over us anyway? We're the normal people in this drama. My father worked as a factory foreman for forty years. He retired and moved with his wife—the only one he ever had—to live in rural contentment, away from the noise and fury of urban living. Is there something wrong with that?"

"No," he murmured, restraining a sudden desire to grin.

"And my brother is an athlete who could have lettered in three or four sports but fell in love with ice hockey when he was eight years old. So he went to college in a country where you could play ice hockey, and he got so good at it that he was drafted and is now a pro. What's wrong with that? Somebody has to do it. Why not a boy from Baltimore who spent every afternoon, weekend, summer and winter vacation trading work for ice time at the local rink?" Her cheeks were red with anger.

"Why not?" Sutter agreed evenly, finding it harder and harder to keep a straight face. Sarah Dunning certainly didn't like him picking on her family.

Sarah, glaring furiously, leaned toward him in her zeal. "And I suppose a woman who likes to train dogs is the ultimate in bizarre behavior! Well, let me tell you, I love dogs, Mr. Sutter. I wish I knew as many people whom I like as I do dogs that I like. And I find dogs much easier to work with, much more honest, much more loyal and kinder hearted. I also happen to have a knack for obedience training and was lucky enough to work for one of the best trainers in the country when I was growing up. She taught me everything I know. She was my summer job, my after-school job, my job that paid my way through university classes."

Sarah took in a breath and gathered herself to finish her defense of her family.

"I know we seem . . . unusual to more conventional people. I mean, my sister was working in Florida as a bartender when she met Lorenzo and went to live with him on a boat—not a usual choice. My parents sold their home and now live in a two-room cabin in Alaska where bears pass through on migration. Not everybody does that. But does that make us an object of humor for people who sit in their stuffy little offices, smothering in cigarette smoke and government statistics?"

Alex's initial amusement had faded as Sarah had so passionately harangued him. There was an odd light in his eyes as he looked at her. His voice was almost kind when he spoke.

"I never said that I thought you were peculiar," he reminded her softly. "Personally . . ." He hesitated, but decided to be honest with her, a little honest anyway. "I prefer people who know themselves and are true to themselves. The ones who change their spots to suit their surroundings are the ones who are dangerous."

Sarah leaned back against the seat and sighed. "No one's ever accused any of the Dunnings of hiding our spots," she declared, giving a half-smothered laugh at the very idea. She sobered and turned a thoughtful glance on him. "That doesn't mean we aren't capable of being as manipulative and deceitful as we have to be, if someone's safety is at stake."

He wasn't completely convinced of that. "You mean you could carry on a masquerade, an overt deception, without much difficulty?"

Sarah bit her lip. Then she nodded and looked straight into his dubious black eyes. "Yes," she told him firmly. "I could."

The car had been slowing down for some time, and now they began stopping and starting. They were obviously driving through the heavily congested traffic of city streets.

"We're in Washington, aren't we?" Sarah asked. It was frustrating peering through the darkened windows.

"I can't answer that."

He felt a tug of admiration for her, and wished he could tell her where she was and exactly what she was voluntarily walking into. But Jones had been explicit. Alex was not to tell her anything that Jones had not given permission for. Not until everyone had agreed to the plans. Including Alex himself.

Alex studied her profile and wondered about the man in her own past that she hadn't mentioned yet. Sarah was an attractive young woman. So why hadn't she married the guy she'd let live in her house?

"You said you preferred dogs to people," he reminded her.

She gave him a startled look. So he *had* heard what the sheriff had said earlier, she thought, recalling the amused gleam in Alex's distant eyes. "Yes."

"Is that why the man who was living with you didn't marry you?"

Sarah's eyes chilled. "My relationship with Robert is personal."

He reached over then and pulled her jaw around, forcing her to look at him. His grip was firm but there was no anger in his touch, so she made no effort to resist. A strange heat flowed between them.

"You don't have a personal life anymore," he said, his eyes hardening. "There can be no secrets in a situation like this," he told her grimly. "I want to know how you met him. Who he is. Why he left. And whether he or anyone else is likely to notice your absence if you fly down to the Caribbean."

Sarah blinked and tried to calm down. He'd frightened her, and she didn't know exactly how. There was something predatory about the way he'd reached out and touched her. It had stirred a primal, female fear within her, something she didn't remember ever feeling before.

She got a grip on her unraveling nerves. "You probably know most of it."

"Humor me," he ordered. Slowly, his gaze still locked with hers, he withdrew his hand and sat back in his seat.

Sarah exhaled softly and bit her lower lip. "Robert's the son of a Baltimore merchant. His father sponsors one of the obedience trophies in the mid-Atlantic dog trials. I won the trophy one year and Robert presented it. He…asked me out later and we started seeing each other. One thing led to another…." Sarah couldn't keep looking at him and tore her eyes away. "We decided it would be easier if we lived under the same roof. I didn't want to live under his roof, so he moved under mine." She pressed her lips together uncomfortably. "We… just weren't compatible," she concluded in a rather faint-hearted voice.

"The file said he wanted to get married and you didn't."

"That's true."

"Why not?"

"It…it just didn't quite seem right." She closed her eyes. "I knew it was a mistake the night he moved in, but I was too proud and too guilty to admit it. He'd wanted to get married to begin with, but I kept dragging my feet. I never should have let us get so involved. It was…a disaster." She grimaced and glared at Sutter. "I don't suppose you've ever had a disaster in your personal life, Mr. Sutter?" Why did he keep staring at her like that? It was unnerving.

He looked away from her and frowned. "That depends on your definition of disaster."

Sarah's annoyance at his cross-examination wilted a little. She sensed he had been dissatisfied once. She wondered if he'd be willing to talk about it. If he would, he might seem less distant and threatening to her, she thought. That might be a welcome relief.

"Have you ever been married?" she asked him cautiously.

He gave her an amused glance. "No."

"Lived with someone?" she asked, a little more boldly, encouraged by his apparent humor.

"Yes," he admitted softly. His gaze wandered over her face with a distant kind of appreciation. "I lived with a woman once." His gaze returned to her curious brown eyes. He added softly, "And I suppose you could call it a disaster."

The car came to a full stop and they heard the motor turn off.

"We're here," Alex told her.

The doors were electronically unlocked from the driver's console. Alex opened the door and held it for Sarah as she crawled across the seat and followed him out. Their eyes met and Sarah felt the slight sting of heat racing through her.

Alex Sutter, you are dangerous in more ways than one, she thought uneasily. She whistled and the dogs bounded after her. She only wished they could protect her from Alex Sutter's unnerving effect.

"This way, Miss Dunning," Raymond was saying anxiously. He cast nervous glances at her dogs. "They'll never understand upstairs," he muttered fretfully. "Never."

Chapter 4

They didn't pass anyone on their way to Jones's office. The parking lot was located inside the building, and they'd parked right next to a stairwell, which he insisted they use, ignoring the elevator. Sarah presumed it was the route less traveled and that he was taking it to avoid running into people along the way. They climbed three flights of stairs before arriving at Jones's floor. He opened the door with an electronic credit-card-shaped key, cautiously stuck his head into the hall to insure that no one was wandering around and then led them to the second door down the hallway on the right. He hustled them inside, closing the gray metal office door after them with an expression of profound relief and motioned for them to put their coats in the closet.

"Anybody care for a cup of coffee?" he asked solicitously as he rummaged through a corner cabinet and poured water into his instant coffee maker.

Sarah looked around the drab little room curiously. It adjoined two others, but the doors were closed and the glass in the upper half of each was thick and convoluted, so she couldn't make out anything when she tried to look through them. There were water stains on the ceiling and the wall-to-wall carpet was threadbare. It certainly could pass for a government office, she thought wryly. They were all alike: dismal, gray, worn, characterless. Then she saw a photograph on a glass-enclosed bookcase. It was a picture of a woman and two children playing at the beach. And Raymond Jones was literally up to his neck in sand as the two gleeful little girls piled it on.

"Your family?" Sarah asked him, warming to him for the first time.

"Yeah," he said with an embarrassed grin. He shook his head. "They're little rascals." He looked at the picture of his family affectionately.

Jones pulled material from various cabinets and drew Sarah over to one corner of the room. He spread out aerial photos, maps and several cryptic reports on a long conference table there.

"I think these will help answer some of your questions, Miss Dunning," Raymond suggested. He took off his coat and hung it in a nearby closet and went to pour coffee into the cups by the coffee maker. He winked at Alex encouragingly. "Cup of coffee, Alex?" he asked diffidently.

"Thanks." Sutter took the cup and lifted one of the files from the table. He took a swallow of the hot drink and began looking at the contents, scanning each paper with razor-sharp attention.

Sarah watched him lounge against the nearby wall, reading, and wondered who he really was. She doubted that Raymond would be giving her any files on Alex Sutter, and yet, if she went along on this mission, her life would be in his hands. To depend on the judgment and trustworthiness of a total stranger . . . Sarah hated the idea.

As if sensing her regard, Sutter looked up from the paper he was studying.

"You don't look very happy to be here, Ms. Dunning," Sutter told her dryly. "If I were you, I'd stop worrying about who to trust and start studying those maps and reports." As if to underscore the importance of her doing that, he added, "I've already seen them. After you've examined them, you'll begin to see why Raymond knows what he does. And why speed is essential."

Sarah took off her coat and sat down. The dogs curled next to her feet. The building they were in was as cold and silent as a tomb. Sarah shivered, surreptitiously rubbed one foot against a friendly canine shoulder, and began reading files.

An hour later Sarah still didn't know exactly where Raymond fit in the intelligence community, but she no longer had any doubt that he fit in somewhere. Secret and Top Secret were stamped all over every radio transcript, handwritten summary and photograph. There were aerial photos that had to have been taken from spy satellites or very high-altitude reconnaissance aircraft. There were communiqués in code or so cryptically stated that for all practical purposes they were unintelligible to the naive reader.

Sarah went back to some of the blowups of the fortified island and wondered how anyone could escape it unnoticed. "It looks like a fortress," she murmured despairingly. "How on earth can we free her?"

Raymond rubbed his hands together happily, encouraged that Sarah was beginning to accept the facts and would now listen with an open mind. Patiently he laid out the steps that could be taken to free Gabrielle Lorenzo.

Sarah listened intently, trying to absorb every nuance and detail, trying to determine what he was leaving out as well as comprehending what he'd explained. When he finished, she turned to gauge Sutter's reaction, but he didn't even look as if he'd been listening.

He was staring at something in the file in his hands and his face was perfectly blank. Too perfectly blank, she thought. He'd seen something that had bothered him so much he'd eliminated every vestige of emotion from his expression.

"Sutter?" she asked. "Is something wrong?"

His expression eased a bit and he closed the file, replaced it in the cabinet and came over to join them at the conference table.

"Old memories," Sutter murmured enigmatically, shrugging it off as nothing. He picked up one of the aerial photos and stared at it intently, tracing the fortifications with his fingertip as if he were committing it to memory.

The phone rang and Raymond walked over to his desk to answer it. From his short, awkward responses, it quickly became apparent that someone was asking him about the progress of the case.

"Er, well," Raymond stuttered uncomfortably, "I made him the offer but he wasn't interested. No. He's not completely turned it down yet, but he's not too, er, thrilled about it, either.... Yes. We've talked to her. We're working on that. All right. Yes. If you'll authorize me to make the offer, I can tell him." Raymond glanced across the room at Sutter and grimaced humorously. "I can ask him right now. Yes, sir. I'll let you know."

Raymond hung up the phone and motioned for Sutter to join him at his desk. "They want to up the money. They're offering you one and a half million now," Raymond murmured apologetically. He shrugged. "They think money buys everything. If you turn them down again, they'll probably offer you more." He rubbed his forehead tiredly. "I've been awake for thirty hours, Alex. I'm gonna have to take a nap soon. I'm too old for this."

Sutter felt the same. He was too old for this, too, but he was about to step waist deep into it all again anyway. There were a number of reasons, but the last straw had been seeing the name of the copilot of the downed airplane in the file he'd just read. It was a young man he'd known ten years ago. The kid hadn't realized what was in their cargo. He'd been used by Moreau and his associates. Now that handsome young man was dead. And he'd left a bride of nineteen a widow. She was expecting a baby in three months, the report said. The boy was the son of a man who'd once saved Sutter's life. And that old man was now all alone in the world, except for a pregnant daughter-in-law who was doubtless in dire need of the old man's help.

Damn it all, he was surrounded with debts from his past, Sutter thought angrily. Like a fisherman's net, they drew him into Jones's trap. And then there was the naive young woman with her dogs curled protectively at her feet. He didn't like the idea of her going on this mission, but if he turned it down, he had a fairly good idea whom they'd ask to go in his stead. He didn't relish having Sarah Dunning's life depend on that man's ability to make snap decisions correctly when things started going wrong on the island later. If there was one thing that

Sutter had learned over the years, it was that things always went wrong.

Sutter looked at Jones and said, "Tell them to wire the money to this account in the next twenty-four hours." He withdrew a pen and paper from inside his coat, wrote something down and handed it to the thunderstruck intelligence analyst.

"Shut your mouth, Raymond. It doesn't look dignified," Sutter advised him, managing a laudably straight face.

Raymond's mouth snapped shut and he walked back to his telephone to relay the information.

Sarah had overheard enough to know that Sutter had accepted an offer. She knew she shouldn't be surprised that he'd accepted the assignment when he'd been offered more money, but she was surprised all the same. Surprised and . . . disappointed. She had begun to think that Alexander Sutter wasn't the kind of man to be swayed by money. Obviously her impression had been wrong, she thought uncomfortably. His eyes met hers and that peculiar tingle of electricity sizzled between them. How did he do that? she wondered.

"They finally found your price," she observed coolly, annoyed that he had such an unnerving effect on her, especially now, when she'd just been so graphically shown that he was a man whose loyalty could be bought.

He nodded, his face carefully devoid of emotion. "Everyone has a price, Ms. Dunning," he pointed out, annoyed that he was stung by her subtle criticism. He worked for money just as everyone else on the planet did. In this case she was damned lucky he was willing to take what they were offering. "They found *my* price," he observed, anger tinging his words. "And it would appear that they've also found *yours*."

At first she didn't understand and she stared at him red cheeked with the implied insult. Then she realized what he must mean and her anger faded. She felt almost embarrassed. He hadn't intended to insult her. He'd been referring to her sister. "Gabrielle," Sarah murmured awkwardly, acknowledging his meaning.

"Precisely." His eyes held hers. "Are you going?"

"Yes." Sarah didn't hesitate. She'd made her decision the moment she'd seen the blowup of the building where her sister was being held, the one with the blurry picture of Gabrielle's face behind a barred window high on the stone wall of the fortress. "I presume that means we'll be partners, then." She refused to look away from his unyielding regard.

"Apparently so," he agreed. "Partners." Sutter looked at Raymond and frowned slightly. "Did you tell her exactly what form our . . . partnership will have to take?" he asked.

Raymond ran his finger around his collar and cleared his throat.

"Uh . . . I didn't quite get to that part. I told her you'd take a boat from Grand Cayman and would strand yourselves just off of Moreau's island." Raymond turned toward Sarah to explain. "You and Alex are supposed to be . . . in love." Raymond cleared his throat. "We're hoping that Moreau will believe you two are so genuinely involved with each other that you couldn't be agents. We're counting on that to make him relax his guard a little with you, just enough to give you room to maneuver on the island a little. He has a reputation for giving lavish entertainment and taking great pride in that island of his. He brings people in on pontoon boats from Jamaica for weekend parties from time to time. If he believes you're who we want him to believe you are, he should slide from suspicious drug lord to charming host. Then you're halfway to finding and freeing Gabrielle Lorenzo."

"Tell her the punch line, Raymond," Sutter told him dryly. "She may still have a change of heart after she hears exactly what kind of partnership you have in mind for us."

Sarah looked from the faintly ironic Sutter to the pinkly uncomfortable Jones. "What does he mean?" Sarah asked Raymond. She tried to allay Jones's discomfort by smiling at him reassuringly. "For heaven's sakes, it can't be *that* bad. Just tell me."

Raymond gathered himself and told her. "We don't think it'll be convincing if you show up merely as vacationing tourists or . . . temporary lovers." He ignored Sarah's widening eyes and trudged on. "While there are a lot of those down in the Caribbean, that kind of a front is something that would arouse Moreau's suspicions too much. It would be the kind of thing agents might pull. We . . . we decided that it might be more convincing if you were . . . honeymooners."

Sarah took a deep breath and reminded herself it was all pretence and that Alex Sutter and she were perfect strangers and always would be. "I don't see any problem with that. So we pretend we're on a honeymoon." She tried to be game about it.

Raymond looked as if it was premature for him to relax. "We need to convince Moreau that you are *genuine* newlyweds. We want to stage a ceremony up here and make sure a photo gets into the island papers."

Sarah glanced at Sutter who was watching her with obvious entertainment. He probably thinks I'll faint in shock, she thought, irritated. She shrugged as if the plan were no problem at all.

"Well," she declared as optimistically as she could. "Sutter and I already agree that our personal relationships have been disasters. We ought to be perfectly suited for a sham marriage and honeymoon." The dogs sat up, unsettled by the slight tension in her voice. She hesitated. "You're sure that this is really necessary?" she asked faintly, as the potential sleeping arrangements for the farce finally occurred to her. "I mean, pretending that we're married is really the best plan?"

Sutter fastened his raincoat and headed for the door.

"It's only necessary," he growled, "if you wish to have a fifty-fifty chance of getting to Moreau's island alive. If you wish to lower the chances, skip the wedding. And the honeymoon."

Sarah glared at him. "There's no need to be nasty, Mr. Sutter," she snapped. "I have no problems with marrying the devil himself if it'll get my sister out of that man's clutches."

"Why, thank you, Ms. Dunning," Sutter told her with a sarcastic look and a bow. He turned toward Raymond. "I have a couple of things to take care of before I leave town. If you need to reach me, call me at Sarah's tonight."

Sarah lifted her eyebrows considerably. "You're coming to my house tonight?" she asked, taken completely by surprise this time.

He grinned like the devil she'd swore she'd willingly marry. "Of course. Where else would a groom stay on his wedding night?" And with that parting shot, he walked out of the office.

Sarah was still staring at the door a full thirty seconds after he'd closed it after him. "Wedding night?" she echoed faintly. She directed a startled glance at Raymond. *"Tonight?"*

Raymond smile crookedly. "We don't have much time," he reminded her apologetically.

"No," she murmured. "Of course not." She looked down at the black-and-silver German shepherd and the coal-black Labrador, their liquid brown eyes gleaming up expectantly at her. She patted them each rather wanly and said with a sigh, "Which of you wants to give me away and which wants to be my maid of honor?"

Raymond clapped his hands and then rubbed them together enthusiastically. "Everything's all arranged. There will be nothing to it. You'll see."

Sarah didn't want to think about it. Married to that black-eyed gun for hire! She'd rather be tied to a snake. At least she wouldn't feel so peculiar and odd around one of those. As if something electrifying might happen if she weren't very, very careful.

Alex slipped out of the drab twelve-story building unnoticed and caught a cab to the closest metro station. There he picked up a pay phone and dialed Grant Macklin.

"It's Alex," he told his partner. "I'm going to be leaving the country tomorrow morning, about dawn. An old problem is festering and needs my attention."

"Does the old problem have a name?" Grant asked.

"Antonio Moreau. Antonio Muerte to his friends."

"Cute. Where'd he think up that handle?" Macklin questioned.

"His father disowned him and his mother never had the same last name for more than a month at a time. Moreau picked the nickname that would bother people the most: Death."

"A real charmer. Do you need any help?" Macklin asked.

"Maybe," Sutter told him. "I don't have much time to talk right now, though. I'm getting married tonight."

"Married?" Macklin shouted, forcing Sutter to pull the phone a little away from his ear. *"To whom?"*

"To a lady dog trainer named Sarah Dunning. It's nothing personal. Strictly business. And *very temporary*."

There was a slight pause, then Macklin said, "I see," although he didn't sound as though he particularly did. "So what can I do to help?"

It wasn't yet dark by the time that Sarah finally got back home, but she felt as though she'd been walking around for days. She'd been all right until she'd reached the safe, familiar surroundings of her broken-down house. Then everything had hit her at once. Someone very dear to her was in terrible danger. She was putting her own life in the hands of total strangers. She couldn't talk to her family about it. And she was sailing off on a fake honeymoon with a man who looked as if he'd been eating little girls like her for breakfast since he'd reached puberty.

She fell across her bed and closed her eyes. The dogs whined softly and licked her hand.

"It's okay, guys," she told them, her voice slurring softly as exhaustion overtook her. "I'm just going to close my eyes for a little while...."

The dogs paced around the bed, circled and lay down.

"Whoever you are, Alexander Sutter," Sarah murmured to herself sleepily. "I sure hope you're as good as Raymond Jones thinks you are."

Sarah drifted into a shallow, restless sleep haunted by a shadowy pair of annoyed black eyes and the mesmerizing memory of Alex Sutter's electrifying presence.

It was the scratching and whining of the dogs that finally awakened her. Night had fallen, and at first Sarah couldn't see a thing. She heard her two guard dogs pacing over to her bedroom doorway and growling softly. Groggily she sat up and tried to shake off the lingering muzziness of sleep. Outside she could hear a car engine being turned off, a door opening and closing and footsteps approaching the house. Whoever it was had a long, brisk stride. Sweet Pea was tied. The visitor wouldn't be stopped.

She slid off the bed and stumbled out to the living room, her dogs bounding silently ahead of her. The solid knock at the door was greeted by two bared set of teeth. Sarah put her hand on the knob. She peered through the peephole, but her eyes weren't focusing well yet and all she could see was a man's shadowy figure in the darkness.

"Who is it?" Sarah asked as she felt around for the front porch light switch on the wall next to her.

"Sutter."

Sarah relaxed and opened the door, telling the dogs, "It's okay. He's a friend." Light flooded the front porch illuminating Sutter as he walked inside.

Alex nodded, looking mildly impressed that he had been elevated to the category of "friend" as far as her guard dogs were concerned.

"Thanks," he said dryly. "Since I'm now a *friend*, don't you think you should finally introduce us?"

Sarah closed the door after him and followed him into the small living room. She noted with some annoyance that he seemed to feel quite at home in her house, even in the dark. He was casually looking around as if the place were newly his instead of longtime hers. Of course, maybe he automatically cased every place he went to, she thought darkly, recalling his occupation.

"The shepherd's name is Groton and the Labrador's name is Wiley," she replied.

Sutter squatted and held out his hand. The two dogs approached and thoroughly sniffed his wrists and fingers; then each graciously permitted him to scratch their ears and pat their heads. He grinned slightly and raised his eyes to hers.

"Groton?" he asked, playing with the German shepherd's ear. When Sarah nodded, he turned to the Labrador and said, "Then you must be Wiley, eh? Nice boys." He rose and walked over to turn on a light on the wall. "Are you trying to save on electricity?" he asked.

"I took a nap when I got back," she explained, feeling a renewal of antagonism. She frowned. "Can't you ask a question without being sarcastic?" she asked, more testily than she'd intended.

Sutter shrugged as he strolled around turning on lights here and there. "Usually," he admitted. He glanced at her, taking in her appearance in one all-encompassing look. She had a point. He usually didn't antagonize women. He managed them, very smoothly. But Sarah . . . Just driving to her house had annoyed him. He managed an olive-branch smile. "Sorry. Why don't you get dressed?"

She looked at him blankly. "I'm already dressed," she pointed out. Then she realized that in comparison to him, she was decidedly underdressed. He was wearing a suit. A fresh one, too. He'd changed since they'd parted earlier in the afternoon. Memory returned in a flood. The fake wedding. She glanced at the wall clock. "Oh! I guess we're dressing for the wedding pictures," she murmured fretfully.

Sutter aimed his index finger in her direction. "Very good, Sarah," he said. This time the gentle sarcasm had an underlying note akin to affection that took some of the sting out of it.

Sarah stared at him. It was the first time he'd called her Sarah, she realized. The seductive sound of his voice saying her name kept reverberating in her head. A barrier going down? Well, they *were* getting married. Even in a pretend marriage you could hardly go around calling your wife by her last name. And she could hardly go around calling him Mr. Sutter anymore, she realized, too. Alex. Why did it seem riskier to call him Alex?

Sarah shook off her fanciful thoughts and wondered if this sudden rescue attempt was causing disruption in his personal life. Had he had to explain his sudden departure to a woman? Poor woman. What a nerve-racking life-style to be involved with. She was probably worried sick every time he took off. Well, she'd be getting him back very soon. In the same condition he'd left her, unless Moreau saw through the charade.

Sutter was calmly looking Sarah over, taking note of her slightly oversize red sweater, faded jeans and generally rumpled appearance. And all the interesting shapes beneath.

"It doesn't matter to me," he told her, drawing her galloping thoughts back to the subject of getting dressed. "Personally I think you look very attractive as you are. Sort of...garden nymphish."

Sarah's mouth fell open. "Garden nymphish?" she repeated, appalled. "You think I look *garden nymphish*?" It sounded so...immature...frivolous...male-playthingish. Sarah wasn't about to be some man's erotic-fantasy plaything! She ignored the ripple of fierce curiosity that coursed through her. Of course she didn't want to be seen that way! Definitely not.

Sutter ignored her dismay and continued his sentence. "But Raymond was adamant and very specific. He wants us photographed in front of a justice of the peace looking as if we've just come from someplace elegant." He looked her over thoughtfully. Sarah wasn't exactly the elegant type. She was more the natural, clean, country-girl type, he decided. It was a little late to argue with Raymond about that, though, so he suggested, "Put on your favorite dress." He frowned. "You do own a dress?"

She stared at him as if she surely couldn't have heard correctly. "Of course I have a dress!" she said indignantly. What kind of a woman did he think she was anyhow? She caught her breath just in time to keep from launching into a blistering objection to his comment. She had two dresses, to be precise. And she just remembered what they looked like. Neither of them were the kind of thing a bride would be wearing. "When are we supposed to be . . . getting married?" she asked, rather more meekly and stalling for time as she tried to think of where she could find something suitable to wear on such short notice.

Sutter glanced at his watch. "In two hours. It will take about forty minutes to get to the justice of the peace from here, so you've got about an hour to get ready."

"Two hours," Sarah murmured, her heart sinking. She could forget shopping, obviously. "I won't need long." Not long at all, considering what was in her closet.

Five minutes later Sarah was standing in front of her open closet with Groton and Wiley sitting solemnly at her feet. All three were staring forlornly at her thinly hung clothes. There wasn't much to choose from. She hadn't bothered with dresses and flashy feminine wear since she'd taken over the business a few years ago. It wasn't that she didn't like nice clothes; she'd just been unwilling to spend her money that way. Other things had been more important to her, or simply more pressing in order to keep the business afloat.

There were a few classic items, of course—an attractive beige suit, a flashy red silk blouse with ruffles, a slinky little black dress, some neatly tailored wool slacks. And she had a couple of pairs of heels that could go with several outfits. But she didn't have anything that a woman would wear to get married in, unless she was being married by a bartender at a cocktail party.

She felt a firm hand on her shoulder and turned to come face-to-face with Alex Sutter. "You scared me," she breathed, wondering why her heart was still beating so fast now that she knew who was behind her. "Don't creep up on me like that."

"Sorry."

Their eyes met and held and Sarah watched as his jaw tightened almost imperceptibly. His eyes dropped to her lips. His dark brows drew together in a frown and he dropped his hand from her shoulder quite abruptly.

"Having trouble picking out a wedding dress?" he asked, dragging his eyes away from her lips to stare at the contents of the closet.

"I guess I am," she admitted. She swallowed and shook her head. "This just isn't going to look like a wedding picture, I'm afraid." She felt the heat from his body; he was standing so close they were nearly touching. And there was a subtle, spicy scent about him, like after-shave.

Alex reached out and pulled the little black dress from the rack, holding it up to her and looking her over with an experienced eye. A slow grin spread across his face and a soft gleam settled in his dark eyes. Sarah felt a tingle of fear and anticipation in the pit of her stomach.

"Stop looking at me like that," she complained sharply.

"Like what?"

"Like you're a hungry wolf and I'm the rabbit you're hunting for dinner."

"Is that how I look at you?" he asked interestedly.

Sarah glared at him. "Yes."

Sutter shrugged unrepentantly. "Wear this," he suggested. "That's the kind of dress a woman would be wearing if she married me." He tossed it casually across her rumpled bed, looked around her room and then, realizing she was still standing there staring at him, he glanced pointedly toward her bathroom. "I thought you said this wouldn't take long?" he challenged her.

Sarah, who'd been wondering what kind of a woman would marry him in a drop-dead black cocktail dress, caught hold of herself and jerked open her drawers. "I'm not used to having

a strange man in my bedroom while I plan what I'm wearing,"
she pointed out.

He seemed amused to hear that, which didn't help her simmering temper at all. The fact that she didn't know why she was
so annoyed with him made it even worse. She snatched tiny
black silk panties, a strapless black bra, a black satin half-slip
that only reached halfway down her thigh and black hose em-
broidered with an enticing sprinkling of tiny black stars. Her
cheeks were dark pink with embarrassment, but she refused to
try to hide her intimate garments. They were both adults. There
was nothing to be nervous and uptight about. She was sure he'd
seen women's undergarments before. Many times. Of course,
Sarah wasn't used to displaying hers, but she tried to be blasé
about it. She refused to hear any more of Sutter's comments
about her being naive.

Sutter was only mildly curious, it was true. He'd seen enough
women's lingerie over the years to more than dull his interest in
that area unless he was personally taking it off a woman. The
Spartan contents of Sarah's closet, on the other hand, were revealing and therefore of greater interest to him. She had obviously selected clothes needed for working with her dogs, and
little enough of that.

The dogs followed Sarah to the bathroom and lay curled
protectively in front of the closed door. When Alex stepped
around them, they growled, although this time they didn't
bother to raise their heads. He lifted a brow in amusement.
Friends apparently merely got threatened to a less violent de-
gree, he thought. The dogs were still wary of him and very
protective of her. That was just as well. She'd need all the protection she could get for the next few days.

Alex stood in the middle of the dark kitchen listening to the
muffled sound of the shower running in the bathroom. The
view through the windowpane into the dark fields and woods
outside was not particularly inviting. She lived in a very lonely
place, he thought. It was not the kind of place that he'd have
expected a young woman would want to be.

It obviously was more than she could keep up on her own,
too. The buildings were sadly in need of repairs. It was probably a miracle the pipes worked and that she still had safe running water. He listened to the water and visualized Sarah

standing under the shower. If she weren't so annoying, he would have enjoyed certain aspects of this assignment. He wondered how she would react if he made a pass at her. A smile curved his lips. It might be interesting to find out.

An owl hooted and Sutter curbed his thoughts. Some things were better left unexplored, and he had the feeling that Sarah Dunning fell into that category, at least as far as he was concerned. She certainly seemed stubborn and independent. He hoped those qualities would be enough to see her through this.

The shower cut off, and a short while later he saw her dash down the hall, wrapped in an old yellow terry-cloth robe. The robe was wearing thin, however, and he could see the outline of a dark half-slip beneath it. His gaze slid down and he couldn't help but admire her black-stockinged legs.

He wandered back into her living room and methodically inspected her meager possessions. He was here to get as thoroughly acquainted with Sarah Dunning as possible within the limited time they had before leaving. As he leafed through an old high-school yearbook, the image of Sarah clad in black lingerie leaped unbidden to his mind. Feeling warm, he loosened his tie a little. Maybe his problem wasn't just jet lag, he thought grimly. Hell.

He reached for one of her photograph albums and thumbed through it. As her "husband," he'd be expected to know more about her and her family than Jones's men could scrape together for a report in a few days. He'd ask her about them again tonight. Before and after the "wedding."

When Sarah joined him, however, he almost forgot she had a family to discuss. She wasn't beautiful, exactly. So what was it that had him staring at her as if he were a man who'd never seen a woman before? he wondered, annoyed at himself. That fresh, clean-scrubbed face of hers with just a little blush and lipstick wasn't what you saw on magazine covers. So why did it make his body temperature rise a notch? She looked good in the dress, but he'd seen women in less that hadn't made him want to... To what? He wasn't sure he wanted to know the answer to that.

His eyes followed the dress's plunging neckline as it fell from Sarah's shoulders down to the provocative swell of her breasts. The sultry black silk was swathed and folded at the waist and clung discreetly to her small hips and shapely legs. As she walked nervously around the room, her knees peeked out from behind the curved slit in the front of the dress. Sutter dragged his eyes back upward. When his eyes reached hers, he smiled.

Only this smile was different. Sarah couldn't quite put her finger on exactly what was different, but something was. "Are you sure this is going to be okay?" she asked uneasily, nervously gesturing to the dress. "I feel like I'm something the devil took from a cocktail hour and threw at some unsuspecting man as part of a deal for his soul."

Sutter wasn't sure he liked her analogy. "You may be right," he muttered. "You look terrific," he said, dismissing the subject as he searched the coat closet for the one wrap that looked as if it was intended for going out. He removed it and held it for her to put on. Their bodies brushed as she slid her arms into the sleeves and pulled the coat closed. For a moment, he stood behind her, unmoving. She smelled fresh and clean. She'd used some perfume, too. A soft, sexy scent. But then he was beginning to think anything might smell sexy on Sarah Dunning.

Sarah glanced up at him questioningly. When she saw the dark look in his eyes, she became very still. A ripple of unease flowed over her body and pooled deep inside her; she moved a little away. She suddenly didn't want him to touch her, not in any way. And at the same time she knew that that wasn't what she wanted at all. She wanted him to put his hands on her, everywhere, in every way.

"Shall we go?" he suggested, breaking the silent tension between them as he nodded curtly in the direction of her front door.

"Yes." The sooner the better.

Chapter 5

Forty minutes later they were walking out of an elevator in a five-story neoclassical building. They looked more like two people going to their execution than to their wedding. At least, that was what Raymond Jones thought they looked like as he caught sight of them and hurried forward to offer welcome.

Sutter bemusedly endured Raymond's manly slap on the back, while Sarah looked as if she'd swallowed something disagreeable and was trying not to show it as he gingerly hugged her a few seconds later. Raymond's wife, looking just like her picture, had come to help make Sarah feel more comfortable with everything. "Raymond thought you might feel better about it if another normal person were around," she said with a soft laugh.

"Normal meaning someone not in their line of work?" Sarah guessed.

"Um-hm." Cecilia Jones put her arm around Sarah and drew her into a nearby room with a frosted-glass door and justice of the peace emblazoned on it in scarlet letters.

Sarah swallowed. She felt as if things were closing in on her. Going too fast. Everything was becoming too real.

She knew the marriage wouldn't be legal. They'd explained that to her. Alex and she hadn't applied for a marriage license. No matter who they said their vows before, they wouldn't be legally married. All the same, it felt strangely believable to her.

She glanced over her shoulder and saw Alex deep in conversation with Raymond and two other cloak-and-dagger types. She straightened her back and stopped thinking about it. Just do what has to be done, she told herself philosophically. And stop thinking about it.

The justice of the peace was a little, blue-haired lady with spectacles. As soon as everyone had finally gathered in front of her desk, she smiled cheerfully and looked at Sarah. Her silvery eyebrows raised at the daring little black dress.

"A bride in black?" She laughed. "Am I presiding over a funeral?"

Sarah paled and glanced at Alex. He didn't appear perturbed by the misplaced attempt at humor. Sarah had never been superstitious, but under the circumstances, that offhand remark upset her. She did look more like someone going to a garish funeral than to a first wedding. She dearly hoped that wasn't a portent of what was to come. Why had the woman said something stupid like that?

"Smile!" urged a man wearing baggy trousers and a battered baseball cap. He was sporting a camera with a big flash attachment. The photographer. Sarah smiled.

"Let's just get through the formalities," the justice of the peace was saying. "You two—" she eyed Alex and Sarah "—stand side by side here in front of me. That ought to make a nice shot, Raymond, whether you use it or not." The photographer scrambled into position, shooting as the mood struck him. "Dearly beloved: We are gathered . . ."

Sarah barely heard the words as the justice of the peace briskly trotted through the pro forma ceremony. It all seemed very mechanical, including the touch of Alex's hand as he slipped a ring on her finger. She didn't look at it. They'd measured her finger for a ring at Raymond's office that afternoon, and someone had probably grabbed a plain gold band at the nearest jewelry store.

"I bet most brides don't feel like I do right now," she said, trying to laugh about it.

"Don't be so sure," Alex said.

She looked at him. "You think they feel shell-shocked, numb and as if this is all happening to someone else?"

"I wouldn't be a bit surprised." He was looking like his old slightly cynical, amused self.

Raymond, standing behind them, laughed. "That's how the groom feels, Alex." He laughed, then grunted as his wife shoved a sharp elbow into his ribs. He gave her an apologetic look. "Not me, honey. Other grooms. Not me."

The photographer, chewing gum a mile a minute, was beginning to look irritated. "You said you wanted some hot kisses," he reminded Raymond.

Jones choked. His wife giggled. Alex lifted an eyebrow. Sarah looked at the photographer as if she wouldn't have minded if he'd fallen through the floor and disappeared forever.

His gum snapping faltered as he caught her hostile expression. "Sorry, Miss . . . uh, Mrs., but that's what he said."

Alex pulled her around to face him. "You *have* been kissed before, haven't you?" he asked, as if unconvinced that she had.

Sarah's glare shifted from the rumpled photographer to the tall, smooth-talking man she'd just "married." "Many times, I can assure you," she said as witheringly as she could. She threw her arms around his neck and let her lips hover just above his. "And I trust this won't be your first time, either," she added.

He laughed and shook his head as he drew her close. "Now what kind of a kiss would look convincing, do you think? Since we're both so experienced, we ought to be able to come up with some pretty good ones. Don't you agree?" he murmured.

He was letting his lips move against hers as he talked, hoping to relax her. He felt her stiffen in his arms the moment the photographer shifted position. He wished they didn't have to stage this. Holding her close may not have helped her relax, but it certainly made him more than comfortable with the idea of kissing. Suddenly he could think of nothing he'd rather do than give Sarah Dunning a kiss. A long, slow, how-do-you-like-to-do-this kind of kiss.

He was ready to do it, audience or not, but Sarah wasn't ready. She was shy. He thought she was a little unsure of him.

This was going to be difficult for her. She'd have to relax if the photo was going to be any good. He wondered if it would be easier for her if she felt she had control of the kissing. Maybe then she'd relax and give it her best effort.

"Forget about these voyeurs," he suggested in a low, amused voice. "You said you could playact if you had to, well, here's your first chance to prove it, Sarah." He looked down into her wide, brown eyes and pulled her up against his chest until she was at his eye level. He lowered his gaze to her half-parted lips and watched her tongue nervously wet those tempting surfaces. "Kiss me," he challenged her in a low voice that was as much a caress as a command. "I dare you."

Sarah's world slowly dissolved; she was only vaguely aware of anything or anyone else around them. There was just Alex Sutter standing toe-to-toe with her, waiting for her to respond to his husky taunt. His eyes were like a raven's, she thought, piercing and black, yet now the piercing was a sweeter, more compelling kind. His black eyes were really a very dark, chocolate brown. Standing this close, she saw them clearly for the first time. *Beautiful, beautiful brown eyes...* The haunting old melody played silently in her mind. *I'll never love blue eyes again.*

She felt his hand slide a few inches down her back to rest near her waist. "I dare you," she heard him whisper again, and Sarah felt his sweet, warm breath on her mouth, making her hungry for his touch on her lips. When he'd first spoken, she had realized that he was going to try to guide her through this awkward intimacy, but then the rational part of her gave way to an overwhelming curiosity. What would it be like if this man truly wanted her? What would it be like to be kissed by Alex Sutter? Mysterious, experienced, suave Alex Sutter?

"I'm not afraid of you," she lied. She pressed closer to him and looped her arms around him more comfortably. Something glittered in his eyes and Sarah swallowed. It was like taking dynamite in your arms. Fear and the thrill of living dangerously raced through her. "There's nothing very hard about kissing," she declared as steadily as she could manage. Why was it suddenly so hard to breathe? Why was everything fading away? How had Alex's face become so close, his strong arms so all enveloping, his hard lips so softly warm against hers? And yet he waited for her, tempting her to finish what was so agonizingly well begun. "I've been kissing since spin the bottle in sixth grade," she murmured in a mesmerized whisper against his lips. Ah, his lips. That was where the electricity was coming from now. His lips. And his arms and his eyes and every strong, well-knit inch of him.

Sarah tilted her head back and pressed her mouth fully against his. Sweet, rolling pleasure flooded her. Ah, the relief of it. And then heat built and she tightened her arms around him and slanted her mouth against his to seal the intimate bond more satisfactorily. The warm fire of it poured through her body and she relaxed into his strengthening embrace. Sarah opened her mouth a little and the pleasure of his immediate, intimate possession made her yield a little more. There was strength and tenderness and a simmering fire in the kiss, in being in his arms.

Where have you been all my life? Why has it taken so long to find this yearning, this peace, this heart-stopping pleasure? Sarah was only distantly aware that she shouldn't be reacting to Alex Sutter with such dangerous thoughts. And as he folded her closer still, kissing her even more thoroughly, she stopped thinking of anything at all.

The photographer was shooting pictures, but to Sarah it no longer mattered. She was only vaguely aware of the rapid snapping and brilliant flashes of light. The camera's actions were totally eclipsed by the flashes of fire and light bursting to life within her.

Somewhere a man began carefully clearing his throat. Sarah felt Alex begin to relax his arms and ease the intimacy of the kiss. She had to drag herself away from the awful temptation to tighten her arms and keep kissing him anyway. As a result of the effort it took to control herself, she jerked back from him as if she'd been singed. She opened her eyes and blinked at his tie a few seconds, recovering her dignity before facing him. What had happened to Sarah, the girl whom men couldn't arouse? she wondered in dismay. If spin the bottle had ever been even remotely like this, she'd have a dozen kids by now. Her cheeks warmed in embarrassment and she forced herself to look at the stranger who had just burned away the ice around her heart. He was staring down at her, and to Sarah's surprise, he looked stunned, as if he no longer recognized her. Then his expression cleared and a familiar, mocking look appeared in its place.

"Not bad for your first performance," he conceded.

Sarah blushed darker. Sutter *knew* she hadn't been performing. She was certain of that. She'd been responding to him, and he was sophisticated enough to be fully aware of that. He'd made her respond. Boy, had he known how, she thought in mournful alarm.

"Thank you," she muttered. "I told you there was nothing to kissing. Any schoolchild knows how."

He took a half step away and lifted an eyebrow skeptically. "I guess so," he agreed. "Spin the bottle must have been a hell of a lot more fun at your school than it was a mine, though."

Sarah choked.

"I doubt that," she said uncomfortably.

She nervously fluffed her hair, a feminine gesture she hadn't used in years. She put it down to female hormones suddenly roused by Alex's expert kissing ability. Down, hormones, she commanded. This isn't the right time for you. Go back to sleep. She glanced around the room to see the photographer checking over his lenses and stuffing his gear in his bag. People were beginning to drift toward the door. The blue-haired justice was locking her desk and reaching for her coat on its stand behind her chair.

Alex walked away to pick up their coats from two men standing by the door, leaving Sarah with Jones and his wife. Raymond looked rather peculiar, she thought. As if he'd suddenly had new information that he hadn't expected and wasn't certain what to do with.

"Are you all right, Raymond?" she asked, concerned.

"Yes," he replied, frowning slightly as he stared at her. "I'm fine. I just hope you are." He glanced at Alex who was returning with their coats and Sarah's purse.

"Well, if you got enough 'hot shots,' I'm ready to go," Sarah said briskly. Ready to go was a tremendous understatement, though. She slipped into her coat, trying to ignore her awareness of Alex's closeness as he held it for her. "Do you have any last-minute advice?" she asked, trying to focus on Raymond and forget about Alex Sutter.

Raymond glanced at Alex and then back at Sarah. "Uh . . . not just now. If we think of anything else, we'll be in touch after you get down to the Caymans." He chewed on his lower lip as he escorted them to the door.

On the elevator ride to the bottom, there was utter silence. No one seemed able to think of a thing to say, yet everyone was obviously nervous, shifting from one foot to the other, fidgeting, clearing their throats, staring intently at the lights flashing from one floor number to the next.

When they finally reached Sutter's silver-gray sports car, Sarah was relieved to see the last of them.

"Good luck," Raymond said, just before he closed Sarah's door and stepped back to stand on the curb to wave goodbye.

"We'll certainly be needing it," Alex muttered. He gunned the engine and shot down the open street.

Sarah smiled and waved at the receding figures. Her smile faded quickly, though. "Any words of advice?" she asked Alex.

He glanced at her. "Yeah. Don't kiss me like that again."

She turned sharply. "What was wrong with the way I kissed you?" she asked defensively, appalled to feel her cheeks warming in embarrassment.

Nothing. Absolutely nothing. "You ought to know," he growled. "You said you were an expert on kisses," he reminded her grimly. He shifted the car into a higher gear. His jaw was fixed and he was staring into the night-darkened road ahead.

Sarah studied his chiseled profile. "You aren't usually this enigmatic," she pointed out.

He shot a brief, scowling glance in her direction. "There's nothing enigmatic about what I just said. Don't kiss me again like that. That's pretty plain, don't you think?"

Sarah crossed her legs, clutched her purse and seethed. She was annoyed, confused and a little hurt by his rejection. She knew that she should have been relieved, and she was upset that she couldn't feel relief at all. So he didn't want her kissing him again, did he?

"Well, how do you want me to kiss you, then?" she asked angrily.

"I'll let you know the next time the situation arises," he told her in an unusually tight voice.

"Fine," She lifted her chin defensively. "I just did what you wanted me to," she pointed out indignantly. "You *dared* me to kiss you, remember? You wanted something convincing."

"I certainly got it."

"You don't have to be sarcastic."

"I don't think either of us would appreciate the alternative."

Sarah heard the underlying threat in his voice and fell silent. He'd been affected by that kiss just as she had. And he didn't like it one bit. She closed her eyes in misery. "This is just great," she said mournfully. "And we're going to be together for days."

"Try not to think about it."

"Thanks. Is that the best advice you can come up with?"

"You're welcome. And yes, it is. If you've got better advice, I'm willing to hear it."

Sarah, unfortunately, couldn't think of a thing. "I'll work on it," she muttered darkly.

"You do that." He made the turn onto the road leading back to Sarah's house and checked his watch. "The plane leaves in three hours. You've got about an hour to grab what you're planning to take."

Sarah pulled a slip of paper out of her purse. "I've already got my checklist," she pointed out. "Don't worry about a thing."

Alex fell silent. He was going to worry about everything. That wasn't like him. Damn it. He was used to working alone. He didn't like having to do the thinking for both of them. He didn't want her life hanging in the balance if something went wrong. Damn Raymond Jones. Why in the hell couldn't they have come up with another solution to the electronic monitoring problem? He focused on the bony shadows of deciduous trees overhanging the unlit country road. What was done, was done. There was nothing to do but get on with it.

As they pulled into Sarah's drive, she turned to him and murmured, "By the way, Raymond didn't tell you about Wiley, did he?"

Sutter pulled in front of her house and killed the engine.

"No. What about Wiley?" he asked suspiciously.

Before Sarah could answer, a man approached the car. Sutter was out and facing him before Sarah could open her door. The man held his hands up, palms forward, and grinned harmlessly.

"I'm Cal," he said. Wiley bounded up behind him and wagged his tail in greeting. "Jones got me on loan from the army." He was the military dog trainer temporarily assigned to take care of Sarah's dogs while she was gone. "Glad to see ya."

Sarah scrambled out of the car and joined them. Sutter relaxed and turned back toward Sarah.

"What about Wiley?" Sutter asked impatiently.

Sarah braced herself. "Wiley's going with us." She was standing there in glittering black, her coat hanging open, her hands clenched at her sides in determination, waiting to argue with him about it to the bitter end, if necessary.

Sutter stared at her for a long minute, made a few choice comments about Raymond's parentage and put his hands on his hips as he stared at the tongue-lolling Labrador at his side. He looked at Sarah after a long minute, and he was frowning as fiercely as he had when he'd told her she was too inexperienced to go on a mission like this.

"Why?" he demanded.

Sarah was surprised. She'd thought he'd start off with a simply roared *no*. Her fingers uncurled and she caressed the Labrador's silky black ear. "Wiley and I are partners," she explained. "He's trained to defend me and to attack or guard whatever I want him to. He'd be a terrific addition to our team." Sarah swallowed. "Besides, I had a long talk with Raymond, and I know one of the things I can't afford to feel is fear. I'll feel safer if Wiley is along. If I feel safer, it'll be easier for me to pretend that I feel safe. That ought to be pretty crucial to our getting onto the island and getting off it alive."

Sutter fingered his keys and considered her demand. He didn't relish the added complication. They had more than enough as it was:

"Why didn't Raymond say something to me about this at the justice of the peace's chambers?" he asked angrily.

Sarah smothered a nervous laugh. "I think he was afraid to."

Sutter's dark expression grew even more forbidding. "He certainly should have been," he growled. "Damn it. First he wants an amateur along. Now a dog. This is turning into a three-ring circus."

Sarah laughed. "Wiley would lay down his life for me," she explained, on a more serious note. "And he'll protect you, too, on my command. He'll protect you to the death, Sutter."

Alex stared at her long and hard. He didn't like it, but he could understand Sarah's reasoning. He imagined that if he'd been in her position, he might have suggested the same thing. Her dogs were her weapons. She wanted to take one with her. He recalled her opening reason—to feel safer.

"You don't feel safe with me?" he asked neutrally.

Sarah was rather ambivalent about that. She did in some ways. She chose to be less than honest with him. "No. Not particularly."

There was a long, taut silence as Sutter turned over the possibilities mentally. The dog would be a nuisance in the water after they sank their boat, but it was conceivable that the Labrador would add to their credibility. Who would take a dog on a boat if they were planning on sinking it? Or planning to escape through the water later? If Moreau had doubts about he and Sarah taking a cruise in the midst of their honeymoon, perhaps the dog along would be a convincing touch. It was . . . domestic.

The more he thought about it, the more he was inclined to let the dog come along. Besides, if Moreau struck up a conversation about Sarah's dog, he might ease into some comments about his own, which might prove useful to them in planning the details of their escape. It might offer the excuse for a tour of the island and give him a chance to survey the guards and Moreau's dogs.

It was a long shot, but then the whole mission was a long shot, in Alex's opinion. If it wasn't for the dangerous consequences, Alex would never have agreed to it. The consequences were real, and Moreau was real. There wasn't really much of a choice.

Sarah was staring at him with an expression bordering on hostile determination. The sparkle radiating from her made him temporarily forget his advice that she not kiss him. He was sorely tempted to pull her into his arms and grind his mouth against hers in a kiss that would break the growing tension between them and force the warmth back into her eyes. That brought to mind one other good reason for taking Wiley along. It might remind him to keep his hands off of her. After that exquisitely nonplatonic kiss in the justice of the peace's chambers, he could use all the reminding he could get.

Sutter frowned. "He's trained to defend you?"

"Yes. No one can touch me if I tell him to keep them away."

Sutter nodded. That could come in handy, all right. Assuming they got that far in the plan, of course. He glanced at his watch. They were running out of time arguing about it. Raymond had obviously already agreed to it, so he must have seen some potential also. The next time he saw Raymond, however, he intended to tell him what he thought of his cowardice in not telling him about the dog face-to-face. To hell with it. What was one more amateur at this point? At least the four-legged amateur acted like a pro.

"All right," Alex agreed. "Bring him along." He ignored her dropping jaw and startled brown eyes. "Now, if you haven't thought of anything else...?" He paused significantly. Her jaw snapped shut and she shook her head in the negative. He nodded and told her "Then let's go. We've got a plane to catch."

Chapter 6

We'll be landing in ten minutes." It was Alex's enticing tenor-baritone voice. His announcement was accompanied by his slight jostling of her shoulder. Sarah stretched and struggled awake.

"Ten minutes," she mumbled as she pulled the blanket off her and sleepily refolded it. Outside all she could see was bright blue Caribbean water all the way to the horizon. They were landing in ten minutes? "Where?"

Alex reached across her and pointed ahead of them. Looking through the small window at an angle, she was eventually able to make out a small, very flat island. It looked about as big as a postage stamp. She hoped the waves were small. A big one could probably wash right over it.

"It's . . . small," she observed, surprised.

"You've never been here before?" Alex asked, equally surprised.

Sarah shook her head. "No. Gabrielle has lived here for several years, but the few times I've come down to dive with her, we've rendezvoused on other islands, usually the American Virgins or in the Florida keys."

"You've dived, then?" he asked. It wasn't a casual question.

"Yes. Down to a hundred and fifty feet." She watched as the flat island spread out, growing larger before her eyes as the plane approached in a straight-on descent to the landing field. She tore her eyes away from the spectacular view of the pale aqua water surrounding the island and looked at Sutter. "Are we going to have to use diving equipment?" she asked, frowning. "Raymond didn't mention that."

Alex was noncommittal. "I don't know. It's not in the plans, but you never know what you'll end up having to do in situations like this." He shrugged. "When you're surrounded by an ocean, it never hurts to be prepared to use scuba gear." He lifted a dark brow slightly. "I don't suppose Wiley knows how to snorkel?"

Sarah gave him a flat look. "No. But he's trained to use a flotation jacket custom-made for him." She smiled sweetly. "And I remembered to pack that, too, for your information."

"He'll appreciate it."

Sarah glanced at her watch and bit her lip. She looked at the great empty sea again. "She's out there somewhere, isn't she?"

Sutter didn't reply.

Sarah forced herself to ask the question that had come to mind. "Do you think Gabrielle is...still alive?" Her hands were clenched in her lap, balled together like two warring fists.

"Yes."

The plane engines droned more loudly. The plane began to skim over land. One-story buildings were scattered about in clusters beneath them. The airport's runways sprawled in welcome.

"How can you be so sure?" Sarah asked.

"I checked." He grinned slightly at her doubtful expression as she swiveled to look at him suspiciously. "We've been getting information every day from people down there. It's not just my wishful thinking, if that's what's worrying you. I wouldn't tell you a lie, Sarah."

She wanted to believe that, and for a long moment Sarah gazed into his eyes. She wished she could see his soul. When he called her Sarah, it just made things harder. Something softened inside her. She thought she must be losing her marbles under the pressure. She looked away. *Sarah. Sarah.* It had been her name all her life. Why did it sound different when he said it?

"I want to believe that," she murmured seriously. "That you wouldn't lie to me. Not even to be kind." She felt his hand cover hers, warming her cold, stiff fingers. She awkwardly attempted to loosen her hand and slip from beneath his. She felt embarrassed taking comfort from him. "We're partners," she said awkwardly. "Don't worry about me. I'm okay." Her pride drove a little more force into her wriggling fingers, but she found that Alex merely tightened his hold. He wouldn't let her go.

"We're on our honeymoon, sweetheart," he murmured in her ear. "And we're about to land and start acting like it. We might as well start getting into the role now."

Sarah laughed a little. "Sorry. I forgot." *I thought you were trying to comfort me. How stupid.*

"Besides," he drawled, "landings always make me nervous. If you hold my hand, it'll help."

Sarah looked at him in surprise. He didn't look the least bit nervous to her. She frowned. "I'll bet you've never been nervous about anything in your life," she said under her breath.

He looked mildly offended and stretched out his legs a little. "If I'm not nervous, then why am I more relaxed when you hold my hand?"

She looked down at their hands. "You're holding mine. I'm not holding yours."

He grinned and laced his hand with hers. "You are now."

Sarah stared at her left hand, entwined in his, and for the first time noticed the wedding band on her ring finger. It wasn't the plain gold band she'd expected to be there. It was a gold band embedded with four respectably sized diamonds. Her mouth fell open in shock.

"Are those real?" she asked, shaking her head as if they couldn't be, although her eyes kept insisting they were.

"If they're not, somebody's swindled the insurance company for a bundle," Alex said in amusement.

"I can't wear this," she protested. "What if it falls off in the ocean or..." She tried to free her hand from his, but he wouldn't let her go.

"Sit still and leave the ring alone. An expensive ring looks more convincing than a cheap one. It looks more permanent."

Sarah leaned back in the seat. "I suppose you have a point," she murmured unhappily. "But don't come after me for the money if anything happens to it."

Sutter was grinning again. "Don't worry about it."

"And please don't tell me how much it's insured for," she breathed prayerfully.

"My lips are sealed," he swore, trying not to laugh.

The wheels bumped and screeched as the big plane set down. Engines roared, wing flaps lifted and Sarah felt herself being pulled forward slightly by the jet's braking action. She clenched her hands as anticipation rushed through her veins. They'd arrived at Owen Roberts airport. It was a little after ten in the morning. They were getting closer. Danger was getting closer. Her palms felt cold.

"I guess this is where we get off," Sarah said, trying to laugh at her limp joke as the jet lumbered down the runway to the terminal.

Alex looked heavenward. "I'm putting up with your amateur status, your dog and your spin the bottle kissing technique, but for God's sake don't try to make me laugh at your lame jokes!"

Pink cheeked from his reference to her kissing ability, Sarah unbuckled her seat belt and strove to be philosophical. "Just trying to relieve the tension," she explained. She gave him an apologetic smile that failed to soften his forbidding expression.

His gaze dropped to her mouth; he frowned a little more.

"Come on," he muttered, getting up from his seat. "Let's go."

Sarah had only a brief glimpse of the island of Grand Cayman, most of it from the airport, the rest from the air. As had been obvious from the plane, it was very flat. Scrubby, flowering bushes and gently swaying palm trees were scattered across the grassy lands and along the island's few narrow roads. The buildings were mostly low to the ground and of square or rectangular construction. They looked as if they were made of solid cement blocks coated with the colonial pink, blue or white plaster commonly seen in the Caribbean basin.

Alex, a garment bag slung over one shoulder, guided her through the short immigration and custom lines. As they showed their identification and chatted with officials, he casually draped an arm around her shoulders and smiled down at her as if he were a man utterly fascinated by his enticing female companion.

"Your wife!" exclaimed one of the customs inspectors in surprise. His light brown face was immediately swathed in smiles. "Congratulations, Alex! I never thought . . ." The man caught himself before he could say something that might prove offensive to Sarah. He smiled at her apologetically and closed her bag. "Sorry, Mrs. Sutter. But you certainly caught a fish that no one thought could be hooked."

Sarah smiled cheerfully and gazed at Alex with an expression she hoped approximated rapt adoration. "Believe me, I know just what you mean."

Alex tightened his hold on her shoulders and pulled her away. "Come on, *darling*. We've got better things to do than stand in the airport and talk to Randal." The intimate look in his eyes left no doubt about what he meant.

The customs inspector's chuckles brought an even deeper blush to Sarah's cheeks. As soon as they were out of the man's sight, Sarah indignantly dropped her bag on Alex's foot. He grimaced and fixed her with a hostile smile as she lifted it back up again. "I'm sorry, *darling*," Sarah said unapologetically. "I guess I lost my grip."

"Right after I lost my head by suggesting we head for bed?" he guessed as they walked into the main part of the small terminal.

"Right about then," she agreed cheerfully.

"How in the hell do you want your new husband to look at you?" he demanded, forcing a smile between gritted teeth as he limped along.

"Not like that," she muttered. "Not in public."

"All right," he agreed tightly. "But I'm not a eunuch and don't expect me to act like one. I'll save those looks for the bedroom."

Sarah stumbled and would have lost her balance if it hadn't been for Alex's strong arm.

"Did I say something unsettling?" he asked unsympathetically.

"Not at all," Sarah lied in self-defense. "Bedroom. Bedroom. Bedroom. See? It's just a word. No problem." *No problem?*

Alex laughed and shook his head. "I'm glad *you* feel that way," he said fervently. He certainly wished that he could say the same about himself. Sleeping next to her in the plane, feeling her warmth, smelling her scent, seeing the curves and shapes of her, had done nothing to lessen his memory of that spin-the-bottle kiss. Bedroom. He had to think about something else. Bedroom. Bedroom. Bedroom.

A man in a short-sleeved airport security uniform approached them and explained that Wiley would have to be loaded directly onto the next plane. He wouldn't be allowed out of his cage till then.

Over the man's shoulder, Sarah noticed a baggage attendant wheeling an animal travel cage toward them.

"Wiley!" she exclaimed, running around the security man to kneel beside the dog's cage.

The Labrador whined excitedly and clawed desperately at the cage floor. While Wiley eagerly shoved his wet nose against the wire door and frantically licked Sarah's hand through the mesh, Alex settled a few details with the crisp-sounding Caymanian official.

"Come on," Alex told her as he turned abruptly back to her. He pulled Sarah to her feet. "We've got an hour before the flight to Cayman Brac. They'll take care of the dog. We'd better get something to eat and check in with Raymond."

Sarah gazed forlornly over her shoulder and called out, "'Bye, Wiley. We'll get you out soon. Don't worry." Alex, holding her by the arm, firmly pulled her around a corner and she lost sight of her faithful friend. Her heart sank. "'Bye, Wiley."

It didn't take Alex long to find out that Raymond had nothing new to report. That taken care of, food was the next item of business on Alex's list. Sarah thought that lunch probably would have tasted much better if she could have felt even a little hungry. After pushing her pasta salad around her plate a few times, she shoved it away and gave up.

It was easier to watch the departing and arriving lines of passengers and the glimpses of life on the island afforded by the airport than it was to swallow food.

People were walking along the roadside. Small cars traveled down the airport roads. The people, whether residents or tourists, looked relaxed, relatively unhurried and casually dressed in cotton clothing suitable to the island's year-round warm climate. The island's atmosphere, like its clothes, might not have been as vividly colorful as some other areas of the Caribbean, but it projected a safe, stable image. These were not a people who had been subjugated under a colonial rule. These were not the embittered grandchildren of plantation slaves. They were a free and seafaring folk moving into the postindustrial age with a relaxed and appealing dignity.

Of course, there were also those who looked as if they were flying through on international business, heading straight from Geneva, London or Miami into George Town to pay a visit to one of the sixteen thousand banks on the small, reef-encircled tax haven.

"Do you live here much of the year?" Sarah asked Alex, who was lost in his own thoughts as they finished their coffee.

"I come and go."

She smiled. He certainly avoided being informative. "I suppose it's a terrific financial advantage to live here."

He nodded and smiled slightly. "Do you know how the Caymans acquired the blessings of avoiding taxation?"

"No. How?"

"By saving the lives of His Majesty's sailors when their ship struck a reef and was sinking several generations ago."

Sarah brightened. "What a noble reason. I had no idea."

Alex smiled cynically. "I'm sure a lot of people benefiting from that act of heroism certainly don't deserve it." He shrugged. "But that's the way the world turns. The courage of one man often reaps benefits for other, less deserving ones."

Sarah tilted her head considerably. "You sound as if you have a personal experience in mind," she said softly, watching his hardened expression and the anger of his eyes.

He pushed his chair back and put some Caymanian money on the table.

"I think we'd better go back," he said, abruptly terminating their conversation. He pointed to a plane coming in for a landing. "I think that's going to be our next plane."

Sarah frowned as she followed along. He *did* have a personal experience in mind. Maybe more than one. She wondered what it was. When it had happened. Why it had left him hard and cynical.

Time passed at a slower pace on Grand Cayman, and it was almost two hours before the small jet took off, taking them to their next destination. One of the stewardesses knew Alex and amiably chatted with them between takeoff and landing. Sarah was fascinated by the woman's lovely accent, a pleasant mixture of Jamaican lilt, Scottish burr and British clip rolled together to sound purely and uniquely Caymanian.

When they arrived at Cayman Brac, one of the two small islands that comprised the Caymans, Sarah found herself repeating a phrase from earlier in the day. She stared pensively through the window of the plane at the compact mass rising slightly above the glistening sea.

"It looks... very small," she murmured, thinking it actually looked a *whole lot* smaller than Grand Cayman. On the other hand, it *did* jut comfortingly higher above the water than the larger island had.

She could see buildings clustered near long ribbons of lovely white-sand beaches kissed by pale aqua water. Most of the structures looked fairly new. Well-kept lawns, flowering bougainvillea, hibiscus and periwinkle wandered in flattering backdrop around the stark-white limestone and cement houses. Here and there a palm-thatched roof appeared, giving an added tropical touch to the atmosphere.

"Do they get blown away in hurricanes down here?" she asked worriedly. In the distance she saw what looked like a school. There were children here. Families.

"Some do," Alex conceded. He wasn't particularly interested in discussing the islands at the moment. He was thinking about the details of the plan. Supplies had to be checked, the boat okayed, Sarah and Wiley prepared psychologically for what was to come. The small landing strip on the Cayman Brac airport grew larger as the plane descended. The moment the wheels touched down, Alex had his hand at his seat belt.

"Welcome to Cayman Brac," said the cinnamon-skinned stewardess in the lilting brogue of the islands. "We hope you've enjoyed your trip with us, and that you'll be travelin' again with us soon."

Her black eyes and curly black hair gave her a uniquely Caymanian appearance. Sarah glanced surreptitiously at Alex, watching his nearly black eyes, his dark hair with a hint of curl about the ears.

"Something wrong?" he asked, spearing her with the same dark eyes she'd been staring at.

Sarah cleared her throat. "I just was thinking that you look a little like some of the Caymanians."

His mouth softened into the merest semblance of a smile and he leaned toward her, teasingly intimidating. "That's because I am Caymanian, my dear. At last, half." He straightened and reached up to drag down her case from the overhead compartment.

"You're . . . very attractive people," she hesitantly observed.

His teeth flashed white as he grinned at her. "A dangerous compliment," he said softly. "They say we're the descendants of the pirates, the men of Cromwell's army in Jamaica and the Scottish, Irish and Welsh adventurers who sailed the Caribbean four hundred years ago." He handed her case to her.

"Great," she muttered. "I'm sailing off with a pirate."

"Son of a pirate," he corrected, turning away, still grinning.

Sarah smiled. "Son of a pirate? Hmm. That's got a nice ring to it. Son of a pirate. Son of a pirate," she mused aloud.

"Watch your language, Sarah," he said in amusement. "It sounds like you're saying son of a . . ." The rest was thankfully drowned out by the sound of a plane taking off.

They descended from the jet and collected their luggage, an anxious-looking Wiley and Alex's car. When they let him out of the cage and into the small back seat, Wiley looked as delighted as a prisoner freed from twenty years' confinement.

"Is this yours?" Sarah asked in surprise, referring to the car, as she fastened her seat belt. She had been expecting some sort of rental arranged for the "honeymoon," but this didn't look like that kind of car. It was too well kept. And it had the feel of a car used by just one person. Besides, the scent of it was familiar to her.

Alex nodded. "Yes," he answered curtly.

He put the small white vehicle in gear and within twenty-five minutes they were pulling to a stop in front of a small, neatly kept house. The cottage also looked like a privately owned property, rather than a rental acquired as part of their cover.

Its solid whitewashed walls gleamed cleanly in the bright sunlight. Dull red tiles framed its four oblong front windows. A palm tree bent picturesquely over a winding limestone walk that led to a solid mahogany front door. Sand and scrub grass encircled the building like a private beachscape, broken here and there by small, luxuriant semitropical bushes. Their broad, shining green leaves and large, dark pink flowers rustled softly in the gentle sea breeze. Behind the house, down a moderately steep slope, she could see beautiful, clear, blue-green water lapping gently at the rocky edge of a pristine beach.

"It's beautiful," she told him as they put things down inside.

Alex pocketed the key he'd used at the front door and smiled slightly. "Thank you."

Sarah noted the proprietary pride in his voice and as her gaze wandered curiously around the interior, she asked, "Is this *your* home?"

He'd disappeared into one of the other rooms, taking their bags with him. "Yes," he called out to her. "If you want to change, come in here."

Sarah did as he suggested, with Wiley excitedly wagging his tail at her side, sniffing everything in sight as quickly as he could in passing. The interior was as unaffectedly charming as the exterior. In a way, she supposed it was typical of the furnishings in an island home. There were two large wicker chairs with thick, red-patterned cushions on the seats. Across the room stood a matching white-painted wicker sofa with a long glass-and-mahogany frame table in front of it. The kitchen was open and airy. A large oval dining table sat comfortably in between, straddling the living room and kitchen areas. Both rooms were done in shell whites, colonial beiges and sea-green colors. Off to one side, she could see a tall, red lacquer display case with what looked like black coral sculptures, two on each of its four shelves. Beside it sat a bookcase full of hardbound books. She was too far away to make out the titles, but they looked like nonfiction; technical books of some sort.

By the time she and Wiley joined him, Alex was at a two-way radio set up in one corner of what otherwise looked like a bedroom. He had just made a connection with someone as they reached the big king-size bed that filled a quarter of the room.

"We're here," Alex announced to whoever was on the other end of the radio. "We'll be down in—" he glanced at his watch and frowned "—about thirty minutes. Is everything on board?" A man's voice replied in the affirmative. "Good. See you in half an hour. Out."

He turned away from the radio and opened the dresser drawer, pulling out a small cellophane-sealed box of contraceptives. Sarah, who had been waiting until he finished talking on the radio to ask him where she could change, felt a small wave of embarrassment. He glanced at her and correctly interpreted the strange look on her face.

"We're supposed to be sexually active," he pointed out. "It won't hurt to take along some props."

"That makes sense," Sarah agreed, as if it were perfectly natural for her to be standing in a strange man's bedroom saying something like that.

He unwrapped the box and threw away the cellophane. Then he tossed a couple of the foil packages into the trash after it. "We wouldn't want them to think we hadn't gotten around to using them."

"I suppose not," she agreed, rather faintly. "Uh, do you think you should throw away more?"

He looked at her in amusement. "How many do you usually go through in a night?" he asked curiously.

Sarah blushed and nervously removed her heels. Her feet were killing her. "I don't go through any," she retorted sharply. "I wasn't speaking from experience. I just thought . . . people on their honeymoon might . . ."

"Do it more often than twice a night?" he supplied with a straight face.

Sarah could have cheerfully stomped on his foot. "Yes," she said with as much calm as she could muster. "It always says that in the women's magazines in the grocery store."

Sutter tried to look impressed by her source of information. "I suppose they ought to know." He lifted two more packets out of the box and dropped them in the trash, then turned to look at her inquiringly. "Is four enough...in the opinion of the women's magazines?"

"I suppose," she said tightly. "I would have thought you'd be the expert on that anyway."

"Really?" He was enjoying teasing her.

"Really."

"Now why would you think that?" he asked with a grin.

"You just look like that kind of man," she retorted bluntly.

"What kind of man is that?" he demanded, grinning even more.

"The kind who would go through more than two in a night!" she declared, more loudly than she'd intended. Her eyes flashed dangerously, warning him not to continue the conversation unless he was prepared to take the consequences.

Alex shook his head as though he just didn't understand how she could think such a thing. Then he dropped the box of contraceptives into his suitcase. "You sound like a couple of men I know," he said in amusement. "I don't know where this image comes from," he said with a sigh.

Sarah watched in relief as he got up and disappeared into the house.

"You can change in there," he called out from the other room. "You have my pirate's word I won't look, but lock the door if that's not reassuring enough for you."

She heard him laugh and made as nasty a face as possible in his direction. She closed the door but was too obstinate to lock it. "I'm not a sissy, you pirate," she muttered as she stalked over to her suitcase on his bed. "A pirate's word! You arrogant . . . son of a pirate!"

She jerked open her suitcase and rummaged through the top layer, finding the swimsuit, shorts and blouse she'd planned to wear on the boat. Raymond had insisted she take at least a few new things. He thought it was necessary if she was to be convincing as a woman sailing off on her honeymoon. He'd had them sent to the house in Maryland before they left.

She fastened the top of her bikini, pulled a pair of shorts over the bottoms and put on a short-sleeved cotton blouse, while

Wiley sat obediently at the doorway, standing guard and staring at her intently.

"Come on, Wiley," Sarah said, walking in sandaled feet past her dog to open the door. "Let's go find Alex." She picked up her gear and slung it across her back.

Sarah found Alex in the living room, pulling some flotation equipment from a closet. He'd changed into crisp white cotton shorts and a bright print cotton shirt. He looked terrific, Sarah thought, as she let her gaze wander over his lean, muscular body. His long legs looked strong. The muscles were smooth and lank, like a swimmer's. There was a light dusting of fine black hair on his legs, forearms and chest that she hadn't noticed before. It made him look even more masculine—and more dangerous—than he had looked in a suit. It wasn't hard to imagine him wearing loose-fitting, calf-length pants, a white shirt open to the waist, a red sash and a sword in his hand.

Alex glanced up at her. "Ready to go?" he asked.

"Aye, aye, Cap'n," she said. "Which way to the boat?"

He hefted some bright orange life jackets in one arm and grabbed a yellow nylon travel bag with the other. He glanced around the room, as if making sure that he hadn't forgotten anything, checked the time on the waterproof black diver's watch on his wrist and frowned.

"Follow me," he said abruptly. "The boat's a little way down the beach. We can walk to the pier in a few minutes."

Sarah followed him in silence, trying to soothe Wiley with an occasional pat on the head. Nothing was calming Wiley down, however, and he pranced and leaped exuberantly at her left side as they slid down the sandy bank in big stumbling strides.

Warm sunlight had washed over her as soon as they had stepped outside of Alex's cottage. Sarah, however, felt a chill encase her heart. The beautiful clear waters of the Caribbean that Gabrielle had come to love stretched out as far as she could see. She remembered clambering down a clean white beach much like this one nearly a year ago with her sister. They'd been vacationing on an island two hours away by plane from here. It had been a rare and much enjoyed break for both of them. They'd laughed together. They'd cried together a little, too, that last night there.

Come back, Sarah. That's what Gabrielle had told her as they'd hugged each other goodbye at the airport. *Come back.*

"Please let us get to her in time," Sarah murmured in a barely audible voice.

Alex turned and for a moment their eyes locked. Hers were tormented. His hard and unyielding.

"We'll know soon if we're in time," he told her evenly. He hesitated, then added, "I told you I'd never lie to you, Sarah. I can't tell you if she's still in one piece. We haven't had any news in over six hours. For a man like Moreau, that's a long time." A lifetime, he could have said, but didn't. "Come on. The boat's over there. You can see it as soon as we get around this rock."

It was there, all right. A beautiful forty-foot cruiser waiting for them at anchor not far from shore.

It was a boat fit for a pirate. Fast, sleek and ruthless.

Chapter 7

They climbed around the jutting rock face and descended the sandy slope to the shore. As Alex had promised, Sarah saw a long, neatly constructed wooden pier extending from the beach well out into the clear water. Ropes were coiled near two of its tall wooden pilings. At the far end, an empty flat-bottomed dive boat was tied. Out in the cove, she heard a boat engine chug to life.

Sarah slid down the last few feet of scrub-studded hillside and stopped when she reached the beach. Squinting against the bright sunlight, she could make out a small boat motoring away from the big cruiser. There was a man at the helm. He swung the boat around and headed straight for the pier.

"Is that the person you were talking to on the radio?" Sarah asked breathlessly. Weathered wooden planking creaked softly under her feet as she hurried to catch up with Alex.

"Yes," Alex answered without breaking stride.

"He looks like he's coming toward us," she pointed out.

"He'd better be."

"Is he a friend of yours? Or is he one of Raymond's people?"

He glanced over his shoulder at her through narrowing eyes and replied in a discouraging tone, "He's a friend of mine."

"Does that mean that Raymond doesn't have any contacts here?" she persisted. "Or that you don't trust them?"

Alex tightened his jaw and said with deceptive smoothness, "Raymond has contacts anywhere he needs them." He gave her a discouraging stare. "And you're not supposed to know about them, so you can quit asking." He didn't address the issue of trust.

Sarah wasn't about to be kept in the dark. "Well, if Raymond has contacts here and you didn't use them, it sounds like you don't trust them." She met his stare stubbornly. "You're not in this alone," she pointed out. "My life is on the line, too. I don't like being kept ignorant."

He hated to admit it, but she had a point. He would have felt the same way if their positions had been reversed. He frowned at her, annoyed she was being so persistent.

"It's not exactly that I distrust them," Alex told her with great reluctance. "It's that I prefer to deal with people whom I know personally." He looked away from her and scowled even more. That was especially true now that he was retired. He didn't want to get sucked back into intelligence work, not even by accident. Keeping away from as many people in Raymond's world as possible would help with that. It added to his credibility, at least as much credibility as possible in a world constructed of duplicity and lies.

Sarah saw him withdraw into himself and wondered what he was thinking. The small surge of pleasure she'd felt when she'd thought he'd begun being candid with her began to ebb. He was gone from her again. And he didn't want her to follow. The stubborn man.

"I see," she said. "Well, I certainly hope that you aren't throwing away important resources for us simply because you like to handpick your team," she said crisply. She hoped the implied criticism in her comment would annoy him enough that he'd explain himself further.

Alex halted at the end of the pier and dropped what he was carrying at his feet. He took the things that Sarah was carrying and dumped them unceremoniously on top of the growing pile. Then he put his hands on his hips and turned to glare at her.

"My astute judgement is what I'm being paid for, in case you've forgotten," he said coldly. "If you don't care to rely on it, don't get on the boat."

Sarah glared right back. "If I don't get on that boat, you cut your chances in half, maybe more." She smiled in satisfaction at his instant fury. "I remember your telling me that. Did you think I wouldn't? You need me, Alex Sutter." Her voice softened a little, but she stubbornly stood her ground. "I just don't want to be left in the dark about you and the people we're putting our trust in."

Alex swore and nodded. "I'll tell you as much as I damn well want to. I need you. That's true. And I don't like that one damned bit." He leaned forward, his body taut in anger. "I've always worked alone, Sarah. I've never wanted a partner. I don't want one now. But I've got one. And damn it all, I need you. But I don't like it. Do you understand? I don't like being responsible for whether you'll live or die. But that's the plan. I agreed to it. I'll honor the contract I made with Raymond. But don't push me, Sarah. I work my own way. If you don't trust me, don't come. It's that damned simple."

Sarah would have dearly loved to slap his face for his arrogant stubbornness. But she knew he was being completely honest with her, and that was worth something, too. She swallowed her anger and lifted her chin.

"I trust you," she said slowly. "I don't know why. You certainly don't make it easy. But I do trust you, Alex. I hope before this is all over, you can trust me just half as much."

With graceful dignity, she turned and watched the approaching boat, now grumbling close to the edge of the pier.

"What's our friend's name?" Sarah inquired. She used the word *our* with the intention of including herself as a partner whether Alex Sutter was ready for one or not.

"George Ebanks." He checked his watch. *Our friend!* She didn't let up, he thought. It was damned irritating listening to her. And the fact that he sympathized with her didn't help his temper at all. He was beginning to feel guilty about keeping her in the dark. Hell.

Wiley bounded into the scrubby grass and made a last-minute pit stop while Sarah searched for and found her sunglasses in the canvas shoulder bag Raymond had thoughtfully supplied among her "honeymoon" trousseau.

"Have you known George long?" Sarah inquired.

"Awhile."

Sarah blithely ignored the fact that he obviously didn't wish to talk about George Ebanks. He had made it clear he didn't want to talk about a lot of things. Well, he was going to before she was through, even if he was madder than a beached whale.

"How long is 'awhile'?" she probed. She smiled sunnily at George Ebanks's grinning face. He was standing in the cockpit and preparing to throw a line to Alex. "He looks like an island fisherman," she observed.

"He is," Alex said curtly. "I've known him for several years. And if you ask exactly how many years that is, I have absolutely no intention of remembering."

She turned her sunglassed eyes on him. "It's too bad that you don't like to talk about yourself much, you know, because I find you absolutely fascinating." She tilted her head to one side thoughtfully. "Is your aversion to talking about yourself a matter of habit or are you hiding all kinds of sordid things?"

Alex looked at her as if he seriously considered taping her mouth. He gritted his teeth and smiled at her acidly. "Why it's the raping, pillaging and murdering, my dear," he admitted with a touch of humility. "Now toss me that line over there and give your imagination a rest."

Alex helped George tie up his motorboat, literally and figuratively turning his back on any further personal inquiries from Sarah.

Undeterred, Sarah mused aloud. "You've lived down here for a number of years, then. So, do you know a lot of people in the Caymans by now? And on the other islands down here? Jamaica?"

George, who'd just killed his engine, heard the last two questions and grinned at her. He was wearing cutoff black pants and a white-and-red striped shirt. His skin was darkly tanned from the sun and the black mustache and stubble of a beard framing his grinning teeth made them look as white as bleached bones.

"Sure he does, mum. Alex knows a lot of folks. But hardly any of them know him." George chuckled as he reached up to take some of the items Alex was handing him from the pier. George didn't look any more concerned about the glower that Alex was giving him than Sarah had. "No one can figure this man at all, 'ceptin' me of course. Most thinks him a canny pirate with business-suit manners. Me, I know him better'n that. And I guess mebbe you do, too." He snatched a folded newspaper from his back pocket and opened the fourth page, interrupting the flow of baggage handling from Alex to the boat. "You're in the *Caymanian Compass*, mon," George exclaimed with an admiring laugh. He jabbed a stubby forefinger at a photo at the bottom corner. "Congratulations to you both," he told them, his eyes gleaming teasingly. "And be sure to ask me to the first christenin', eh, mon?" George threw back his raggedy black-haired head and laughed with great good humor.

Alex, not amused, held the paper and quietly studied the black-and-white photo and its caption.

Sarah peered curiously around his shoulder and immediately recognized the picture as one that had been taken in the justice's chambers. It certainly looked convincing to her, she thought uncomfortably. They were wrapped in each other's arms and kissing quite thoroughly. She could even feel the memory of the flash and sizzle begin to filter back. And the sensation of his body pressed against hers. Trying to find something more businesslike to think about, she tore her gaze away from their entwined figures and looked down at the caption below.

Mr. Alexander Sutter, longtime resident of the islands of the Caribbean, was married yesterday in the United States. He will introduce his new bride to the Caymans, where he has most recently resided, and the neighboring Caribbean in a honeymoon cruise. Mr. Sutter, a businessman, is well-known in jewelry and banking circles on Grand Cayman and Washington.

Sarah glanced up at Alex. "Is that true? About your long-time residence in the Caribbean, I mean."

"More or less," he said.

"You're such a gushing fountain of information! What's the harm in admitting that to me?" she asked with a laugh.

"Probably nothing, but I'd rather not find out, frankly." Alex tucked the newspaper into one of the waterproof bags attached to the flotation equipment and handed them to George. "Thanks for the paper, George," he told the fisherman.

George was standing in his boat, still grinning, but obviously prepared to take them out to the cruiser whenever Alex was ready. "No problem, mon," George said cheerfully.

Sarah took his outstretched hand and hopped lightly into the boat. Alex followed, with Wiley close behind him. Alex looked at Wiley with increased respect. The dog hadn't rocked the boat when he'd jumped in.

"I see you weren't exaggerating about Wiley's sea legs," Alex said with begrudging admiration.

Sarah grinned from ear to ear and sat down to hug her faithful four-footed friend. "Yep. The best you've ever seen," she promised.

George let out the throttle and shook his head in bemusement all the way to the big boat. "I gotta tell you, mon, I never heard of anyone takin' a dog with 'em on their 'oneymoon."

Alex grimaced and shook his head like a man resigned to his fate. Then his eyes changed expression slightly and a cool grin glimmered beneath his stoicism. He reached down to scratch Wiley behind the ears.

"Sarah's very attached to her dog, George. I had to promise to bring him along before she'd agree to marry me."

George roared with deeply male laughter. "Good for you, Sarah!" he shouted to her over the sounds of the engine and the rushing seawater. "Alex has always been too handsome for his own good. No wonder he married you. He finally met a woman who wouldn't throw herself at his beautiful feet!"

Alex, who sat a little across from Sarah, moved closer and casually draped his arm over her shoulders. Sarah looked at him in surprise. He massaged her shoulder ever so slightly with his fingertips, a slight smile on his hard mouth.

He was still angry with her, but he couldn't very well fight with her, much as he was tempted. He thought perhaps he would tease her into submission. She didn't seem to be afraid of him, and that was really too bad. Because she had a lot to be afraid of.

"Sarah's not about to fall at my feet," he agreed with a smooth piratical grin. His eyes met and held Sarah's and he challenged, softly, "I have no effect on her at all. Isn't that right, Sarah?"

Sarah felt the warmth of his nearness, the pleasure of his touch, and wasn't so sure about that. He exerted a powerful, effortless attraction. She felt her knees weaken and her mouth go dry as she stared back into his dark challenging eyes. Sarah was too proud to admit the effect he had on her, so she smiled at him with icy sweetness.

"You're absolutely right," she lied. "Falling at your feet is undignified. It holds no appeal at all for me. Besides, I would hate to be just another notch in your sandals."

George laughed and slapped his hip appreciatively.

"She's a spunky one, isn't she, Alex? Not like Eliseaux at all."

Alex turned a brief look of irritation at his laughing friend, but when he turned his attention back to Sarah, his expression softened slightly. He smiled slightly and it was one that Sarah could almost believe was sincere. It made him look breathtakingly handsome, she thought, riveted to him in spite of herself.

"That's one of the things I admire about you," he murmured, running a fingertip up over her shoulder and slowly, suggestively, down her spine. "You don't back down. You rise to meet a challenge."

Sarah tried to ignore the pleasingly warm sensation his slow caress was producing in her back and hips. "I'm glad you find *something* to admire," she said, a little breathlessly.

He let his gaze wander down across her face. Her square jaw and well-formed cheekbones gave her a look of confidence and strength that he found very appealing. Her eyes were hard to read behind the sunglasses, but her mouth was temptingly parted. Her lips soft . . .

"I find a lot to like about you," he told her. He lifted one brow in irony. "If you promise to stop digging into my personal life, I'll promise not to show you just how appealing you are."

The heat she felt enveloping her had nothing to do with the sun blazing overhead or the warm sea surrounding them. It had to do with the effect Alex Sutter had on her. Period. Sarah looked away and tried to tell herself it was just the adrenaline pumping through her veins, just the pressure and tension of the mission they were on, just his physical attractiveness and his experienced way with women. She knew she was trying to save herself with all those excuses, but she clung to them anyway. Because the other explanation was too frightening to be faced. She couldn't be drawn to a man she didn't know. She couldn't want a man who refused to reveal his life to her. She wasn't that stupid. Surely not.

George pulled the small motorboat around to the rope ladder hanging down the side of the large boat moored in the peaceful little cove. Between the three of them, everything was loaded and a final check of provisions made quite rapidly. Wiley wagged his tail and lolled his tongue in excitement as he stood next to the rail with Sarah, watching the fisherman motor away.

Just behind her, Alex said crisply, "Let's go."

Sarah turned to look up into his dark, inscrutable eyes and her heart turned over. He was so much physically bigger than she was. Why did it suddenly seem so much more noticeable?

"I feel like I'm going to sea with a pirate," she told him, trying to joke away the sudden tension in every nerve in her body. Somehow Wiley didn't seem like much of a chaperon anymore.

A grin slashed his handsome face and he nodded. "The son of a pirate," he corrected.

He let out the throttle and the cruiser surged through the waters. Wind whipped his dark hair and flapped his shirt against his skin.

Sarah sat in the soft padded seat next to him and helped spread out the nautical chart on the board in front of him. He pointed to a small dot in the middle of the blue.

"That's where we're going," he said over the engine's smooth whine. "Moreau's island. ETA: four hours."

Sarah glanced at the clock on the panel in front of him. They'd get there just before sunset.

"Why don't you go below and put things away?" he suggested, glancing at her. He grinned. "Make it look nice and lived in. Give it the woman's touch I keep hearing about."

Sarah nodded. That made sense. Then she recalled something that George Ebanks had said. "Didn't Eliseaux have a woman's touch?" she asked.

He frowned. "I don't remember." George had a big mouth. He'd have to remind him to keep it shut. Even around his "bride."

Sarah dangled a foot off the top step and braced her hands on the railing, staring down into the cabin section of the boat with a pensive look on her face.

"Eliseaux. I don't think I ever heard that name before. Where did she get it?"

"From her mother, I presume," Alex muttered. His frown darkened. "If you want to keep probing, you'd better be prepared to take the consequences," he warned. He looked at her and the slow, desultory way his hard eyes wandered down to her mouth and breasts were a graphic warning of the kind of punishment he was threatening to inflict.

Sarah pursed her lips. "Raping and pillaging? I don't believe you'd do it. It's all a bluff."

He pulled the throttle down and turned to look at her as if he couldn't believe she'd just said what he'd heard.

"Are you daring me, Sarah?" he asked softly.

The gleam in his eyes could have been amusement, but Sarah's nerve began to quail and she decided not to find out. She shrugged and shook her head. "Not at all. But...I think I'd better get to work. We put a lot of gear down there."

He nodded his head and gave her a cynical smile. "We certainly did. And after you've stowed it, contemplate the sleeping arrangements for tonight."

Sarah tossed her head and swung down the stairs. "No problem. I'll get right on it, Cap'n."

He stared at her in irritation as she sauntered down the stairs into the cabin area below. Sauntered was the only word for it, he thought in annoyance. Did she swing her trim little hips like that on purpose? She surely wasn't that foolish, or naive. It had to be out of defiance. Well, that was just too damned bad. They weren't going to get acquainted if he could help it. No telling each other the stories of their lives. No tender comradeship. No emotional intimacy that could easily lead into the kind of sexual intimacy that would definitely get out of hand.

A mental picture of being completely intimate in every way with her materialized vividly in his imagination. Alex swore like a sailor for a solid thirty seconds. He yanked his gaze away from the empty passageway and put it forcibly into the open sea straight ahead of him. His hands tightened on the wheel and he grimly tried to repress the image of Sarah's sexy little body.

Wiley whined next to him and began licking his ankle.

Alex scowled at the dog.

"Why in the hell are you up here?" he asked the uncomprehending animal. "When a man thinks the things I'm thinking about your mistress, you'd damn well better be down there standing guard over her."

Wiley whimpered, as if asking for a translation into dog language, then perked up his ears and stared down into the cabin.

"Yeah. Right down those stairs. Great guard dog you are," Alex muttered. "You're fraternizing with the enemy, pal. She's counting on you, you idiot. You don't want to let her down, now do you?"

Wiley cocked his head to one side and let his tongue loll. He stared up at Alex with a look of rapt interest. He obviously was willing to listen, but he wasn't clear on the details.

Alex shook his head and sighed. "It looks like she's gone to sea with *two* pirates, if you ask me, mate."

Wiley whined again, licked his chops and lifted his wet black nose to scent the wind. Then he curled up near Sutter's feet.

Sarah popped her head and shoulders into view and saw Wiley.

Sutter gave her a jaundiced look of amusement. "*You* may not fall at my feet," he said, "but apparently your dog isn't so particular."

Sarah smothered a laugh. "It would be easier to understand if Wiley were a she," she said, shaking her head.

Alex looked mildly offended. "I've never gone in for bitches," Alex muttered. Well, maybe one or two could have been characterized as that. He glared at the dog for making him remember.

"Where do you want me to put your things?" Sarah asked pleasantly.

He gave her a devilish smile. She had no right to sound so pleasantly relaxed while he was standing up here trying to forget what her mouth tasted like. "Why, right next to yours, dear heart," he said smoothly. "Right next to yours."

Her face fell a little. "You mean...in the same sleeping quarters?" Her heart sank. She knew what he was going to say.

He nodded and grinned more broadly. "Absolutely. I have a reputation to maintain. You said yourself I look like the kind of man who, well, I won't embarrass you by being graphic about it."

"Thanks," Sarah muttered.

Sutter chuckled. "Don't mention it. But think about it. You wouldn't want people thinking that I don't sleep with my own wife, now would you? And considering my reputation, if I didn't, that would raise a lot of doubt about our honeymoon, don't you agree?"

"I suppose you're right," Sarah said. She backed downstairs. "I'll...put your things with mine."

"Terrific," Sutter said tightly. He glanced at his watch. If they were lucky, maybe Moreau's men would pick them up when they patrolled tonight. He'd prefer that to waiting. Especially since he'd be waiting in bed. With Sarah. "Just terrific," he muttered again.

They dropped the sea anchor and battened down the cruiser for the night. The skies had clouded over and there was the possibility of a storm.

Sutter checked the sonar and picked up a school of fish. He flipped on the radio at the designated time and picked up the coded signal from the navy. Moreau's two high-speed boats were leaving their berths on the island and preparing to make their usual sweep of the surrounding ocean. He checked his watch. That ought to put them in his vicinity in about an hour and a half, if they followed their normal routine. He turned off the electronic equipment and went down into the cabin.

"Something smells very good," he said, looking expectantly in the direction of the small galley.

Sarah shrugged. "I can't do much harm to fresh fish and tossed salad," she pointed out. She pulled the potatoes out of the oven and switched off the electric grill under the flounder. "I hope you didn't bring me along to cook, though," she added. "Home economics was my worst subject."

Alex pulled a bottle of blush wine out of the refrigerator and put some oil-and-vinegar dressing on the table.

"I'm an excellent chef," he said with an immodest grin. "If you'd like to pilot the boat, I'll stay below and cook."

Sarah gave him a considering look. "Do you think you could teach me soon enough to save us from breakfast?"

"Have you ever handled a boat this size?"

"No. I sailed a catboat once," she offered hopefully.

Alex swung one muscular leg over a nailed-down stool and sat down at the table. "I'm afraid that won't help." He poured the wine and rubbed his hands together enthusiastically. "I'm starved. The sea always brings out my appetite."

Sarah brushed against him as she put their plates on the table and squeezed into the seat across from him. His eyes flicked over her and she felt her own appetite begin to evaporate.

"Well, since I can't pilot this thing, I certainly want you to stay healthy and well fed," she said fervently. She offered him a basket of rolls fresh from the microwave.

"All pirates should have such a devoted crew," he said in amusement. He lifted his glass of wine. "To our success."

Sarah lifted her glass and touched it to his. Their eyes met and held as they swallowed the wine. Sarah had never felt so close to a man in her life as she did to Alex Sutter for that long, silent moment.

As they began eating, she asked lightly, "So how did you become a good cook?"

Alex was too hungry to become angry at her continuing efforts to unearth his background. "It was a matter of self-preservation," he said between bites.

"Did your mother teach you?" she asked innocently.

He glanced at her in amusement. "Good try. You slipped that in quite smoothly. But I have no intention of discussing my upbringing. Or my mother."

Sarah laughed. "All right." She caught her lower lip between her teeth and looked at him pensively. She frowned, then snapped her fingers when she thought of a solution. "If you won't tell me the truth, I'll just have to invent a past for you."

He took another swallow of the wine. "That's ridiculous," he pointed out. He speared another piece of fish with his fork. "What good is a fictional biography going to be to you?"

Sarah lowered her eyes. "Well, you see, it bothers me that you know so much about me and I know nothing at all, really, about you. It . . . seems so lopsided. Besides, a wife would be expected to know something about her husband." She glanced up at him hopefully.

He chewed his fish and stared at her. He washed the food down with another healthy swallow of the wine.

"I don't think anyone would be surprised if you knew very little about me," he said slowly. "People who've known me for years would find that quite understandable."

Sarah pulled her roll apart and buttered it. "All right. It will just be for me, then." She ate the roll and watched him eat. He did that the same way he did a lot of things. No nonsense. Right down to business. Neat. Clean. She wiped her mouth with a napkin and finished her wine. After they'd cleaned up the dishes and disposed of the garbage, she asked, "Are you ready to hear your life story?"

Alex followed her up onto the deck to watch the sun set in a sky turned blood-red near the horizon. He leaned his forearms on the rail and stared at the rich celestial palette of colors. Overhead and to the east, storm clouds continued to gather like a heavy gray shroud.

"All right," he agreed. His mouth twisted in mild amusement. "Tell me the story of my life." He was curious to hear what she'd imagine for him.

Sarah leaned her elbows on the rail and formed a steeple with her fingertips. "Well, let's see. To begin at the beginning. You said you were half-Caymanian. Was that on your father's side?" She looked at him questioningly. He shrugged as if he didn't know, but there was a flicker of surprise in the depths of his dark eyes that made her think she just might have guessed correctly. She had a fifty-fifty chance of guessing right. She grinned at him triumphantly. "I'll bet he was a Caymanian. A seaman, a man who traveled the world. A sea wolf who plundered the hearts of women on five continents."

Sarah warmed to her fantasy in spite of her subject's mildly amused reaction.

"I suppose that's where I've inherited my four-package-a-night tendencies," he suggested dryly.

Sarah blushed, but she was relaxed from having drunk the wine, and from being able to talk to Alex as if they were friends. "Definitely," she agreed with a laugh. "Now don't interrupt."

"Sorry," he murmured with a grin.

"One day he sailed into a port and met your mother. She was a beautiful woman from…let's see, where could she have been from?"

Alex shrugged. She punched him lightly on the arm in reprisal, making him laugh softly.

"She was from . . . Not Miami. You're not the Miami type. Perhaps from Galveston or New Orleans. Anyway, they fell madly in love, but her family didn't want her to marry a man from the islands and leave them to raise a family elsewhere."

Alex stared silently at the red sun sliding into the deep-orange sea.

"But she loved him madly," Sarah fantasized. "So she followed him anyway. They were very happy and had a son named Alex."

"Of course," he said dryly.

"Your father taught you how to swim and fish and sail a boat, just like all the island boys." She thought she saw a

shadow pass over his face, but it was gone so quickly, she
wasn't sure it had really been there. She turned, facing him, and
leaned one elbow on the rail. "It was hard to see him gone so
much, but that was a sailor's life. You...never had any brothers
or sisters?"

He turned to look at her, and his eyes were cool masks. "This
is your fantasy," he reminded her. "I had—I have whatever you
imagine."

Sarah fell silent and wondered if somehow her little story was
hurting him. "Do you want me to stop?" she asked softly. She
reached out and laid her hand on his arm. He was warm beneath her touch. Warm and very solid.

He looked down at her hand and back up at her face. "No.
As a matter of fact, I'm finding it . . . enlightening."

Sarah took a deep breath and wondered what he meant by
that. Was she so close that it unnerved him? Or was she so far
from the mark that it offended his sensibilities in some unknown way? She turned away, staring out to sea.

"You had no brothers or sisters. You grew up rather lonely.
Your mother..." She glanced at him. She didn't want to say
that his mother was dead. If she were alive, it would sound
awful, she thought. "You haven't seen your mother or your
father in many years." She left it at that. "You ran away to sea
as a teenager and became a prowling jack-of-many-trades in the
Caribbean. You're a self-taught man. You've lived on the edge
of what's legal, taking money from whoever could pay your
price for...the kind of work Raymond used to ask you to do."
Whatever that really was, she thought to herself.

The last sliver of red was swallowed up by the black night. A
gull cried in the distance. Water splashed as a fish broke the
surface and then dove again.

"You have quite an imagination," Alex said, now turning
cool eyes on her. She was so far from the mark, it almost hurt.
He would have taken her scenario any day over the reality of his
past.

"Ah, but now I get to the current part," she announced with
a proud grin. "You work in black coral." She could remember
seeing some pieces in his cottage on Cayman Brac. It was as
good a guess as any she could come up with. "You're a trader.

A businessman. Making your fortune. Smuggling a little on the side, perhaps?'' she added teasingly.

The corners of his eyes crinkled a little and his hard, straight mouth softened into a slight curve. "So I'm a smuggler on the side."

Sarah laughed. "And that's why Eliseaux left."

His head snapped around and he stared at her.

"*Is* that why she left?" Sarah asked in amazement. She couldn't believe that she might have guessed the real reason.

Alex frowned. "No. As a matter of fact—" He bit off the rest of what he was going to say. He wasn't going to tell her a damned thing. He had to remember that. It would be easier that way. For both of them.

Sarah waited, holding her breath, hoping he might give her a morsel of the truth after all that. When it became obvious that he wasn't going to, she sighed and let her imagination run wild again.

"Where was I? Oh yes. Eliseaux. You met her...in a bar...on...Haiti or Martinique. Someplace where they speak French and the women are beautiful and lissome and have elegant names and long, shapely legs."

He grinned at her description in spite of himself. It wasn't really a bad description of Eliseaux. But she'd made up the name herself. She wasn't any more French than he was.

Sarah found she didn't relish having to talk about the next part. "You had a mad, passionate love affair all over the Caribbean."

Alex looked at her in surprise. "That sounds exhausting," he pointed out, trying not to laugh.

She smiled at him confidently. "You were strong. And you were young."

"I must have been," he agreed. He looked at Sarah questioningly. "Is that it? The end of my biography?"

"You're quite over the hill," Sarah announced sadly. "Only your legendary past burns now. You've settled on a mousy little wife from a cold, marshy climate. A woman who likes dogs better than men, of all things!"

He grinned at her and shook his head. "I think that's been much overstated. I seem to recall a kiss not so long ago..."

Sarah shook her finger at him admonishingly. "Gentlemen never kiss and tell," she warned. "Besides, this is your biography, not mine."

He grabbed her hand and pulled it around his waist, forcing her to step close to him to keep from falling against his chest as she lost her balance. His dark eyes no longer gleamed with amusement. His mouth was hard and unlaughing. "But you're in my biography now, Sarah," he told her huskily.

She could feel the warm strength of him and she put her hand on his chest, as if to hold him off.

"What's the matter, Sarah?" he teased her softly as he gently rubbed his thumb over her captured hand. "Did your fantasy suddenly become a little too real for you?"

She swallowed and looked helplessly into his eyes. She had the most awful desire to lean into him, to curl her arms around his neck, to see if his kiss could possibly be as devastating as she remembered it to be. She forced herself to fight the temptation.

"I was just trying to fill the time," she whispered huskily, knowing that wasn't quite true. "Please..."

He leaned toward her, pushing her against the rail so he could trap her there. His body pressed against her and he put an arm around her shoulders. His eyes were as black as the night sea, and right now he looked just as dangerous. He slid his hand into her hair and brushed his lips against her warm cheek.

"Please what?" he murmured harshly. "Please be what you imagine I am?" There was an undertone of bitterness in his voice and his hand tightened around her still-captured wrist at his back.

"I didn't mean to tease you," she whispered. "What did I say? I'm sorry, Alex."

His mouth hovered above hers and for a long, agonizing moment, Sarah thought he was going to kiss her. Her mouth ached. Her whole body ached. Ached with wanting him to do it. Ached to be held tenderly in his arms, to listen to him whisper love words in her ear.

"Sweet heaven," he murmured unsteadily. "What in the hell is happening?"

Through eyes half-closed with desire, she saw him struggle to stop what he'd begun. It didn't matter that he was a virtual stranger anymore. It didn't matter that he didn't want to tell her a thing about himself. It didn't matter that they would probably never see each other again. The only thing that mattered was to be one with him. To be wrapped in his arms and feel the heat of his love blazing over her.

"No," he muttered. He grimaced and, clenching his teeth against the jaws of desire that had so savagely gripped him, he pushed away from her. He stood with his back to her, his hands clenched tightly into fists at his side, his eyes closed, his head tossed back. "Why don't you go down to bed," he said curtly.

He lifted his head sharply and turned to look off the starboard side. From the tense set of his shoulders and the intense expression on his face, Sarah guessed what he was looking for.

"Moreau's men?" she asked faintly. She wrapped her arms around herself and tried to stop her teeth from chattering. She felt cold.

Alex nodded. "Yeah. Moreau's men." He pointed to a boat in the distance.

The sound of its engines grew a little louder. It hovered in the darkness for a while, never coming any closer. They watched for nearly half an hour. Eventually the boat left.

Sarah breathed a sigh of relief. She preferred facing them in the daylight. She felt a little limp as Alex pushed her firmly in the direction of the cabin stairs.

"They saw us," he said tersely. "They'll probably be back in the morning to see if we're still here."

"Great," Sarah murmured gamely. "Just like we wanted."

Alex looked around for Wiley, only to find the dog curled at the foot of the stairs. "A fine protector you've got," he muttered. "He sleeps on the job." He motioned for Sarah to go down into the cabin. "Go ahead. I'll be down after I check for any last-minute communication from our many friends."

In the distance Sarah heard the sinister rumble of thunder. A jagged streak of lightning pierced the sky far off in the east. She wished Alex had let her stay with him.

Thinking it would look more convincing for Moreau's men in case they returned before dawn, she pulled out one of the sexy lace negligees Jones had had the nerve to give her. She was glad to be under the covers before Alex came downstairs.

What was sleeping in the same bed anyway? No big deal. They could be adult about it. Sarah's thoughts got muzzier and muzzier. She turned over onto her stomach and closed her eyes. She wished Alex would hurry. She couldn't stay awake much longer.

Chapter 8

It was dark, and Sarah was being gently rocked by the slow, ageless rhythms of the sea. She vaguely sensed the warm male body stretching out beside her, and she snuggled more deeply into the pillow, relaxing because he was finally there with her. "Alex," she murmured sleepily.

"Hmm?"

"Just Alex . . ." Her words slurred, and she fell back into a deep sleep, a soft smile on her face.

The way she said his name made his belly tighten. There was a naive trust in her voice that made him feel peculiar. It drew him to her, made him want to protect her. Protect her. That was a dangerous inclination. His jaw tightened. He'd spent a lifetime walking tightropes. Alone. For the first time, he wondered if perhaps there could be more to his life than that. He wondered what it would be like if he and Sarah had met under other circumstances.

She was fun to be with. He grinned, wry and self-mocking at the word that had sprung into his mind. Fun. When had he ever had time for that? Running in the shadows, keeping out of sight. He'd spent most of his adult life as the invisible man. Most of his youth had been much the same, living on the fringes of polite, acceptable society. Fun. There had never been much time for that.

How different her past was from his. She'd had a close, loving family. Parents who'd raised her. She'd earned an honest living.

Alex's gaze drifted down across the smooth creamy skin of her face to the soft curve of her neck and shoulder. Farther down, he found the gentle rise and fall of her breasts beneath the cotton sheet. A handful, he thought. She'd be soft and warm against his palm. He wanted to reach out and slide the sheet down and cup her warm flesh with his hand, rub her nipple between his fingers.

He inhaled and closed his eyes. If he didn't stop thinking about it, he was going to do just that. He wondered what she would do if he did. He remembered the way she'd softened in his arms when they'd kissed, the way her skin had warmed and her mouth welcomed him. He had no doubt that she was physically attracted to him, although he doubted she was comfortable with that fact. Hell. He couldn't blame her. *He* was uncomfortable with that. That was a laugh. Mr. Stud had developed a conscience. He remembered telling Blake and Grant that his ideal definition of involvement with a woman was a weekend in bed. He'd been exaggerating, mainly to get them off his back. But there was a kernel of truth there, too. He hadn't found many women who interested him enough for anything more than a casual acquaintance.

Alex rolled over onto his stomach and smothered a groan in the pillow. If he succumbed to the temptation to try to seduce Sarah, he was sure she would end up in tears over it eventually. In spite of her independence, her spunk—as George had so amusingly put it—she just wasn't the casual bedmate type. She was too innocent, too inexperienced, to make love with him without feeling badly about it later. He didn't think she could accept being a one-night stand, no matter how much they were attracted to each other.

He'd never been a cad where women were concerned, and he was determined not to start with Sarah Dunning. In spite of the fact that he found her annoying and persistent, he liked her. He genuinely liked her. He didn't want her to be hurt.

He rolled back onto his side and crossed his arms in front of his bare chest, trying to take up the least amount of space on the bed that he could. There was a foot of space between them. Hell. It wasn't enough. He felt the warmth from her body. He heard the soft, tantalizing sound of her breathing. Damn. He'd shared a bed with a woman before. But never had he felt as if every nerve in his skin was tuned to her wavelength, aware of her every movement.

He could smell the tantalizing scent of her clean skin. His body tightened every time he drew a breath. The virginal white lace of her nightgown made her look like a bride on her wedding bed, a thought that made his loins begin to ache. The diamonds on her ring flashed as her hand moved slightly. He remembered her worry about the expense and half smiled. It looked good on her. As if it belonged there. He wondered how much of an argument she'd put up if he insisted she keep it after they got back, as sort of a souvenir. Hell, Grant had already charged it to his account at Malone's. If he wanted her to keep it, she'd keep it.

Her dark blond hair was fluffed around her head. She looked vulnerable lying there. No smart comebacks. No bold stares. No promises of how courageous she could be when the time came. She just looked like an unspoiled, innocent young woman. He reached out and lifted a few strands of the dark burnished gold and rubbed it softly between his fingertips. Soft, sweet Sarah.

He pulled his hand away with an effort. He wasn't used to sleeping with a woman in his bed. He hadn't done that for a long time, not since he and Eliseaux had politely parted company. Watching Sarah's gently curled form, he thought he could learn to enjoy sleeping with her.

That was irrelevant, of course. She had to go back to her world when this was over. And he had to go back to his. As tempting as it was to consider making love to her, he knew it would eventually bring them both more pain than pleasure. He closed his eyes. He'd been alone too long. That had to be his problem. Sarah Dunning was just an attractive young woman. He was making a mountain out of a molehill.

He wished the molehill wasn't having the effect on his body that she was, though. Because there was nothing he could do about it, lying next to her in the cabin, growing hard with desire, wearing nothing but a pair of pajama bottoms. He swore under his breath and tried to forget about her warm brown eyes, her soft, kissable lips, her lighthearted smile, her shapely body lying a foot away beneath two thin layers of cotton.

He should be old enough not to react like this to a woman, he thought, grimly amused. He was beginning to think she might have him pegged right. Maybe he was a four-package-a-night man. He certainly hadn't noticed it before. Not until this trip.

Softly, Alex swore himself to sleep.

It was the cool breeze across her bare thigh that awoke Sarah a little after dawn. She felt warm everywhere else. It didn't take long to discover why. She was sprawled across Alex. His arm was around her shoulders and she could feel every inch of his chest, belly and thighs as she pressed down against him. She opened her eyes and found his disconcerted black-eyed gaze on her.

"Sorry," she mumbled as color flooded her cheeks. His body felt delicious against hers. She shifted her weight slightly and realized what the ridge of flesh pressing against her thigh was. Her cheeks darkened and she tried to move away.

He laughed and put his arms around her, holding her in place. "Good morning," he said, grinning at her obvious embarrassment. "Didn't you ever wake up and find that boyfriend of yours in this condition?"

Sarah tried to tug the nightgown down over her bare thigh and shook her head. "We, uh, never discussed it," she mumbled.

He raised his eyebrows. "No? I suppose discussion isn't usually what's needed when a man's in this condition," he conceded.

Sarah felt even more embarrassed and she was angry that she was embarrassed. She wished she had more experience with men—and other things. She wished she could sit here and make off-color jokes with Alex and not feel herself growing pink.

"We didn't discuss it. We didn't do anything else, either," she snapped defensively. She tried to pull away, but was met with the iron grip of Alex's arms holding her still. She laid her face on his shoulder so she didn't have to see the frown on his face. Or the question in his eyes. "We didn't do much of anything," she mumbled against the bare skin of his chest. "That's why we broke up. I just . . . couldn't get that excited about it."

Alex stared at the cabin ceiling and frowned. She was obviously embarrassed. But what she was saying was hard to believe. "Are you telling me you didn't sleep with him?" he asked incredulously.

She pushed herself up on both hands, facing him fiercely. "Yes. That's exactly what I'm telling you. Is that a crime?"

He shook his head. "The poor son of a bitch. Why did you let him move in with you?"

"It's none of your business," Sarah said, trying to wriggle free of his steely grip. She pushed against his warm, hard ribs with her palms, arched her back against his strong, unyielding arms, doubled up her legs until he entangled them with his and flipped her onto her back, holding her down with his body.

He held her hands, laced in his, beside her head.

"Yes, it is my business," he said harshly. "Anything I want to know about you is my business." His eyes glittered dangerously. He pressed his lips against hers, burying his hard male flesh against her soft, flat belly. "Do you get off teasing men?" he asked angrily. "I didn't just *wake up* in this condition, my luscious little bedmate. I spent the whole damned night like this. Now I want an answer to my question." He shifted his weight across her, easing off her chest a little so she could breathe more easily. "Why didn't you sleep with him, Sarah?" he asked more softly.

She swallowed and licked her lips. She didn't have much experience dealing with a man who was sexually frustrated, as Alex obviously was. She tried not to aggravate him further. She'd wait till they were out of bed and dressed for that.

"I...tried to...but...I never could get past the kissing and caressing part." She looked away, stoically staring at the portal. "We thought... We thought that if he spent more time with me doing every day things together, I'd relax with him and enjoy... being more intimate. He wanted to get married. He said I would feel differently about being intimate with him if we were legally married."

"You didn't agree?"

She shook her head. "He . . . was a very good friend. But he just wasn't the man for me." She turned to look accusingly at Sutter. "And he never got as upset about it as you are. I don't think he had a very…strong libido." Sutter was frowning. And she could feel the hard, throbbing pressure on her belly. There was nothing weak about Alex's libido. She wondered if he were in pain. Anxiously she tried to soothe him. "I'm sorry if you spent all night like that because of me." She blushed again and asked in a soft voice. "Does it hurt? Can I do something to make it easier for you?"

He half closed his eyes, trying not to think about how good it felt to be pressed against her soft belly. How fiercely he wanted to be inside her. "It aches, but it's not fatal. Hell." He sighed in exasperation. "It's not your fault, Sarah." He inhaled sharply, trying to slow the heavy beating of his pulse. Having her under him like this wasn't helping at all. But it felt so good, he couldn't drag himself away. "I can't believe you didn't want more than kissing from a man," he murmured, looking at her with the hunger for her growing in his eyes. "You're a hell of a good kisser," he pointed out with a husky laugh.

Sarah felt her heart contract as she looked into his face. His unshaved jaws were slightly darkened by a light morning shadow. A muscle in his cheek jerked tensely as he stared down at her. His lashes were very dark and the pupils in his eyes were expanding, making him look more vulnerable than she'd ever seen him. His hair was boyishly mussed, and she reached out to touch it lightly, smiling a little. The sensation of his bare warm skin against hers was unbelievably enticing and she snuggled against him, unconscious of the devastating effect it had on him. Her mouth went dry and she stared at him with her heart in her eyes.

"You're not a bad kisser yourself," she whispered rather unsteadily.

His mouth grew taut. "Don't look at me like that, Sarah," he muttered grimly. His eyes dropped to her mouth. It was too late, and he knew it. Oh, God. He knew it.

"Like what?" she whispered back. Her breathing was becoming very shallow. She watched his eyes darken as he let his gaze wander over the delicious curves of her shoulders and the delicate shapes of her breasts. She knew he could see a lot through the thin eyelet cotton. She felt her skin begin to tingle as goose bumps rose in the wake of his hot, steady perusal. Her nipples tightened as he stared at their pouting shapes beneath the fine white material. "When you look at me like that I feel like you're touching me all over," she whispered unsteadily. "Touching me all over with fire . . ."

He groaned, released her hands and lowered himself back down onto her, sliding his fingers into her hair, holding her head in his tender grasp. His body throbbed and his skin felt like molten metal. His mouth ached to kiss her. Her breath was sweet across his lips. He stared into her wide, unfocused eyes, and he saw surrender. His control slipped another notch as the blood in his veins turned to fire.

"Don't look at me like you want me to kiss you," he muttered as he lowered his lips to teasingly brush hers. He felt another hot surge of desire wash through his loins, and he knew that he wasn't going to have the strength to stop. He wanted her too much. Much too much. "Sarah," he muttered hoarsely. "I'm sorry . . ."

His mouth was hot and demanding and Sarah felt the fire in him as it burned against her skin. She had a distant memory of wondering why he was sorry just before every form of thinking became utterly impossible.

His hands were sliding down her body, lifting the thin cotton, moving over her bare skin. Everywhere he touched her she seemed to come alive. He made her feel wanted. Truly, desperately wanted. She moaned and arched against him, opening her mouth and welcoming his warm, sensuous invasion.

He desperately broke off the kiss and buried his face in her neck, panting as if he'd been running hard. He started swearing softly, and she felt a tremor rack his tense, lean body. He heaved himself onto his side and yanked the nightgown off her. His face was dark and taut as his hungry gaze traveled slowly down her nude body. She bent her knee and tried to turn away from him then, as embarrassment began to wash over her. Gently but firmly, he pushed her back down.

"I've seen you in my imagination stripped as bare as you are now," he murmured. He lowered his head to place a long, soul-wrenching kiss on her mouth. When he felt her relax again, he gently broke the kiss and lifted his head to gaze down on her. "As luscious as I saw you in my mind, Sarah, you're even lovelier in the flesh." He ran a fingertip slowly across her breast, then followed the path with his mouth. "You're soft and smooth and as warm as a fire in winter. Don't turn away. You're beautiful, Sarah."

His hot gaze frightened her, but it was an exciting kind of fear. A part of her warned that it was the kind of thing a man might be expected to say at a time like this, but she cupped his face in her hands and searched his eyes and saw nothing but honesty staring back at her like a slow, steady flame. And his low, soothing voice eased her fears, working on her like a hypnotic trance. He was mesmerizing, dissolving her resistance before it could begin. She wanted to believe him.

"Beautiful?" she murmured, pressing a soft kiss along his jaw. "You make me feel very beautiful," she whispered.

Pain flickered inside him. She was so young, so trusting. He tried to stop, but she pulled him down onto her breast, relaxing into his arms and he lost the last thread of his self-control.

Slowly he caressed her breasts and ran his hand over her belly, sending whispers of excitement rushing over her. She closed her eyes and moaned softly. All the years of icy resistance to this deep, primitive pleasure melted in the heat of his slow, steady onslaught. When he withdrew his hand, she whimpered in protest and reached for him, trying to bring him back, to continue the miracle. He pressed a soothing kiss on her throat and murmured reassurance, but again moved a little bit away. The bed dipped, and she opened her eyes to see him toss his pajama bottoms away.

He was magnificently naked as he turned back to her. Sarah swallowed and uncertainty began to creep into her eyes as she suddenly realized very clearly what she was about to do. What they were going to do. He saw the flicker of doubt in the depths of her soft brown eyes and he both wanted to comfort her and to distract her. It was too late to back out. He wouldn't let her go. He needed to make her his, to forge a bond with her. Every male instinct for sexual conquest rose up within him. He didn't give her another moment to think about it. He covered her with his body, and kissed her until she was pliant and eager and nearly as senseless with wanting as he was.

"It's all right, Sarah," he muttered huskily against her mouth.

His tongue traced a warm, enticing trail over her lips, along the sensitive interior of her mouth. His conscience was trying to shout at him that it wasn't all right at all, that he was seducing an innocent young woman, that he was going to regret this, but the blood coursing hotly through his veins drowned out the pleas.

He slid his hands into her soft, silky hair and cupped her head tenderly. He kissed her lips, gently, sweetly, oh so persuasively. Each skillfully drawn-out kiss was a cajoling plea convincing her to join him in the pleasure that he so intensely wanted to share with her.

Sarah didn't know when the last twinge of anxiety dissipated. Slowly she put her trusting arms around his strong, warm back. This was the first time, but it seemed as if it had always been meant to be. She knew his touch, she remembered his kiss. She felt as if she were coming home.

He bent his head and gently tongued first one taut nipple and then the other. Fierce, daring pleasure radiated from the place where his warm mouth teased her. Fiery arrows shot deep into her abdomen where he gently massaged the ache with the heel of his hand. The ache settled deeper, between her thighs and she raised her hips instinctively, trying to ease the discomfort against his thigh, which had slowly pressed between her legs.

He caressed the velvety skin of her inner thigh with his warm, knowing hand. She stiffened, roused from the erotic haze by the sudden intimacy of his touch. Alex wasn't about to let her think anymore, and he found the places that made her forget everything but the need to be in his arms. Sarah dug her nails along his back, moaning in pleasure. He laughed softly and kissed her ear, making her even wilder.

"Sweet, sweet Sarah," he whispered.

She felt him move over her, slide his hands under her hips and renew his command of her mouth with another devastatingly thorough kiss. If the world had been hit by a comet, she wouldn't have known or cared. There was only one thing that she cared about at that moment and it was being completely possessed by the man whose every touch was like a poignant memory of love. She heard his harsh, sobbing breaths as he broke the kiss for a moment and buried his face in the side of her neck, striving to regain control for a few more minutes.

"You're like a fire in my blood," he whispered harshly. And as he said it, it sounded almost like a bitter accusation, an admission reluctantly forced from his unwilling lips.

He wanted nothing more than to bury himself in her sweet, warm body. He was shaking, balancing on the edge of ecstasy. He shook his head in one last desperate effort to resist the temptation to just go ahead and take her. Flesh against flesh. Without precautions. He groaned and turned away.

Sarah felt him twist his body and then heard the sound of a packet being ripped open. She felt his hips shift, and then he was turning back to her. His mouth found hers and his hands ran slowly up and down her sides. He kneed her thighs apart and settled himself so that there was no pleasure point untouched. The slow grinding motion of his hips made her grow wet and warm and she squirmed against him, panting and almost crying in frustration.

"Easy, honey," he murmured to her. His voice sounded strained. "Do you like that? There. Easy..." He groaned.

"Please," she sobbed, rolling her head back and forth, not knowing why it felt so terribly close yet so far away. Something had to happen. "Please, please, please..."

He wanted it so fiercely for her that he could have died holding off his own pleasure. He felt her begin to go rigid under him and he held her tightly until the last wave eased up.

Then he entered her, barely able to think anymore, so desperate was his body for release. He pulled her thighs up around his hips and plunged all the way in. He felt Sarah stiffen at the invasion and he shook with the effort to hold himself still for a moment.

The brief, splitting pain made her go rigid, but she'd been so deeply and satisfyingly relaxed when he'd entered her that the pain was slight and soon gone. She sensed he was waiting for her to let him know she was all right, and she pressed her lips to his hot, damp cheek, lifting her hips in an unmistakable message. She felt his whole body untense for a split second as relief overwhelmed him. Then, as if he'd lost his last ounce of control, he began thrusting into her. She felt something building deep inside her. His breathing became hoarse and his hips were thrusting hard and fast. Suddenly they were kissing desperately and he was convulsing against her, groaning and crushing her in his arms, carrying her with him into the white-hot fires of ecstasy.

In the aftermath, the fires died down to a deep, warm glow.

Sarah hadn't expected the afterglow. But then, she hadn't expected the raging fires, either. Alex lay beside her, his breathing still rough and uneven, his forehead resting against the hollow of her shoulder. Lying there, wrapped in his arms as their breathing gradually evened out, feeling him relaxed against her while that unbelievable electricity sizzled everyplace that their warm, moist skin came in contact, Sarah wished that she could make time hold still for once. She wanted that poignant moment to last.

She was dimly aware of his lips on her throat again, more gently now, as if giving a tender kiss of thanks, or the farewell kiss that a knight might have reverently placed on his lady's hand. She smiled at the unexpected emotional message in that gesture. Alex was a complex man. Hard and cynical. Blunt and ruthless. Yet capable of being gentle, kind and tender. She wondered if he'd be annoyed to hear that was what she thought. She smiled.

Alex rolled away from her and lay with his arm across his eyes, listening to his rarely heard from conscience. He should have stopped. Things never should have gotten anywhere near this point between them. How in the hell had it? In his whole life, he'd never felt so out of control in his feelings for a woman. He wondered if it might be some early form of mid-life male crisis. He was bitterly tempted to laugh. Maybe he was simply losing his mind.

"Alex?" Sarah's voice was tentative. The afterglow had begun to fade as he physically separated from her, making room for her rational thinking to return. She'd turned onto her side and seen the tight set of his mouth, the grim look in his face, the tension in his arm over his eyes. She gathered the sheet, awkwardly trying to cover her nakedness, then she lightly touched his fingers with her own. "Are you all right?" she asked softly.

His mouth twisted wryly and he slowly turned to look at her. "I think that's my line," he told her. After all that had just happened, she was concerned about him. Salt in his wounds.

She tilted her head to one side. He looked like a god to her. As attractive as he'd seemed before, now he was even more so. She smiled awkwardly. "I'm . . . fine," she told him. What an incredible understatement. Her eyes softened and she couldn't tear them away from him. She could look at him forever, she thought wistfully.

He reached out to touch her cheek, tracing its lovely shape with one fingertip. "This 'honeymoon' has become more real than I intended, Sarah," he said slowly. He was never at a loss for words. So why couldn't he find the ones he wanted to say to her?

She saw the frown begin to gather on his face and had an awful thought. What if he was going to say he'd just been carried away by passion? That it was just proximity that had driven him into making love with her? That he didn't want her to feel anything truly deep or, heaven forbid, really lasting? Sarah knew she didn't want to hear those words from him. Not now. Not when she felt so much a part of him. Not when she ached for him to hold her.

She laid her finger across his lips. "It's not real," she said, barely above a whisper. "It's all a memory from some other time, some other place." He must think her crazy to talk like that, she thought. She felt a little crazy saying it out loud. "Would you mind . . . holding me a little while, though? Just a few moments more. Please." She smiled shyly and added solemnly, "No strings. I promise."

Alex closed his eyes and pulled her into his arms, grimly calling himself every kind of a fool there was. She wasn't going to ask anything of him. Not promises of love. Not eternal devotion. She just wanted a few moments more in his arms. Exactly what he'd have chosen for himself. The hell of it was that the feel of her wrapped close, legs entwining trustingly with his, eased his own discomfort. His sense of guilt grew harder to stomach.

"I'm sorry," he whispered, kissing her hair, gently nuzzling her ear. He eased himself free of her arms and got out of bed.

Sarah pulled the sheet over her and watched him with growing dismay as he walked around the cabin, retrieving their inside-out clothing, disappearing in the direction of the head.

When he returned, damp from a shower, she pushed herself up on her elbows and mustered her courage. "Why do you keep saying that?" she asked. She tried to sound calm, reasonable and prepared for any response he might give her. Her heart was beginning to ache, though, and she held her breath as she waited to hear what he would say.

She watched him pull on his shorts and stare at her for a very long moment. He gave every appearance of having no intention of answering. Her heart nearly stopped in suspense. She sensed he was trying to keep bad news from her. She didn't want that. With a little more determination, she repeated, "Why do you keep saying that you're sorry?"

Alex stood there looking as if he wished he didn't have to answer. "I'm...out of your league, Sarah," he said, trying to find a way to explain that would be the least hurtful to her. "You shouldn't be involved with me." A modern robber baron, barely on the right side of the law. He ran his hand over her soft, creamy skin and added, "And I shouldn't be involved with you." A woman who was tying him in knots. A woman who fascinated him like no other ever had. A radiant, passionately loving woman. Something ached inside him as he contemplated what he was refusing to let himself reach out and take.

Sarah took a deep breath. "You're out of my league?" she repeated. As he slowly nodded she managed a small, philosophical smile in spite of the sudden pain that had lanced her heart. "I see." She looked down at her hands as embarrassment warmed her cheeks. She knew he'd found physical pleasure with her. But obviously he wanted other things from a woman than that. He must think her very untutored in the ways of the world. Boring. She was sorely tempted to tell him that *she* was sorry. She seemed to have more to apologize for than he did.

Alex pulled her chin around and forced her to look at him. "You deserve better than this," he said softly, thinking of the roaming life he'd led and the difficulty he'd always had in admitting anyone into the intimate corners of his heart and mind.

He saw the fleeting expression of humiliation in her face and bit his tongue to keep from telling her that she had nothing to feel humiliated about. She was wonderful. She was intoxicating. He held his silence with an effort.

Sarah shrugged. "Thanks." She wasn't sure what he meant when he said she deserved something better. She licked her lips and forced herself to voice the obvious question. "You mean I deserve more than a brief...affair?" Her eyes were honest. She wasn't trying to force him to say something he didn't want to. She just wanted to know the truth.

"Yes." He frowned. No. That wasn't really what he meant. He knew he hadn't made love with her for that reason. He wanted her close to him. He wanted to possess her. He wanted her to possess him. And that was something he could never recall entertaining as a possibility before. Not ever.

His jaw tightened. It had to be some kind of temporary insanity. Maybe a virus. He was truly going mad. He shook his head and got up. "Why don't you get dressed while I make some coffee. We can talk over breakfast."

Maybe then he'd have unfogged his brain enough to be able to handle the whole situation with finesse. Just as everyone always expected him to, he thought dryly. On his way out of the cabin, he stepped over Wiley's sprawled figure and muttered critically, "You were no help at all, you son of a bitch."

Sarah scrambled to find her clothes and get cleaned up. Before she'd swallowed her first sip of Alex's coffee, however, they heard the sound of a powerful boat engine approaching the cruiser at high speed.

Alex bounded up the stairs and grimly stared at the craft closing in on them from the starboard side.

"Moreau's men are back."

Chapter 9

Four men watched them, waiting for orders from the man at the helm. They were dressed in cutoff jeans and tie-dyed tank tops. They looked like rejects from a beach party. She guessed them to be in their late twenties or thirties. And four pairs of eyes riveted on Sarah the moment she joined Alex on the deck.

She waved and smiled at them as if she were delighted to have them stop by. Her stomach felt cold and coiled in a knot as she ignored the blatant interest three of the men paid to her anatomy.

Alex moved a little in front of her. "Hello!" he called out, cupping his mouth with both hands. The boat rocked gently under his feet; he absorbed the motion effortlessly. "Fishing?" There were long poles sprouting from the back of Moreau's boat. Props, but effective.

The man behind the wheel swung the boat alongside Alex's and jumped down into full view. He was blond and blue eyed. He could have been a prep-school student turned ocean yachtsman who'd given it all up for a vagabond life. There was a hard, cool expression in his eyes that made Sarah very nervous. Below her, inside the boat, she heard Wiley growl low as he sensed her tension even at a distance.

The blond man grinned and leaned against the rail. "Yeah. We were out all night." He let his eyes run quickly over everything in sight. Then he took his time looking over Sarah. The smile changed a little, becoming more personal.

Alex smiled back, his teeth white against the light tan of his skin and his wind-rustled black hair. "Catch anything?" he asked interestedly.

The blond man nodded and refocused his attention on Sutter. "Yeah. These are good waters. We always catch a lot." His eyes narrowed slightly. "We saw you last night."

"Is that so?" Alex glanced at Sarah and the cool grin on his face became more rakish. "We didn't notice."

The men laughed. Sarah blushed and resisted the urge to put her arm around Alex and hide a little behind his back. She felt like a piece of meat being drooled over by a pack of male dogs. She hoped that Raymond hadn't miscalculated the potential danger represented by Moreau's men. She felt Wiley slink up beside her. She didn't have to look down to know his ears would be slightly flattened and his eyes on their visitors.

The men stopped laughing.

"Where are you from?" the blonde asked conversationally. His eyes had narrowed considerably upon seeing Wiley.

Alex knew they'd seen the boat's name and home port on the stern. They were stalling for time, deciding what to do with them. He wondered what choices they were considering. Every time one of them stared at Sarah he felt a cold fury twist in his gut at one possibility that sprang to mind. He and Raymond had agreed that he would be unarmed on the boat and going onto the island. It was the only way to do it. But right now he would have changed it all without a second thought. Even a diver's knife strapped to his leg would have been welcome.

"The Caymans," Alex answered. He pulled Sarah up against his side and casually draped one arm around her shoulders. She felt cold even though the sun had heated the deck already. She must be scared stiff, he thought. He kissed her on the cheek and grinned broadly at the boatload of staring brigands. "We're on our honeymoon."

The blonde laughed and nodded his head. "I guess you're not fishing, then," he said, leering at Sarah suggestively.

Alex repressed the sudden urge to leap across the space separating them and knock the man's teeth down his throat. Instead he grinned back and nodded. "No fishing," he agreed.

The blonde motioned toward the dog. There was a cold gleam in his eyes now. "I never heard of anyone taking a dog on their honeymoon," he said suspiciously. He motioned again and one of the men picked up a rifle and pointed it straight at Alex's heart.

Alex's face hardened and he pushed Sarah behind him.

The blonde told one of the other men, "Search them. And the rest of the boat."

Wiley would have leaped straight at the man, but Sarah had given him the hand signal to stay. Through slitted eyes, the Labrador watched the man frisk first Alex, then Sarah. His hands lingered over Sarah and he grinned crookedly.

"They're clean." He hopped down into the cabin and turned things inside out.

"What do you want?" Alex demanded, eyes glittering dangerously as he stared at the blond man calling the shots.

The blonde grinned back and shook his head. "Now, now. Don't get testy. You're in our waters, man. We're just making sure you're not dangerous."

"Do we look dangerous?" Alex asked coldly.

The blonde wasn't sure. "People aren't always what they look like they are. Especially in the Caribbean." He swung back up and got on the radio. After a few short interchanges with someone on the other end of the connection, he called out, "Okay. Get back over here, Reedy."

The lean, darkly tanned man who'd searched them jumped back onto their boat.

Sarah moved closer to Alex, putting her hands on his shoulders. He hadn't put his hands down. The man still held a rifle on him. Sarah didn't have to act at all to let the fear show in her eyes. The thought of a bullet piercing him was horrifying.

The blonde shouted for the gun to be lowered, then shrugged apologetically at Alex. "Sorry, pal. But we can't be too careful. There are a lot of downright pirates in these waters." The men laughed.

"Yeah," Sutter agreed, lowering his arms. He pressed a small button on the panel beneath the railing as the other boat began to back away.

There was a small explosion and Sarah was flung against Alex's back. Wiley skittered across the deck as the boat lurched and began to list slightly to one side. Alex's arm came around her as he steadied them. For a moment he squeezed her hard. She looked into his eyes and saw the determination there. And the confidence that this was going to work. She drew in her breath and focused on what she was supposed to do. Scrambling for the life jackets, she spared a quick look at the smugglers. Guns had materialized in their hands. Expensive ones. With fancy scopes. And they were watching the chaos on Alex's boat with obvious suspicion.

She prayed. Wiley was standing in his jacket. She and Alex had on theirs. Alex was working the cruiser's emergency equipment from the helm while swearing impressively. She desperately did everything he told her to, hoping their audience would believe the act was real. And unpremeditated.

Alex jumped down below and reemerged a few moments later wearing a grim expression. He was picking up the handpiece for his radio when the blond man shouted, "Can we be of any help?"

Alex hesitated. "Help? I'm not sure we want your help." He looked pointedly at the guns.

The smugglers' captain said something to them. The guns disappeared from sight.

"I think we'd be better off calling in an SOS," Alex argued, unimpressed.

The blonde smiled apologetically. "Are you in danger of sinking?"

Alex shrugged. "I don't know. I don't intend to bet our lives on it. It looks like we've got a hole below the waterline, but the boat should be sealed off. Only one fuel compartment is taking water. We ought to be able to limp as far as Jamaica, if nothing else goes wrong."

The blonde looked at the radio in Alex's hand. "Or you could sit here until another boat comes to help," he said, saying what Alex had not.

Alex nodded. "I could do that. There are a few nearby. We passed a naval vessel yesterday evening. It seemed to be hanging around, like they lost something. They might even be able to help me repair the damage, if they're not in a hurry."

The blond man's face hardened noticeably. It was obvious he didn't like inviting the navy any closer, or giving them any excuse to stay in these waters. "Wait a minute," he yelled. "Let me call my boss." He turned to his radio.

"Do you think he's going to take us to the island?" Sarah murmured, shielding her eyes from the sun. She couldn't tell what Alex was thinking. He was completely focused on keeping them afloat.

Alex flicked a look toward the blond captain. "Yeah. I think he will. I don't think they want the navy here if they can avoid it. And I don't think they want to call attention to themselves by doing us any harm."

The blond man jumped down onto the foredeck of his boat and lifted his hand. "We'll give you a tow," he shouted, grinning engagingly, although his eyes were still curiously flat and emotionless.

Alex, not in any hurry to be saved and with grave doubt written all over his face, stood with his hands on his hips and stared back at the man. "At gunpoint?" he asked.

The blond man had one of his men maneuver the boat into towing position. "Naw. Forget that. We just had to make sure you weren't drug runners or that kind of riffraff. You know how it is out here."

Alex lifted an eyebrow. "Yeah. I know." He grabbed the line being tossed at him. "Where are you offering to take us?" he inquired.

The blond man's grin became a little less friendly. "Do you have any choice?" he asked.

Alex was about to say yes, he did, and the other man recognized that. Quickly he threw another line, this time to Sarah.

"You don't want your new bride stuck out here with the U.S. navy, do you, man? Come on. Our island isn't far. Forty minutes away. We can help you repair the damage to your boat and you can pick up your honeymoon where you left off." His eyes ran over Sarah suggestively.

Alex laughed to keep from showing the bastard how angry he was. "Does this island have a name?"

"Tortuga Escondida."

"How did anyone ever find this island to begin with?" Sarah muttered as she stood next to Alex by the helm. "And I thought the Caymans were small." She shook her head and stared, wide eyed.

"Not many did find it," Alex said dryly. He pointed at the sea breaking into white foam over a coral reef that half embraced the small dab of land rising above the clear blue. "And the ones who did ran the risk of being dragged against its reefs. It's not exactly a welcoming oasis."

He pointed to a mast sticking out of the water a few hundred yards off the port bow. "There was water on the island, filtered up through the limestone, but no naturally growing plant life. Until a hundred years ago, if you were stranded here for long, you were likely to develop scurvy. At the very least."

They were using one of the engines; only one of the screws had been affected by the damage they'd inflicted in the explosion, but Alex kept a second shut off for good measure. The tow lines to the other big cruiser had been taut most of the way. As soon as they cleared the reefs, Alex would limp their bark gently into Moreau's port to tie up.

The island rose a mere hundred and fifty feet out of the water, and it was less than ten miles wide. Trees had been brought to it seventy-five years ago and had flourished, bringing a much-needed green to its barren seascape. Coconut palms and Bermuda grass and a few flowering bushes gave it a pleasing appearance. And then Sarah saw the stark cement wall that rose up a hundred feet above the beach like a medieval castle. Forked along its top were what looked like artillery openings. And there were guns bristling out the slits.

"Charming little beach house," Sarah observed. She scratched Wiley's ear and watched the rest of the fortress appear before her as they cruised around the southern circumference of the island. There were three piers, each with a fast ocean-worthy boat tied to it. Boats the size of coast-guard cutters. Boats that appeared to be armed. There was a satellite dish and several large antennae rising from a spot not far from what looked like the main house. "All the comforts of home," she murmured.

Alex laughed but without much amusement. "If you can call this viper's nest a home," he conceded.

Sarah had seen a sketch of Antonio Moreau at Raymond's office and she recognized him the moment she laid eyes on him. She had just jumped off the boat and was trying to make the pier stop swaying beneath her feet when he strode down onto the planking and came out to meet them. He walked with a slight swagger, like a man who was accustomed to acknowledging cheers from the sidelines. His jet-black hair was slick with water. His canary-yellow shirt was wide open and unbuttoned halfway down his hairy chest. Gold glittered rapaciously in the front of his mouth as he grinned at her and held out his hand.

"Ah, the honeymooner," he exclaimed, kissing the icy flesh of her hand, letting his fingers linger a little longer than necessary before he released her. His eyes were coffee colored. They were also quite, quite cold.

Sarah forced a tired smile. She figured she was entitled to look exhausted, all things considered. "It hasn't gone exactly the way I'd always dreamed it would," she admitted. Alex had joined her and she could feel his warmth at her back. She leaned back against him and closed her eyes. "Has it, darling?" she murmured.

It was impossible to argue with that. "No. It's been a rough twenty-four hours." He met Moreau's narrow scrutiny and said, "Alex Sutter." He held out his hand and firmly shook Moreau's. "I don't suppose we could rent a room somewhere around here? I don't think I want to sleep in the cruiser again until we've checked out the damage."

Moreau threw back his head and laughed. "Rent a room? No. But you can be my guests. As you can imagine, we are a little isolated here. As it happens, no one is visiting, and I have several suites I can put at your disposal."

"You are too kind," Alex said smoothly. He frowned. "I'm sorry, I don't believe I got your name."

Moreau motioned for them to come with him. "My name is Antonio. Antonio Moreau. This is my island. And those were my men who found you." There was an arrogant pride in his voice. "And your beautiful bride?" He lifted his harsh black brows expectantly.

"Sarah," she supplied. She glanced back at Alex's boat and then at Alex. "Uh, could we bring along my dog?" she asked Moreau apologetically.

On cue, Wiley poked his head up above the stair.

Moreau was obviously not surprised. "Ah, yes, the honeymooners with a dog." His slit-eyed gaze slithered from Wiley to Sarah to Alex. He grinned from ear to ear and nodded vigorously. "Of course. I love dogs. Just make sure to keep him very close, Sarah. It might be dangerous for him to stray from your side."

She called Wiley, who leaped ashore and trotted alongside her as they climbed the limestone staircase up into the fortress that Moreau called home.

"What could be dangerous, Antonio?" she asked innocently.

"There are some very big lizards on my island," he said slyly. "They could get hungry enough to make a meal of anything that strayed."

Sarah laughed. "Are you pulling my leg?" she asked. She gave him a wide-eyed stare as he glanced at her. When his eyes traveled slowly down her bare legs, she acted as though it didn't bother her in the least.

"Why no," Antonio said with exaggerated solemnity. He glanced at Alex's face and chuckled. "I wouldn't dare. I doubt that your husband would like that at all."

Alex smiled at the drug runner but his eyes were as hard as flint. "I think you are a very perceptive man."

Moreau laughed and led them into a door cut through the limestone rock face.

Alex found Sarah's hand with his. She squeezed his strong fingers and wondered if Gabrielle was still on the island. And still alive.

Their room had one door, and louvered windows that opened out over a fifteen-foot drop to a rocky slope that rolled downward to the sandy beach. The bed was large and covered with cotton sheets splashed with brilliant red and yellow flowers. A large wooden armoire, ornately carved and painted a dull gold, stood along the wall next to a valet, dresser and chair.

Alex watched as two of their "rescuers" dumped their gear in a heap in the middle of the room. "Thank you," he said with a sardonic lift of his brow.

He closed the door. They were alone. Sarah sat down on the bed and let out the breath she'd been holding while Alex glanced thoughtfully around the room.

"I think I'll put a few things away," he murmured.

Sarah watched as he took his time, examining things with a lot more interest then she thought they merited. Instead of studying Moreau's household furnishings, he ought to be planning the next step of their mission. She frowned.

"Don't you think we should—" she began.

"Why don't you put your things on the dresser," he interrupted. He glanced pointedly at the mirror there. "Fix your pretty face, darling."

Sarah crossed her arms stubbornly. "I'm not budging. I want to know when—"

He'd crossed the floor, pulled her into his arms and kissed her before she could finish the sentence. As he buried his face in her hair, she heard him murmur. "There are lots of insects in the islands. Have you noticed how infested it is here?"

Sarah pulled her head back and looked into his eyes. He wasn't kidding. He grinned slightly and nibbled her lips provocatively but the look in his eyes was not seductive. He was trying to tell her something. "Insects?" she murmured. Her eyes lit up. "As in lots of little bugs?"

"Uh-huh." And then he enfolded her in his arms and kissed her.

After a few very satisfying moments, he loosened his hold on her and said with regret, "It must be close to lunchtime. I'll bet our host will let us dine with him." He put a light kiss on her forehead. "Let's get unpacked and out of here in the next fifteen minutes."

Sarah giggled when he patted her bottom. She assumed he was playing for the audience that they apparently had. She tried to keep up her part of the masquerade. Then she saw the small wire running behind the armoire, and the tiny metal disc Alex casually indicated in the lamp.

Their eyes met. Sarah wished she had more experience at this sort of thing. He'd been right. He didn't need an amateur. He needed a pro.

"I wish I could be more help," she told him sincerely.

Sutter shrugged and shook his head. "I didn't expect you to be able to repair boats when I married you," he said.

"Thank goodness for that."

There was a knock at the door. "Señor Moreau would like you to join him for lunch," said a voice. It was a woman's.

Sarah opened the door. The invitation was being given by a gray-haired mestiza woman about four and a half feet tall. Her face was creased and her eyes were soft and worn. She looked as if she'd lived a hundred years, but she couldn't have been more than sixty.

"Thank you," Sarah told her. Glancing at Alex, who nodded, she said, "We'd love to. Could you show us the way?"

"*Sí, señora.* This way."

Raymond had said that Moreau liked to entertain, and it didn't take long to realize how accurate that assessment had been. Fresh fruits and vegetables had been flown in from Florida, meats from Texas, liquors and spices from Jamaica. There was room in the dining room to serve forty or fifty people with ease. And it looked out onto a broad, white-tiled patio that overlooked the sea.

Moreau arrived at the same time they did. The blond, preppy-looking boat captain was with him.

"You've already met Craig," Moreau said, gesturing to his subordinate.

"I don't believe we got around to names," Alex said. He pulled out Sarah's chair and sat down next to her.

Moreau chuckled and sat on Sarah's other side. "Craig Moreton. Of Rhode Island, Connecticut, San Diego and Tortuga Escondida."

Sarah managed to look impressed, and she smiled admiringly at him. "You've traveled a lot," she said.

Craig nodded and gave her a measured smile. "Yeah." He passed the marinated fish appetizer and reached for the cold glass of beer that had just been placed in front of him.

Sarah shook out a linen napkin and turned to try out her most admiring smile on their host. "You certainly like to live in style, even if you are a little cut off from the world here, Mr. Moreau."

He seemed pleased, but he was not a fool and flattery from an easily impressed young woman had obviously not turned his head in many years. "I have always believed that you should enjoy the fruits of your own labors," he explained. His golden smile glinted. "And please, do not call me Mr. Moreau. Antonio. Call me Antonio."

"Antonio," she acceded with a fluttery smile. Smiling on cue was coming naturally to her, she thought in amusement. She looked at the food in front of her and tried to forget what Moreau had just said. She was too hungry not to eat, but she suffered a twinge of acute indigestion as she fleetingly pondered what illegal labors had earned the money that had purchased her lunch.

The conversation drifted from one innocuous topic to the next. Sarah wondered how they had all learned to banter so effortlessly while revealing so little about themselves. She felt Wiley nudge her ankle and she cleared her throat. She surreptitiously slipped him a piece of cold meat from one of her salads.

Moreau slapped a copy of the *Caymanian Compass* onto the table. Sarah nearly jumped guiltily. For a moment she'd thought he'd noticed her feeding the dog and didn't like it. Then she realized he was pointing to their "wedding" photo and article.

"We try to keep up with the news here," Moreau boasted, looking past Sarah to Alex. "Notice of your wedding was a highlight of the islands news." His eyes had narrowed thoughtfully. "I thought your name was familiar when Craig told me who he'd found. When I saw the article, it began to come back to me. You've been around the islands for a long time, eh? I seem to remember knowing someone in the Bahamas who had done some business with you a few years ago. I believe you helped him import some items that had been . . . difficult to acquire."

Sarah heard the subtle insinuation in Moreau's voice. He was hinting that Alex may have given some illegal help. She glanced at her silent "spouse" and said, "Why, Alex, I didn't know you'd worked in the Bahamas." Was it true? What Moreau was insinuating?

He gave her a level stare and an unencouraging smile. "I didn't want to bore you with details of my work."

Moreau laughed and slapped his fork against the tabletop. "Women always want to know everything! You should know by now, Alex, that nothing about their man bores them. It can be...inconvenient!"

Sarah looked mildly indignant and cast a critical look from silent "husband" to their chuckling host. "I beg your pardon!"

Moreau seemed to enjoy her irritation and merely laughed harder. "I'm sorry, Sarah. But what would you know of such things? Being a woman—" he glanced at her meaningfully "—and such a pretty one."

Before Sarah could launch into a blistering retort, Alex interrupted. "She also doesn't know anything about boat repair," he said smoothly. "In the interest of keeping her nose out of that, I wonder if she could take Wiley for a walk while I work on the damage?"

"Of course," Moreau swiftly agreed. His eyes took on a calculating gleam. "I would be happy to show her around."

"You're too kind," Sarah said weakly.

The vision of being alone in Moreau's company was strongly unappealing to Sarah. She wanted to be free to look around without having someone observing her actions all the time. Especially someone as shrewd and observant as Moreau. They'd discussed her taking advantage of any such opportunities that came her way. Moreau's presence would be a complication.

Alex seemed abominably pleased. She didn't know whether she was more surprised or shocked to realize that.

"Thanks," he told Moreau. "I'm sure she won't get lost or fall into the sea if she's with you."

Moreau shook his head. He kissed the hand of a young girl serving him coffee. She blushed and giggled and ran barefooted from the room.

"I have never lost a woman on a walk around this island. Of that I can assure you."

"Isn't that wonderful?" Sarah managed to exclaim as all the men turned their attention to her. "That certainly makes me feel better." She gave Alex a level stare. "I can't wait to go."

Sarah closed her eyes as Alex bent close to kiss her lingeringly on the mouth. Was there a message in the warmth of his lips? Or did she just imagine that he was trying to give her courage? When he squeezed her hand, she no longer had any doubts. Their eyes met as he broke the kiss. There was warmth and something deep and hard in his expression.

"Enjoy your walk, darling," Alex said. "We can trade stories later," he murmured.

Sarah watched him disappear with Craig Moreton. Then Moreau's hand was at her chair back. She was alone with him. Except for Wiley.

"Are you ready?" Moreau asked. His soft, silky voice was different from the one he had used with Alex over lunch. It was the voice of a man who thought he was being seductive, she realized.

Sarah took a deep breath. Ready? She wasn't really sure. But she had no choice. She smiled at him.

"Oh, yes. I can hardly wait to see your pretty island, Antonio. It's very kind of you to show me around."

Chapter 10

Sarah had seen at least sixty different photographs of Moreau's island. Most were overhead shots, blown up to show great detail. She knew what she was going to see. Seeing it at eye level was very different than seeing it from a satellite blowup, however, and it took concentration to connect the reality all around her with the memory of those scattered pictures.

Moreau led her along the "main street" of his complex—a cement strip wide enough for a small car to drive on. It meandered through the sparse trees and sandy rock, always within sight of the sprawling fortress along the south shore.

Wiley sniffed and stopped with helpful regularity, giving Sarah plenty of time to get her bearings and examine landmarks. She saw the easternmost end of the fortress and her heart chilled. That was where Gabrielle was being kept. At least, that was where she was the last time anyone had been able to report it.

"Is that the end of your castle?" Sarah asked innocently, shielding her eyes from the strong midday sun and pointing toward the place where she hoped Gabrielle still was.

Moreau seemed entertained by her choice of words and laughed condescendingly. "My castle? How kind of you to call it that. It's merely my humble home."

Sarah's brown eyes widened at his outrageous humility. "If this is a humble little home, you must have grown up in the Vatican," she exclaimed.

A tic twitched in Moreau's jaw and his eyes became half slits. "No, Sarah. I grew up...in rather different circumstances." There was a cool dislike in every word he uttered. He obviously hated remembering his roots. The moment passed, and he cloaked himself in an attitude of careless charm. "I am the proverbial poor boy who made good. It's much admired in your country, in many countries."

"Yes. Congratulations." She smiled flirtatiously as he gave her a slight bow indicating his acceptance of her praise. There was a dangerous light in his cold, dark eyes as he noted her increased openness to him. Sarah hurried on before he took her light invitation to friendliness more seriously than she intended. "Then you know what a castle this place is. Is it a secret hideaway? How on earth did you find it? Are you going to add on to it?"

Moreau chuckled. He appeared disarmed by her sudden gush of questions. She was just a silly young woman, interested in nest building. "It's not exactly a secret, but no one comes ashore without my permission. Unless there's a hurricane or some emergency."

"Of course." Sarah hoped no one ever had to bet their life on his hospitality in an emergency. She wouldn't have wanted to bet hers. She gave him a cajoling look. "How on earth did you ever find it out here in the middle of nowhere?"

He shrugged and spread his hands, as if it wasn't really so difficult and there wasn't much to explain. "It's been so long ago, I've forgotten, Sarah. To tell you the truth, I'd heard about it for years. It was sold a couple of times. The last time, I happened to have the financial ability to buy it."

"How wonderful," Sarah said with a sigh, great admiration shining through each overstated word.

Moreau was too egotistical to realize she wasn't serious and he beamed and pushed out his chest a little. "I've done modestly well for a poor boy from a big-city slum."

"You certainly have."

They stopped a few hundred feet from the three-story building's end. Moreau rubbed his chin thoughtfully.

"Until just now, when you asked me, I never thought about adding on to it. I made a few . . . modifications . . . when I first acquired Tortuga Escondida, but I've been too busy to think about it since. Perhaps it would be a good idea."

Wiley had returned to her side and was paying very close attention to the bushes around the edge of the building. He'd seen or scented something and was preparing to confront it. A guard and one of the dogs, she thought. One of the dogs she'd trained. Perhaps he already had her scent. She hoped he could remember it. It had been a long time since he'd seen her or smelled her. She crossed her fingers and held Wiley by the leash she'd brought along.

"You've certainly made your own paradise, Antonio," she said.

They rounded the end of the building and came face-to-face with a guard in uniform wearing a holstered gun and heeling a big Doberman pinscher at his left side.

"*Hola,* Friedrich," Moreau said to the red-haired dog handler.

Friedrich snapped to attention and then gave Sarah a slow, interested perusal. Sarah was more concerned with the reception she was getting from the Doberman. He was staring at her through round eyes that betrayed no recognition of her at all. His teeth were slightly bared. And there was a tightness in his stance that warned he was fully prepared to spring at her at a moment's notice.

Sarah's heart fell. Maybe they'd built their hopes on a fantasy. What if the dogs didn't remember her? That spine-chilling thought gave rise to hysterical laughter that she managed to keep frozen deep in her throat. *I'm so sorry, Alex.*

"Sarah, you look very strange," Moreau was saying with touching solicitude. He put a hand lightly on her shoulder, withdrawing it with equal fastidiousness as Wiley growled.

Sarah reached deep and found a light smile for him. "Sorry, I was just thinking that your castle looks very forbidding from down here. I mean, having a guard and dog patrolling..." She tried to appear curious. "Do you have that much trouble?" She sighed and swung her hand around in an arc, encompassing the waving palms and a few small birds singing in the bushes. "It looks like such a paradise."

Moreau had been watching Wiley as she spoke, but now turned his attention back to Sarah. "We haven't had any trouble," he told her softly. "And I intend to keep it that way." He glanced up at the square-cut windows above them and frowned. Someone had appeared in the shadows. He wasn't pleased. He turned back the way they had come. "Perhaps we should see how your husband is doing on the repairs to your boat," he suggested smoothly.

Sarah leaned back and spread her arms, as if she were trying to soak up the warm Caribbean sunlight. "If you insist," she said with a mournful pout. Dimples appeared in her cheeks and she permitted a girlish smile to shine through her disappointment. "But Alex told you that I'm no help at all with any of that. So if you're hoping that my being there will speed him up, I'm sorry. You'll be very disappointed." She shielded her eyes coquettishly with her hand and tilted her head to one side as she continued to grin at him, unabashed. "Now who would have thought I'd be spending my honeymoon strolling on an island paradise with another man? My mother would be horrified!"

He was surprised, but he seemed to accept her teasing as something to be expected. Sarah decided he definitely had the ego and personality of a hard-core Latin-lover type. He turned her stomach, especially since she knew how he'd lived and what he'd done, but she fiercely repressed her revulsion. The key to managing him was flattery and expressions of admiration. That was what Raymond had told her and she was in complete agreement.

He sent a pointed glance in Wiley's direction. "I would enjoy strolling, as you so charmingly put it, arm in arm, but your dog doesn't appear to approve."

Sarah slipped her arm through Moreau's and laughed. "He's a little overprotective," she explained lightheartedly. "Don't mind him. He'd never bite."

Moreau didn't look too sure of that, but he looked into Sarah's eyes, caressing her with his, then pulled his elbow in toward his body, capturing her arm. "I've had chaperons accompany me while I took young ladies for a walk," he reminisced, amused. "But the chaperons never had four feet before."

Sarah laughed cheerfully. "There's a first time for everything, I guess."

He shot an assessing look at her, as if turning over possibilities in his mind. "I suppose that's true. So, tell me, how did you meet Alex?"

Sarah was well prepared to answer that particular question, and she relaxed. She gave Moreau a more personal smile and spun out the imaginary story that Alex and Raymond and she had agreed on. By the time they reached the pier where Alex's boat was being repaired, Moreau was glassy eyed with boredom from hearing about it.

Alex jumped from the deck to the pier and saw her. He also saw the close contact that Moreau was maintaining, keeping her arm tucked in his. His eyes were dark and unyielding as he approached them.

"Did you enjoy your walk?" he asked. He flicked his gaze over her coolly. Wiley wasn't the only one who could act overprotective.

Sarah threw herself into his arms and gave him a big kiss, much to his surprise. And Moreau's.

"Of course. Now is the boat all fixed? Are we ready to go?" She sounded suitably eager and optimistic.

Alex held her against his chest with her toes brushing against the wood planks. "Sorry, darling. Almost. We tried, but the explosion bent a lot of things out of shape. Covering the ones we can't rebend here is taking a little longer than we'd hoped."

Sarah made a petulant moue with her mouth and she sank her fingers in his dark hair, which was already in great disarray from the work he'd been doing.

Alex's mouth tightened. "Don't be a spoiled brat, Sarah," he said sharply. He let her slide down his front, then he slid his hand possessively over her bottom. "Besides, we're together. I thought that's all you wanted from a honeymoon." He managed to look suitably annoyed that she was complaining already in their marriage.

Moreau was trying not to grin too broadly at this display of domestic disharmony. "Perhaps you wouldn't mind if I left you alone? I have some business to attend to."

Alex gave him a level glance. "Go right ahead."

Sarah nuzzled his neck affectionately while Moreau walked back up the trail toward the sprawling house. When she could no longer hear his footsteps, she whispered into Alex's ear, "Can I tell you how much I missed you now?" They needed a safe place to talk. She hoped that he might have found somewhere where they wouldn't be overheard.

Alex bent as if to kiss her ear, but instead he murmured, "Not here, darling. Why don't we find someplace a little more private? Then you can show me."

He covered her mouth with his, and Sarah clung to him. He was comfort and warmth and strength, mystery and excitement and adventure. He was everything she'd ever wanted in a man. Being in his arms was like coming home. When he gently disengaged them, she felt the loss everywhere. She had to concentrate to keep from trembling in disappointment. He was only kissing her as part of the act, of course, but she found that it touched her heart anyway. She put her arm around his waist and walked with him onto the boat.

"I'll show you what we've done," he said casually. "Then you can tell me about your day." He grinned at her rakishly. "Maybe under a nice, cool shower. You look hot, darling."

Sarah laughed and followed him down into the cabin area to see what he was talking about. She stopped laughing when he pulled her into the head with him and began turning on the water spigots of the shower.

"I thought you were kidding," she said faintly.

He put his hands on his hips and frowned at her. "If you want to talk, get in," he said succinctly.

Sarah turned her back and stripped down to her underwear. She was about to say she didn't care to remove anything else, but he saved her the trouble by laughing softly and telling her to hurry up. He was already standing under the water, unashamedly naked and lathering himself with the soap when she stepped into the spray.

"I didn't think you really meant to take a shower," she said in surprise.

He glanced over his shoulder at her and grinned, seeing her two semitransparent garments plastered to her skin. "So I see."

He tossed her the soap anyway. "Might as well, while you're here."

Sarah felt ridiculous, but she scrubbed herself down with the bar, skirting the completely soaked bra and panties.

"Ahh," Alex groaned in pleasure as the water sluiced over him. He opened one dark eye and lifted his brow questioningly. "See anything unexpected?" He pulled her close so that she had to answer close to his ear.

"No. Everything was exactly where it was supposed to be," she said. It was easy to lean forward and rest her arms around him as she talked. And the soothing feel of his hands on her back as the water ran over them in steady rivulets... It made everything a little more bearable. "There was a shadow in the window at the end, like someone was walking in front of it. I couldn't make anything out. I don't know who it was."

"And the dogs?"

Sarah took a deep breath. "I saw one. With his handler." She felt his hands still on her back. He was waiting for more. It wasn't what she wanted to tell him, but she had no choice. He needed to know. "The pinscher would have come at me on command," she said softly. "He wouldn't have hesitated for even a second." Alex was very still as he absorbed what she'd said. She pressed her face against his neck. "I'm sorry, Alex," she said miserably. "Maybe... maybe the next time something will come back to him. Pinschers are strange dogs. He was a juvenile when I handled him. He's full grown now. They aren't always trustworthy when they've reached sexual maturity. Especially the males."

He squeezed her gently and murmured, "I can relate to that."

She jerked her head up in surprise. There was a soft gleam in his eyes. "How can you joke at a time like this?" she asked, somewhat in awe of his relaxed attitude about such bad information. "What if I can't do my part? What if the dogs won't obey me?"

He shrugged. "That hasn't happened yet," he pointed out. He lifted her chin and looked steadily into her worried eyes. "You did a good job." He recalled the arm-in-arm return with Moreau and a frown gathered on his brow. "Don't overdo it getting friendly with the host," he warned softly. "No more locked elbows."

Sarah wondered if that was a good idea or not. "It did make him relax more, thinking I was just another bimbo who admired his masterful accomplishments." She couldn't help grimacing.

Alex's eyes hardened. "Keep your distance from him. Let him think you're so smitten with me that you have no interest in another man's attention, not even for innocent flirting."

He was being very firm about it. She looked at him doubtfully. "If you're sure. But I could keep him distracted...."

Alex began to look downright angry then. "No. I told you that I was out of your league, Sarah," he pointed out bluntly. "Well you're not even in the same galaxy with him. It's too dangerous. Stick with Wiley."

Sarah was slightly incensed that he'd think her so lacking in female sophistication that she couldn't take advantage of Moreau, not even a little bit. But to be told to confine herself to her dog's company! She gave him an outraged glare and stepped away with a violent tug. "Yes, sir," she said emphatically. She stepped out of the shower, dried herself with a rough white towel and tugged on her clothes, mumbling irritably to herself.

Alex was frowning at her and wondering why she was reacting that way. He wanted to protect her, damn it! And he didn't want to risk Moreau's taking a serious, close and personal look at Sarah. Alex was afraid that Moreau might decide she was worth playing with, even if she were on her honeymoon and her husband was on the island with her.

Sarah stomped out of the boat with Wiley on her heels and Alex fastening his pants as he leaped after her.

Moreau ran into them just as Alex was catching up and about to grab Sarah by the arm to give her a piece of his mind. "When I left, you were disagreeing. When I come back, you still look angry. Are honeymoons not all they say they are?" he asked teasingly.

Sarah smiled brilliantly. "I wouldn't know," she said blithely. "I haven't had enough of one to say." She gave Alex a pointed glare and marched off in the direction of their room.

Moreau shook his head and the gold in his teeth glittered in the late-afternoon sun. "I think it is time for a drink." He put his arm around Alex's shoulders and they turned toward the patio and its wet bar. "Tell me. What would you like?"

To shake Sarah's teeth until they rattled, Alex thought, still staring at her disappearing backside. Delectably curved little thing. And wet where her damp underwear was soaking through her shorts.

Moreau noticed the direction of Sutter's gaze and laughed robustly. "Didn't you let her even take her clothes off? Eh, mon! You've got to be more patient! That's no way to start off a lifetime together. You've got to mellow out." He seemed vastly amused by it all. "You need a little anesthesia. It's been a rough honeymoon," he conceded magnanimously. "I'll give you a double. A triple. You'll be feeling no pain in no time at all. What will it be? Bourbon? Rum? Gin?" He looked at Alex expectantly. Moreau did enjoy playing the consummate host.

"A double. Any brand of whiskey you've got." Alex didn't know whether he needed the drink more to dull his concern for Sarah or to ease the distaste of having Antonio Moreau this close without breaking the man's neck. Hell. It didn't make much difference.

"Keekee," Moreau shouted to the young Jamaican woman who was replenishing the bar glasses and draping herself over one of the stools in expectation of a little nightlife with Moreau's second in command. "Bring the bottle of whiskey over to the table, eh, *chiquita*?"

"*Sí*, Antonio," she giggled.

"And the ice. Don't forget the ice."

Chiquita didn't forget the ice.

By the time Sarah and Wiley found their way back to the patio, everyone was feeling very mellow indeed. Antonio was roaring with laughter at some off-color story that Moreton had just finished telling in a combination of English, Spanish and French. The red-haired guard was now off duty and sitting with his boots propped up on the table, gulping down his third beer. Several of Moreau's men were playing cards, smoking and fondling two of the women who'd crept out of the woodwork since lunch.

Sarah stood with Wiley and frowned. "Den of thieves," she muttered to herself. Maybe they'd get drunk enough that she could walk off and let Gabrielle out without anyone knowing what was happening. That was a brightening thought and she was smiling as she sauntered over to the table where Alex was listening to Moreau trying to come up with a tale more outrageous than Moreton's.

Moreau saw her and pushed his chair back to rise to his feet. "The bride!" he called out with a grin. He glanced at the blue-and-red cotton sundress she'd donned and grinned even more. "You look drier than you did the last time I saw you," he said slyly. When she blushed he laughed. "What do you drink, Sarah?"

Normally tea, but she couldn't say that. She didn't want anything to spoil Moreau's relaxed mood. The suspiciousness that had clung to him ever since they arrived had dissipated a great deal. Perhaps it was the drinking. Or perhaps he was becoming more confident that they were merely stranded honeymooners. Either way, she didn't want to rearouse his doubts.

She caught her lip between her teeth and thought about it. "What do you normally drink down here? Rum?"

Moreau added. "Yes. But we have anything you want. I never liked doing without."

Sarah could well imagine that. She touched her tongue thoughtfully to her top lip and then said, "How about a piña colada?"

Moreau smiled paternalistically and patted her on the cheek. He didn't notice Alex's eyes narrow in dislike. "A very tasty choice, Sarah." He had the male waiter, who also tended bar, mix up the frothy yellow concoction.

Chiquita, who'd been drinking vodka tonics steadily ever since Moreton had arrived, plopped herself on Moreton's lap and linked her arms behind his neck. Moreton grinned at her and began to rub the flat of her stomach just below her breasts.

Sarah took the piña colada from the impassive bartender and tried not to pay any attention to the hot light beginning to burn in Moreau's eyes as he watched Moreton tease the young woman sitting on his lap. She stirred her drink and took a very small sip. With Moreau's men loosening their inhibitions, she certainly wanted to stay as alert as possible. Perhaps she was being ridiculously optimistic to assume that they had any inhibitions to loosen in the first place, of course.

Moreau clapped his hands and called for dinner to be served. Everyone was starved and they fell on the grilled fish and spiced rice as if they hadn't eaten all day. They kept right on drinking, though, too. Sarah glanced at Alex. He seemed to be getting as sloshed as the rest of them, she thought in dismay. He was laughing more loudly than normal, and he was joking with Moreton as if they were old buddies! She couldn't envision Alex doing that if he were completely sober. She'd seen his violent dislike of Moreau.

Old buddies. She could have gagged. Everything was going from bad to worse. She slipped Wiley some bread and a couple of small pieces of roasted sea turtle. She glanced down and noticed that Wiley was staring doubtfully at the sea turtle.

"Beggars can't be choosers," she informed him in a schoolmarmish voice. "Don't think about it. Just eat it."

"What was that, Sarah?" Moreau asked.

"I was just telling Wiley he had to clean his plate," she replied easily.

Moreau bent over to look at the Labrador. When he looked back at Sarah, he was perplexed. "This Wiley is a very good dog. You would not know he was there most of the time, he's so silent. Did you have him trained?"

Sarah choked on her sea turtle. Alex handed her a glass of beer after she managed to clear her throat. She hoped he wasn't trying to get *her* drunk, too. Maybe he thought she could hold her liquor. It was a little late to disillusion him on that point, so she gave him a very unblinking stare and handed the beer back to him, hoping he'd get the message.

"Wiley's just naturally good," she said, turning an angelic smile on Moreau, who was listening attentively.

Moreau's mouth fell open upon hearing her startling explanation for Wiley's obedience. He obviously couldn't believe she'd said something so inane. "Is that so?" He cast a slightly sympathetic glance in Alex's direction. Apparently he was revising his opinion of what Alex had to put up with, matrimonially speaking. "That's very unusual. He must be one of a kind."

Sarah grinned. "Oh, he certainly is." And he had the ribbons to prove it.

Moreau was trying to be polite to her, in spite of his some-what lowered estimate of her intelligence. "I wasn't so fortu-nate," he said in amusement. "I had to have my dogs trained by an expert."

"Is that so?" Sarah said, amazed that she could keep as straight a face as she was. "An expert?"

"Yes," he went on. "They're very well trained now. Even better than your Wiley." He gave her a condescending smile intended to soften his arrogant assertion.

"Even better than Wiley," she exclaimed as if impressed. In a pig's eye, you jerk. But you go right along thinking that.

Sarah tried not to tense up or show the wrong kind of inter-est in his choice of conversational material. She pushed her fish to one side and searched for a piece of vegetable. "Did they learn a lot of good tricks?" she asked with utter sincerity.

Moreau leaned back in his chair and shook his head at the idiocy of her question. "They weren't trained to do *tricks*," he explained patiently.

"No?" She sounded disappointed. She smiled and patted Wiley on the head. "Wiley knows lots of tricks. He's very clever. I sometimes think he's smarter than most people I know."

Moreau laughed. He thought she was exaggerating. She wasn't.

Sarah plied the drug czar with another bimboesque smile. "So if your dogs don't do tricks, what do they do? Just walk around with your guards all day?"

Moreau looked mildly offended that she'd put it like that. As if there were nothing to it at all. "Yes," he said, a little an-noyed. "But that's harder than it looks."

Sarah giggled. "No. It couldn't be. What's hard about it?"

Moreau's cheeks darkened a little. Obviously humiliation was not something he was comfortable with. Not even this small pricking of his pride as Sarah questioned his canine corp's ability to perform spectacularly. He turned cool eyes toward one of the men slugging rum and colas at the bar; he snapped his fingers and growled, "Bring in Rocco and Mitla." He ges-tured for the next course to be brought in and the last one cleared away. "They guard whatever I tell them to guard," he said arrogantly.

That gave Sarah an idea. "Anything?"

Alex had stopped drinking and was sitting very still. Sarah didn't want to break eye contact with Moreau. She had him on the line and she didn't want to lose him. She wanted to reel him in. Slowly. Dogs and all.

Moreau was staring at her, as if reassessing her, no longer sure she was quite as dumb as he'd thought. "Yes. Anything," he replied slowly.

"Could you make them guard me?" she asked, her eyes were lighting up at the possibility. "I mean, just like in the movies, where you have to stay put or the dogs growl and won't let you pass?"

He looked at her as if she were crazy, but he relaxed. Obviously no one playing with a full deck would suggest something as idiotic as that. He laughed. "Of course. That would be very easy."

"How much would you like to bet?" she challenged, taking another sip of her drink. Her body was beginning to shake lightly. She was treading on very thin ice now, and she wasn't used to it. The liquor flowed through her like fire. It didn't make her feel more confident, but it anesthetized the fear a little.

"My dear, Sarah," Moreau was saying, sounding paternalistically condescending, "I couldn't take a bet on that. It would be like taking money from a baby." His amused glance went from Sarah to Alex. "Your husband can tell you. Dogs trained like mine are not to be played with. Not even by such a pretty young woman as you. They're dangerous."

Sarah leaned toward him, smiling as if she sensed she'd already won. "You mean you couldn't control them? You couldn't keep them from harming me, once you've told them to keep me in one place?"

He recognized the trap he'd fallen into and for a split second it was obvious he wondered if she'd set it for him on purpose. No. The suspicion cleared away. He couldn't imagine a young woman idiotic enough to play games with dangerous guard dogs. "I can control them," he said confidently. He looked at Alex as if to ask permission. "Do you let your wife play such games, Alex?"

Sarah was afraid Alex might not agree, and she laid her hand on his arm as she turned to look at him. His face was hard to read. He seemed amused by the conversation, but Sarah sensed he was angry beneath that facade.

"Sarah does as she pleases," Alex said. "I don't imagine I can stop her without paying a very steep price for it."

Moreau laughed raucously, obviously thinking the price would be extracted in bed. Sarah saw more deeply and understood. He wasn't crazy about the idea, but he knew she wanted to see the dogs, try to work with them. Doing it this way was probably as good a chance as she was likely to get. It was worth a try. He'd back her up. But he didn't particularly like it. When he looked at her, that showed in the depths of his eyes, only for her to see.

Sarah pressed her lips to his and murmured, "Thank you, Alex."

"You're not welcome," he murmured against her mouth. "Careful, darling. Remember what he said. They're dangerous."

"I'll remember," she whispered. It was nice to think that he cared. That the way he was looking at her wasn't just for Moreau's benefit. Her face softened. Her heart ached a little.

"All right, Sarah," Moreau conceded, his good nature temporarily restored. "We'll play your game. You may be right. It could be...diverting. Here on the island, there isn't much to do for entertainment."

Sarah wondered what the obvious debauchery, satellite connections and full-scale aquatic capability were used for. She didn't ask. She merely smiled and clapped her hands together as if celebrating a victory.

"Terrific!" she exclaimed enthusiastically.

Alex put his empty glass on the table and laughed humorlessly. "Sarah is nothing if not diverting," he observed in a long-suffering tone. He frowned as two big Dobermans were brought into the room on leashes, then he pinned Moreau with a rapier-sharp look. "I would not be amused if my wife was hurt," he pointed out in a deceptively soft voice. "As irritating as she can be, I've grown rather attached to her."

Moreau nodded. He seemed unconcerned that anything would go wrong. "I can understand that," he said with man-to-man sympathy dripping from each word. "Don't worry about a thing. Leave everything to me."

Alex's eyes were hard and so was his smile. There was nothing he wanted to do less than leave Sarah's life in that bastard's hands. He was hating every minute of this charade. His stomach had twisted into the granddaddy of all Gordian knots since she'd started talking about the dogs. It hadn't taken him long to guess what she was planning on trying. Apparently there was going to be a lot more of this to hate, thanks to Sarah and her bright idea. He swallowed the rest of his beer and watched as Sarah rose to face the dogs. He knew it was a brilliant strategy. She was absolutely right to try it. If he didn't care what happened to her, he would have applauded the decision. But he did care. Damn it all. He cared.

"Nice doggies. Nice doggies," Sarah said cheerfully.

Two pair of eyes stared at her with cold malevolence. Mouths opened. Teeth bared. They growled in soft warning.

"Nice doggies." She surreptitiously gave Wiley a quiet hand signal to stay while everyone was looking at her face and the Dobermans. There wasn't anything nice about those doggies, though, no matter how she looked at them. They were sullen and suspicious. Nasty and on edge. Very, very dangerous. "Nice doggies. You wouldn't keep me here if I wanted to leave, now would you?" she cajoled them softly.

Hair stood up on their backs and they lowered their heads warningly.

"All right, Antonio," she said, her eyes now on him. "Where shall I stand? Where are you going to make them keep me?"

Chapter 11

Moreau had her stand in a corner of the room, not too far away from where the patio opened out into the tropical twilight. Rocco and Mitla were posted eight feet away from her. Moreau had their handlers order them to sit. Then he had them unleashed.

Sarah tilted her head to one side and wrapped her arms around herself protectively. "My what big teeth they have," she said with a silly grin.

Alex was lounging in his chair, his long legs stretched out in front of him, his arms crossed in front of his chest. There was a decided frown on his face, though. He was the picture of husbandly discomfort with his beloved's ill-advised adventure.

Moreau was impressed and he told Sarah. "You are so foolishly brave," he said softly, "that it makes me sad."

"Sad?" Sarah wasn't certain what he meant.

"Because you are going to lose your bet," he reminded her.

"But you said you wouldn't bet with me," she pointed out in surprise.

"Ah, but I've changed my mind. Just a little bet." He grinned. The alcohol had dulled his brain, and he tottered a little as he walked toward her, past the dogs. He put his hand on her cheek, smiling.

Sarah struggled not to shrink from his touch in disgust. She gave him a sly, cautious look and ventured, "And what did you want the stakes to be?"

His rough, cold fingers were like a harbinger of death, she thought. There was a smell of horror about the man, and it became very noticeable when he was this close. She moved a little away, glancing shyly at Alex sprawled in the chair, watching intently.

Moreau knew she was trying to remind him of her "husband," but he'd never spent a great deal of time worrying about the stability of marriage, especially other people's marriages. He sensed that it would be wiser for him to not press her, however, so he withdrew back behind the dogs.

"*I'll* name *my* prize. *You* name *yours*," he suggested with a grand gesture of one hand. He grinned broadly and his thoughts were written in his expression. He was absolutely certain he would win. He could afford to be arrogant and let her name her stakes. She'd never get them.

"And what would you choose as a prize?" Sarah asked, holding her breath.

"A walk in my Garden of Eden by moonlight," he said slowly. "'With you. My charming guest."

Alex didn't like it. He straightened in his chair and his eyes bore into Moreau's back like two knives. He knew what Moreau wanted to do in the garden. Walking was not the word for it. He shot a sharp glance at Sarah. Their eyes met and he was infuriated to realize that she was actually considering taking him up on his offer.

Moreau waited. "And what will be *your* prize?" he asked in amusement. Not that it mattered what she said. He was confident she would never win.

Sarah glanced at the dogs. They weren't quite as hostile as they had been at first. They were staring at her, but without the animosity of earlier. That didn't necessarily mean they were any more disposed to her than earlier, of course. Alex didn't look too pleased, but if she could position them for their escape plan, perhaps he'd cheer up.

"I know!" she exclaimed, snapping her fingers as if it had just occurred to her. "I'd like a midnight cruise around your island." She smiled at Alex and struggled to hold back a giggle. "With my husband."

Moreau shrugged. "Done." He had eyes that would have nailed a coffin shut, and they impaled her with the force of his entire personality. "I shall hold you to it."

"Agreed." She caught her lower lip between her teeth. "How far will I have to go to be considered the winner?"

Moreau couldn't have cared less. He doubted she'd get more than a step away from her starting position and it was obvious to everyone in the room. "Past the dogs. Either one. Past his back." He grinned, and added, "Without being bitten."

Sarah laughed nervously. "Of course. If they bite me, I lose." She had rarely been bitten by a dog, but she didn't want to think of the damage the Dobermans could do to her arm, throat or face if they sank their teeth into her.

Drinks were being poured all around, and the motley gathering was watching through a mild haze of booze as Moreau directed the handlers to order the dogs to keep her at bay. Sarah was hoping that the heavy drinking would be to her advantage. They might be too misty eyed to realize exactly what she was doing; they might misconstrue her few silent commands as merely the motions of a distraught woman trying to win a bet. It might mean the difference between being discovered and going free. *Have another drink, boys. You, too, Chiquita.*

Her back and stomach were damp; so were her legs. The handlers wandered over to join the guffawing card players and a couple of the women. She was on her own. *Come on Rocco, Mitla. Remember me.* "Nice doggy," she chirped, bending down slightly, smiling at the two fiercely staring dogs. "Nice doggy..."

Alex watched Sarah bend down and slowly extend her hand and he felt a wave of nausea hit him. The image of her, rent and bleeding on the tiled floor, rose up in his mind's eye. If the dogs tore into her, she would be defenseless. He wouldn't be able to get to her in time. They'd be on her too fast. Besides, the closest thing to a weapon he possessed was his knife and fork left from dessert. How in the hell had he ever let Raymond talk them into this fiasco? The dogs didn't look as if they gave a damn about her. He had no idea if there was even the glimmer of recognition in their murderous eyes, since their backs were toward him. The stiffness of their posture and the slight growling and ruffling of hackles were far from encouraging.

He looked over the small crowd in the dining room through half-closed lids. At least they all thought he was three sheets to the wind and annoyed with his idiot of a wife. That would make them less suspicious of him. And Moreau seemed to have eyes primarily for Sarah, now that she was challenging him with the dogs.

He wondered if Raymond's contact in Jamaica had been able to drug the drinks handed out to the crew pulling night duty along the island's perimeter. If he had, that island cruise Sarah was trying to win might turn out to be a very fine addition to their plan. It would mean they wouldn't have to worry about hijacking a boat from the pier or repossessing his. It would mean they'd have one given to them on a silver platter.

There would be the little inconvenience of the crew, of course. But Alex figured he and Wiley ought to be able to dispatch most of them without too much difficulty. Especially since a couple of them were losing at the card table and drinking steadily to try and forget it.

He heard a dog growl and his eyes shot back to Sarah, crouching low to the floor, at eye level with one of the dogs, still in her original spot. His skin felt cold and he began to sweat. If the dogs went after her, he'd pull them off with his bare hands if he had to. With his bare hands, damn it.

Sarah was completely oblivious to anything but trying to connect with Rocco. He was the more distrustful of the two dogs. Mitla, less paranoid, was showing slight signs of confusion. He was beginning to remember her smell, her voice. He didn't understand why he was being asked to guard her. But Rocco was more detached. In that, he reminded Sarah of his owner, Moreau. There was something missing in them, both man and dog. Perhaps it was just a tiny scrap of genetic material, the infinitesimally small piece that carried the ability to form strong attachments, the sense of loyalty, the essence of a conscience. That was the piece that wasn't there in either of them.

Rocco's ears flipped straight up. He wasn't softening, but he was beginning to hesitate. He licked his chops and his brow wrinkled as if he were thinking hard.

Sarah smiled and said, "Good boy. Good boy." She sat back on her heels, wrapping her arms around her knees and holding her skirt around her legs; she sang to them softly, hoping that might bring something back. It was a little crooning tune she used with the dogs when they were stressed out. While she sang to them, she jiggled her fingers, first this way and then that way. It was the signal to obey her and her alone. She wasn't certain they'd recall it anymore. Or if its meaning had been corrupted by their present handlers to mean something else. She doubted that, however. These handlers looked like meatheads with no knowledge of sophisticated animal training. They'd probably been told a few straightforward commands and been handed the dogs.

Sarah felt a surge of guilt for having trained the dogs only to turn them over to such dangerous, ignorant men. She hadn't known that then, of course. The lawyer who'd negotiated with her had been well connected and he'd answered all the questions she'd asked, leaving her with the impression that the dogs would go to responsible owners. She just hadn't known. *It's too late to worry about it now, Sarah.* She kept crooning and quickly glanced around to gauge the situation.

The men weren't paying much attention. It was obvious that none of them expected her to move an inch without having ninety-five pounds of black-haired fury standing over her. Even Moreau was allowing himself to be distracted by Chiquita's laughter and cloying attentiveness. Moreton apparently had no problems sharing her with his boss; Chiquita seemed to think that two men were better than one.

Sarah watched as some of Chiquita's clothing was loosened and Moreau settled her comfortably across his lap, intent on fondling what he'd set free. Sarah blushed and glanced in Alex's direction. At least he wasn't rolling around with the hired help, she thought in relief as she struggled to keep her frazzled nerves from unraveling completely.

Alex... Sarah focused her eyes on him, soaking up some reassurance from his solid, reclining figure. She knew that her feelings were probably plastered all over her face, but she couldn't help it. For a split second, she just needed him to see. *Sorry, Alex. I guess I can't act all the time.* She gazed at him and she wished he could be close to her, close enough for just a quick, light hug. Or a reassuring kiss. She thought she saw a small glimmer of amusement in his face, and she wondered if perhaps he'd guessed what she'd been thinking. It was hard to tell, since he looked so relaxed he might be falling asleep. Maybe it was just a dream. Or the effects of the food and drink. Or maybe he *could* read what was in her heart. *Alex*...

Sarah dragged her eyes back to Mitla and stopped humming. She got down on her knees and crept a step forward, calling Mitla's name softly. *Mitla*... *Nice little Mitla*... *Easy, Mitla*... Sarah wiggled her fingers, and she kept her gaze steady and clear. She held the dog with her will, with her eyes, but gently. You couldn't rush an animal like this. You had to draw them out gently.

Alex was stretched out in his chair and smothering a yawn, but he was watching every move that Sarah made through his half-closed eyes. He saw her flinch as Rocco came up off his haunches, and he tensed, ready to spring out of his chair if the dog moved any closer to her. Then she laughed softly and made that funny gesture with her hand again, and Rocco settled back down again. Alex slowly expelled his breath and swore at the fact that the pounding in his chest refused to settle down as quickly. *Come on, you son of a bitch. Recognize her! How could anyone, even a dog like you, forget her?*

How was he going to be able to forget her? If the situation had been less dangerous, he would have laughed. Unless they got off this island in one piece, he wouldn't have to worry about trying to forget Sarah Dunning.

He watched her kneel in the direction of the other dog, the one that seemed a little less hair-trigger violent, in his estimation. The dog blinked and whined softly. Then it started licking its chops quite rapidly. Nerves. The animal didn't know what to do. It was torn in two directions and at a loss to decide which it was supposed to follow.

Alex had to fight hard to keep from grinning. *One down, one to go, Sarah.*

Mitla had remembered.

Sarah could have kissed the dog in relief. Good boy, Mitla. That simplified the decision of which direction to head in trying to pass the dogs. Mitla was definitely the path of less resistance here. Sarah began to inch her way toward Mitla's outside shoulder. She spoke softly, hummed a little and occasionally tried a hand signal on the dogs, asking them to stay. It was awkward, though, because she tried to slip in the signals when Moreau and the handlers weren't looking her way. Of course, Keekee and the other girls were doing a wonderful job of diverting the men's attention. Raymond couldn't have provided better support if he'd hired them, Sarah thought in amusement.

Sarah had almost made it to Mitla's nose, when Moreau lifted his head and realized that she was nearly poised to win the bet.

"It can't be!" he exclaimed, dumping Chiquita out of his lap and back into Moreton's accommodating arms, as he rose from his chair. He made a couple of explicit remarks in Haitian French that made two of the men playing cards laugh until they nearly cried.

Sarah, however, was concerned about the effect of Moreau's renewed attention on the other Doberman pinscher, Rocco. Moreau's excited comments fueled the animal's aggressive instincts and he took a sinister step toward her.

Sarah stopped and stared at the dog with every bit of authority she could muster. She couldn't give an authoritative voice command without arousing Moreau's suspicion. But she was going to have to do something and fast. Rocco wasn't willing to bow to her authority. A mere three feet now separated her from victory. So near, yet so far. And she couldn't stay where she was forever. She gauged Mitla's state of mind, and decided that she was willing to bet that Mitla wouldn't attack her, even if she threw herself past the dog. Unfortunately she was afraid that that violent action might trigger Rocco into an assault on her.

She inhaled and crossed her fingers. This *had* to work. If it didn't, she'd be spending the evening in the garden with a serpent. She much preferred to be freeing Gabrielle and getting off the island with Alex instead. She glanced at Alex and saw the tense look in his shuttered eyes, and she gave him a hopeful smile. Crossing her fingers, she sprang forward. She landed in a crouch on the floor just past Mitla's back. The bet was won! Unfortunately there was no time to feel the thrill of victory. There was an ominous sound that she immediately recognized and it turned her blood cold. Rocco was snarling in attack as his nails scratched the floor to get at her.

The moment that Sarah sailed past Mitla, everything moved into painfully slow motion for Alex. His body lagged; the room had become a sea of molasses to struggle through; even the chair was difficult to get out of. The huge male Doberman was already ripping at the back of Sarah's dress by the time he managed to reach her. His mind was a haze of red fury as he yanked the dog off her with his bare hands. As the animal's teeth came down on his arm, he was landing a solid blow on its ribs with his foot. The animal whimpered as it crashed onto its side and whipped immediately back onto its feet, ready to go for Alex's throat.

"Stay!" Several voices screamed the harsh command at once. Moreau. Two of the dog handlers. And Sarah, who was shouting with every ounce of authority she possessed as she struggled to her knees on the floor.

Rocco, scrambling for his balance on the tiles, didn't seem to hear any of them for a moment. The animal's urge to destroy the man who'd attacked him made it hard for his brain to register the sharp commands to halt. Fortunately for Alex, Wiley's reflexes were quicker than the Doberman's. As the pinscher rose to savage Alex, the bristling Labrador landed squarely in the animal's path, fully prepared to defend his mistress's lover to the death.

That surprised the Doberman tremendously. And surprise let him hear the command now being repeated, quite loudly, by his regular handler. "Stay! Rocco, stay!"

Sarah had managed to get to her feet, although her legs were shaking so badly that she didn't know how she was able to stand. She threw herself into Alex's arms, hugging him so tightly that she felt him grunt as the air whooshed out of his lungs. He was laughing unsteadily as he grabbed her arms and loosened her grip.

"Hey," he objected. "I didn't escape being chewed up just to have you suffocate me." Besides, he urgently needed to see that she was truly unhurt. His gaze flicked over her, followed by his hands.

She looked up into his eyes and saw the depths of his own relief that she hadn't been injured. His hand was on her back, gently pulling up the dangling shreds where Rocco's teeth had viciously lacerated the fabric. She felt him stiffen and suck in his breath.

"That could have been your back," he muttered.

Sarah touched his face with her hand in a light caress. "But it wasn't. Thanks to you." She pulled away and gingerly examined his arm. The bites weren't as deep as she'd feared they might be, but blood was trickling down to his wrist from the slash marks just below his elbow. "Oh, Alex..." She lifted eyes filled with apology. "I'm sorry. I never should have made that silly bet."

"Forget it," he said curtly. The arm hurt. He was still knotted inside from the vision of Rocco sailing onto her with his teeth bared. He had no idea if Moreau had recognized the experience and authority in Sarah's voice when she'd tried to stop Rocco from attacking him. All he wanted to do was hold her. Hold her as tightly as humanly possible. Until she sank into his skin and became a part of him, instead of putting herself at risk of heavy-duty injury.

He pulled her back into his arms and buried his face in her hair. He told himself it was a totally reasonable action for him to take. It would be convincing to the spectators muttering all around them. It would also help sooth the ragged feeling in his chest and stop the puerile shaking that was threatening to overtake his control. God, it felt good to hold her, safe and whole, in his arms again. He ran his hand exploratorily over her back a second time, more slowly. It was a relief when he could feel no blood or gaping wounds beneath the ribboned dress.

She sensed his need to make sure she was all right by physically touching her, running his hands over her, holding her against him until the fear had washed away. When he began to relax, she eased herself a little away again so she could try to do something about his arm. *Your poor arm, darling.*

Someone handed her two clean linen napkins and a pitcher of ice water. Sarah was too worried to fret about neatness, so she poured the water over his arm, spilling it onto the floor.

"I had no idea you were so sloppy," Alex teased her.

Sarah didn't bother to look up. "Don't argue with your paramedic," she told him. She wished her fingers weren't trembling so badly. It would make tying the napkins and winding them around his arm much easier.

Moreau had joined them and was more perplexed about Sarah's success in getting by the dogs than concerned about his guest's injury. Obviously no one ever sued Antonio Moreau. You were injured at your own risk here.

"How did you do it?" he asked. He was staring at Sarah with the fixed gaze of a viper watching a field mouse targeted for an afternoon snack.

Sarah swallowed and finished tying the makeshift bandage. "I don't know," she lied with a helpless lift of her shoulders. "I always liked animals. Maybe they just sensed that." She shook her head. "I tried to get right down there with them, Antonio. You know, be like a dog. Maybe they don't pick on people who stay at dog level." She tried to sound a little hysterical and she leaned against Alex's chest as if overcome. It was easy to project hysteria and being overcome. "I don't think I'm going to be up for a midnight cruise after this," she murmured weakly. "How about a rain check?"

Moreau was watching her, and very little of what he was thinking could be seen in his face. "I never heard of anything so ridiculous as that," he muttered suspiciously. "Dogs not attacking something at their eye level or lower!" He spat out an expletive summarizing his opinion of that argument.

Sarah turned on him furiously. "Well, just because *you* never heard of it doesn't mean it can't happen." She wagged a finger at him threateningly. It was ludicrous. She was small, unarmed and outnumbered. It made her look courageous, thoroughly captivating and completely innocent. "I won the bet, Antonio. Now don't be a sore looser." The rush of adrenaline couldn't sustain her indefinitely, and she sagged against Alex, her face very pale. "I think I'd better go lie down, guys. It's getting awfully warm in here." She fanned her hand limply near her face.

Alex sat her in the nearest chair and pushed her head down to her knees. The heat receded and the woozy feeling along with it. After a few minutes, she straightened up and carefully rose to her feet, with Alex cursing her for trying to go too fast and threatening to pass out on him.

Alex looked very angry. He turned toward Moreau and said in a politely crisp voice. "If you'll excuse us, Moreau, I have a few things to say to my wife in private."

The dark look on Alex's face made Sarah pale.

"I can imagine," Moreau said, nodding his head and beginning to grin as his suspicions slid away. "She's a lot of trouble," he observed. A man came into the room and murmured in Moreau's ear. Moreau glanced at his watch and nodded. "I regret, but I have some business waiting for me." He gave them a slight nod of farewell as he prepared to leave. "If you want to take that cruise later, just go down to the pier. Craig will tell them to take you out. There's a crew at the docks all night. They'll be happy to have something to do. It's been rather boring here lately."

Sarah watched him disappear into the night. He was going to see Gabrielle. To turn the screws a little tighter. To try to force her to talk. Sarah lifted her face to Alex and murmured, "Can we go now?"

He nodded. "We most certainly can, darling." There was an ominous ring in his voice and a threat in the way he'd said that last word.

Sarah glanced at him nervously as he thrust her ahead of him. "Uh, what are you going to do?" she asked.

Several men passed them, eyeing her shredded dress and Alex's bloodstained linen bandage with open curiosity.

"My dear, I am going to turn you over my knee."

Sarah drew her eyebrows together in a straight line. "I don't think I deserve that!" she protested. "I mean, you have to consider the whole picture." She felt his hand pushing her into their room and she balked as soon as the door closed behind them. She faced him pugnaciously, her hands on her hips. She was preparing to argue in her own defense while apologizing again for his being injured when he nobly came to her rescue, but before she could open her mouth, he was hurling a vase at the lamp, sending both crashing to the floor.

Sarah looked at him in great alarm and her blood ran cold.

He paced around the room, rampaging from one side to the other, tossing things through the air to smack against the wall, growling at her that she'd better not pull any more stunts if she wanted to make it to her next birthday in one piece. Acting like a man possessed.

At first, Sarah had thought he was going to attack her, and fear for her own safety lanced through her. Alex was a strong, experienced male. He could have done a tremendous amount of physical harm to her if he'd hit her or beaten her. But her initial fear turned into puzzlement as she gradually realized he was ventilating his fury on the inanimate objects in the room, not on her. He was demolishing the place. Then she noticed that the demolishment was selective. Confined to the side of the room where the bugs had been hidden.

He stopped as abruptly as he'd begun and he strolled into the bathroom to unbandage his arm and wash the injury with soap and water as if nothing were amiss. Sarah peered in as he opened his shaving kit and pulled out some antiseptic. He smeared it generously over the bleeding wounds, swearing through gritted teeth as he did so.

"Let me," she murmured, taking the coil of bandage from his kit. He didn't resist. He was looking at her, and this time the dark look in his eyes brought a different kind of fear. A very desirable kind, she thought.

Sarah carefully rebandaged his arm.

"Thank you," he said quietly when she had finished.

They stood together for a moment. Then, wordlessly, he put the things away and drew her back into the bedroom, sat down on the bed and pulled her down onto his lap, cradling her in his good arm. His dark eyes were on her and she felt the heat, the worry, the relief, still there, boiling inside of him, now that they were alone and he could afford to let it show in all honesty.

"I didn't mean to scare you, Sarah," he whispered, tracing the delicate bones of her face with his injured hand. "I needed to be able to talk to you, though." He grinned slightly. "Alone."

She smiled. The shaking wasn't so bad, now that she was in his arms. "I thought that was why you were going berserk. I suppose the others will think you turned me over your lap for a sound thrashing."

He nodded; the grin faded. "I imagine that's the way they would handle this." He pulled her close and buried his face against her neck, sighing as if he was finally sure she was safe. "I thought I wasn't going to get to you in time," he whispered raggedly. He swore softly. "I thought . . ." He didn't want to remember what he thought.

Sarah snuggled against him and wound her arms around his neck. "I'm here, my love," she murmured. "I'm here. We're all right."

Wiley, who'd padded silently after them and then sat in one corner watching Alex throwing furniture around the room, now lay down in front of their closed door. He rested his nose across his paws and let his eyes close.

Alex looked over at the dog. "I owe Wiley a few steak dinners," he said wryly. He turned his attention back to Sarah. "That'll have to wait, I'm afraid." He slid his hand up over her breast in a light, tender caress, smiling a little when she relaxed against his hand. He asked huskily, "Do you think he'll mind pulling guard duty while I have my way with his mistress?"

Sarah laughed softly and shook her head. "No. And his mistress won't mind in the least, either."

"I'm glad to hear that," Alex murmured in amusement. "Come here," he said huskily. "Let me make sure everything's all right."

Sarah captured his head between her hands and kissed him on the mouth. There were no barriers. There was no hesitation. There was just the tremendous rightness of their joining together. The kiss deepened and became intimately thorough and Sarah didn't know how many of the soft moans of pleasure were hers and how many were his. The melting together of their sighs, their groans, their bodies, acted like an aphrodisiac on her already heightened senses. To be one person. To be one heart. To be one.

"Alex . . ." she whispered, her eyes closed in ecstasy as his lips found her jaw and then her throat. His mouth and his hands

and his sweetly murmured endearments made her want to cry.
She heard him choke on her name and then their mouths were
fused. Their bodies straining, and their incoherent murmur-
ings became more desperate.

He brought her back with him down onto the bed and they
rolled together, careful of his injured arm, their mouths finding and fusing, their bodies crushing close. "Let me, Sarah,"
he whispered harshly. "Let me. . . ." It was a demand; it was a
plea.

His eyes were half-closed as his mouth found her breast, and
he tongued the soft skin with stunning effect. His hands roamed
over her, comforting and arousing, reassuring and promising,
making her feel that she was his. Everywhere she felt his hands,
his mouth, his knowing touch. "Yes," she whispered. "Yes.
Oh, yes. Yes."

They were too desperate for each other to strip. Clothes were
frantically pushed out of the way, just enough for access.
Quickly, quickly. The ache was too sharp. Life too short. Death
had brushed too near. Harsh sounds of labored breathing,
pleading noises, panting and cries of pleasure swirled and caressed and incited. They rolled against each other. They rolled
back. He pulled her thigh over his and thrust into her, holding
her fast as she moaned against his cheek.

"Sarah. . ." he groaned. It was said the way a man might say,
I love you. The way a man might say, I need you.

Sarah melted completely. *I love you. It can't be, but it is, my
love. I love you.*

Fused together at mouth and groin, at heart and soul, enfolded in each other's frantic embrace, they felt the ancient fires
build and grow and threaten to bury them in the avalanche of
desire. But when they convulsed together, dying a little even as
they were ecstatically reborn, Sarah felt triumphant. She was
drenched in the white-hot fires of love. Even if it was only for
a while, she was glad. With tears in her eyes, she smiled.

In this moment in time, Alex, you love me. You love me.

That would be enough, she told herself. It would have to be.
He'd made it clear that there wouldn't be anything more. Her
arms tightened around him and she reveled in his tender response.

I love you.

Chapter 12

They lay tangled together on the bed until darkness fell. Reluctantly Alex rolled onto his side. He turned his head so he could look at Sarah.

"Sarah," he whispered softly. "We have to go."

She was tousled and glowing and a little exhausted. She opened her eyes and drank in the sight of him. "I know."

Neither of them moved.

Alex ran his hand over her cheek, down her throat. It came to rest possessively over her ribs, just below her breast. The relaxed, warm look that had been on his face at first began to transform into an expression that was harder to interpret.

To Sarah, it seemed as if regret, guilt, anger and frustration all were there. But uppermost was regret. It made her sad to think he might be regretting making love to her, or having her here now. She knew there wouldn't be much more time left for them. If they were very, very lucky they'd find Gabrielle tonight and slip away in the darkness.

And then they'd say goodbye.

"Don't look at me like that," he said, a little awkwardly as though he were embarrassed. He rolled away, onto his back, and began refastening his pants.

Sarah smiled sadly. "Like I want you to kiss me?" she asked softly, recalling the last time he'd told her that.

He sighed and lay still. "No. Like I'm a combination of Adonis and James Bond," he said. He turned back onto his side and helped her as she struggled to get the rest of the way out of her dress.

Sarah slipped off the bed and found some dark cotton slacks and a dark print blouse in her luggage. As she dressed, she smiled at him affectionately. "How did you know that's what I was thinking?" she teased.

He lifted a dark brow. She was very comfortable with him, he realized. She dressed in front of him as if it were perfectly natural. He felt as if it were, too, as if there were nothing more normal in all the world than their being together, performing the small intimacies of life together without embarrassment. He wondered what it would be like if he simply took her with him after it was all over. Kept her as the woman in his life. He watched her brush her hair and thought how soft it felt to the touch, how sweet in scent. Like the rest of her.

She was packing up her things. His, too, he noticed with a wry grin. She wasn't always as sloppy as when she'd splashed water all over the place trying to clean the bite on his arm. She'd surprised him. He hadn't expected her to be the person she was. Vibrant and passionate and clever.

He wanted her. Damn it. He wanted her. Her smiles and her lame jokes, and her courage and her tender kisses and her sweet fire.

"Don't look at me like that, Sarah," he repeated softly. He got off the bed and pulled her into his arms, forestalling her reply. He pulled her head against his shoulder and kissed her tenderly on the cheek. "Are you ready to go?"

Her heart was pounding, partly because he was confusing her, partly because the most crucial part of the plan was about to happen. She kissed him lightly on the lips and let her hands linger on his face, as if she would memorize the touch of him. "You're the most remarkable man I've ever met, Alex Sutter," she told him seriously. "I'm sorry if it shows on my face when I look at you. I guess I don't have as much talent for acting as I thought I did." She drew in her breath. His eyes, so dark, were warning her not to go on, not to say anymore. She smiled and touched his hard lips with hers, lightly, oh so lightly. "I can't help falling in love with you a little. Surely it isn't the first time you've swept a girl off her feet, is it?" She smiled at him, her trust and her love, there for him to see. "I'm a big girl, Alex. It's all right. *I'll* be all right."

He held her close and rested his chin on her head. "You certainly know how to torture a man," he murmured.

"I don't understand," she whispered.

He laughed humorlessly. "Come on. We'd better continue this discussion after we spring Gabrielle."

The information that Raymond had provided them about Moreau's island was turning out to be very accurate. There were about thirty men and a fluctuating number of women, usually less than ten, on the small droplet of land. Most slept in cottages attached to the main house by small breezeways. Some, like Craig Moreton, slept in the big house, often with a companion. The cook, bartender and housekeeping staff stayed in the southwest corner. Moreau had a big suite of rooms in the center of the fortress.

A guard and dog patrolled during the day. Another guard and dog patrolled at night. The dog that wasn't on patrol was turned loose along the northwest edge of the island, free to attack any stranger trying to come over the barbed-wire fence that stretched for nearly five miles.

It was quiet now, all the carousers having tumbled off to their rooms. There was just the sound of the sea breeze in the palms and the tide kissing the shore.

Alex opened their window and silently slipped out onto the narrow balcony. He held out his hand to Sarah. She looked down the fifteen-foot drop below them.

"I see why they always tell you not to look down," she whispered.

Alex grinned and pulled a long, thin rope from a latch hook on his belt. He made a quick loop and had Sarah put one foot in it, then slid the rope through a pair of pulleys he'd clamped to the railing of the balcony overhead.

"Hold tight," he whispered.

"I certainly will," she muttered. Her fingers were white as she clung to the rope while he lowered her down. She went down very quickly. The moment her feet hit dirt, she looked up at him. He was already shinnying down the ropes, hand over hand. "Where'd you learn to do that?" she asked as he dropped lightly to her side.

He freed the rope and coiled it, then propelled her in the direction that she'd taken with Moreau earlier in the day.

"I hope she's all right," Sarah murmured.

"Yes." It would be a hell of a shame if they'd come this far only to find that she wasn't, Alex thought grimly. He pulled down the thick sunglasses he'd brought along.

"Isn't this the wrong time of day for that?" Sarah whispered in amazement.

Alex grinned. "No. It's the latest in heat-sensing night vision. Just the kind of thing Moreau would have worn to play hide-and-seek with you on your midnight stroll through his Garden of Eden."

Sarah grimaced. "Please don't remind me."

Alex moved some underbrush out of the way and they turned eastward, along the route the guards always took. They'd covered about a mile when he heard voices and pulled her behind a heavily overgrown area behind a palm tree.

It was Moreau. He was talking to the guard as they walked back to the house. And Rocco was with them.

"...keeping her mouth shut like a clam..." Moreau was complaining. "I told her if she doesn't talk tomorrow, no matter how pretty her face is, I'm going to have to do a little plastic surgery on it. Without anesthesia." He was very angry and his voice was as cold as the ice at the bottom of the antarctic.

Sarah was sprawled against Alex and she could feel her heart pounding with fear as the footsteps passed by. She heard a soft whine, and her heart sank. Rocco had scented them and was trying to point it out to his handler.

"What's the matter with Rocco?" Moreau asked sharply.

The footsteps stopped. The dog whined intermittently, as if unsure of himself.

The handler said something incoherent, apparently trying to explain why the dog seemed confused. Moreau snorted in disgust.

"I'm beginning to think the dogs aren't as much use to us as I'd hoped they would be." He swore crudely. "Maybe he smells a bitch in heat in Jamaica and wants to go for a swim!"

The dog whimpered sharply, as though he'd been cuffed in reprimand. The footsteps resumed and the voices disappeared in the direction of the main house.

Sarah was trembling. "They're going to..."

Alex tightened his arms around her and then pulled her to her feet with him. "No, they're not. We're going to get her first," he said.

There was steely determination beneath the warm reassurance. Sarah took heart. Don't give up. It ain't over till it's over. Wasn't that what somebody famous had once said?

Alex held her close to his side and stared in the direction that Moreau, Rocco and the handler had gone. He could still see a faint impression of their body heat through the special lenses. He motioned for her to stay still a little longer.

"I'm scared to death," Sarah admitted in a shaky whisper. "How did you ever get into this kind of business in the first place?" She'd wondered that ever since she'd met him; she wondered if he'd be willing to give her an answer now, since they were...closer.

He looked down at her through the glasses and although she couldn't make out his eyes, she could see the slight tightening in his face. He still didn't care much for the subject. Even now.

He lifted his hand to her hair, letting the dark blond waves slip between his fingers. There was an aura of sadness about him. As if he were remembering why. And wished that he weren't.

"It was a long time ago," he murmured. "I needed the money."

Sarah shook her head. "That isn't all," she whispered. "Tell me the truth, Alex."

He withdrew from her and the frown became hard and determined. "That *is* the truth," he whispered harshly. "I did it for money. I'm paid for my services."

He made it sound like prostitution. It made her stomach churn uncomfortably. She just couldn't reconcile what he was saying with what she felt about him. The man she'd come to know couldn't be bought. Yet it *had* been the money that had decided him in Raymond's office. She'd seen that. Heard it with her own ears. When they'd increased the money, he'd agreed to come. She shook her head, denying the memory. Denying what he was telling her. She didn't want to believe it. And yet she had no reason not to. No rational reason anyway.

"There's more to it," she whispered stubbornly. There was a note of pleading there that she couldn't quite eliminate. She wanted him to tell her that her instincts were right about him. She wanted it so badly she could taste it.

He stepped closer and pulled her up against his chest. His hand held her face; the fingers were painfully hard against her smooth flesh. His anger was palpable, simmering just beneath the surface, hot against her skin.

"Stop romanticizing this," he told her.

His voice was so harshly cold, Sarah barely recognized it. Anger and fury and frustration were there, prodding him on, forcing out the words.

She squirmed a little and whispered, "You're hurting me." Her eyes sought his, but there was nothing beyond the cool glass reflecting her own anxious fears.

"I'm not the man you imagine me to be," he warned her through half-clenched teeth. "I got into this business because I had a facility for it. I'm good at it. And because of that, I was paid very well. I told you that the last time you asked. The answer's the same. It's always going to be the same answer, Sarah. Stop searching for a prettier reason. I'm not a hero. Don't try to make me into one."

He felt her stiffen in his arms at the things he was saying. Good. He wanted her to feel some revulsion for him. When she'd asked how he'd gotten into the business, it *had* made him remember why. And if he'd told her, he could imagine what she'd say, what she'd think.

He didn't want to see that kind of distaste in her eyes. It was better that she think of him as a soulless mercenary than what he really was. He'd lived a masquerade for years, all his life, really. No one had ever known. Not since he was very young. And he didn't want Sarah to know. It was better this way, he told himself fiercely, hating the twist of pain in his gut as he saw her withdraw from him. He'd wanted to hurt her in order to drive her a little away, to protect her from a worse hurt when this was all over and they had to part. Much as he wanted to keep her, he knew it would never work. He was the kind of man who was meant to live alone. She should have a rich life with a husband whom everyday people knew and respected, with children laughing in a yard. He saw children then and, against his will, he wondered what it would be like to father her children. To raise them with her. To hold her in the hard times and laugh with her in the good times. To grow old together. To possess her. And in turn, to be hers and hers alone.

Something cracked inside him then, and he pulled her against his mouth. If he could have let himself have a life like that, he would have chosen Sarah. Only Sarah. The kiss was desperate, plundering, filled with all the things that they could never have together, that suddenly he wanted very fiercely. He was numb with the realization that he would have given years off his life to have that with her. In the desperation of that kiss, his soul was bared to her, although he knew she wouldn't realize why. Thank God for that. She should never know how much he wanted her. Or why he wouldn't let himself succumb to the temptation to keep her. Oh, God, to keep her.

Her sweet mouth, her soft body, her arms around his neck... He softened the kiss without having meant to and when he finally, regretfully lifted his lips from hers, he wondered how much of himself he'd given away. Her eyes were unfocused and her mouth swollen and trembling from his kisses. He felt the blow to his heart and cursed the woman who'd borne him, the man who'd fathered him, the life that he could not give to Sarah because of them. He'd never felt the hatred before. He'd accepted the facts of his life. Until now. He had to force himself not to touch her again. He ached with all the tenderness that she brought into his heart. If he touched her, there was no way he could keep it from her.

He clenched his jaw and fought the impulse.

"Let's go," he whispered harshly. He stepped out onto the path, and pulled Sarah along behind him. "We've waited long enough."

Sarah shakily wiped the back of her hand across her aching mouth. The kiss had been so hard in the beginning, he'd drawn blood. She saw it as she looked down at her knuckles. His? Or hers? Maybe both, she thought unhappily. Why couldn't he tell her what was tormenting him? What could be so bad? A hundred horrifying possibilities paraded before her numbed brain. *I love you anyway, Alex Sutter,* she thought fiercely. I wish...

It was silly to wish. And her loving him wasn't going to make any difference in their relationship. Because he obviously didn't love her. Not enough anyway. And he was reluctant to let her love him. Physically, he'd succumbed to the fire between them. But emotionally...

Sarah brushed away the moisture that had sprung to her eyes and made them burn. It was hard enough to see in the dark without crying, she thought irritably, upset with herself. Everything was coming to a head, though, and the tears helped in a way. Even as the salty trail dried on her cheeks, she felt her strength coming back. The tears had washed away a little of the pain and tension. The rest, well, it was manageable.

Okay, Gabrielle. We're coming to get you. Right now. Sarah's chin acquired a stubborn set.

There was a light burning in the curtained window where Gabrielle Lorenzo was being held prisoner.

Alex crouched and pulled Sarah along behind him, running silently around the far end of the building, away from the moonlight and into the shadows of the building. He found a niche near the patio that led into the section of the building where they wished to go, and he pushed Sarah into it ahead of him, trapping her body against the rough plaster-covered wall with his.

Sarah felt the beating of his heart and wondered if he was exhilarated by this. She watched him scan the area, like a falcon searching every centimeter for trouble. When he straightened and relaxed a little, she knew they were all right. So far anyway.

"If they're doing what Raymond said they're doing, there should be no one with Gabrielle for the next couple of hours except the dog. Let's hope they haven't changed their routine," he whispered.

Sarah crept up the stairs, following Alex's every move, trying not to make any sound in case there was someone close by whom they weren't expecting. Everything unfolded just the way

Raymond had predicted. The guards were downstairs, playing cards and monitoring the dog in Gabrielle's room.

The dog was her guard at night. And he was the only guard.

Alex stopped and flattened his back against the wall. Beside him was the wooden door leading to Gabrielle's room, assuming that it *was* her room. Sarah flattened next to him, her heart pounding, her breath hard to catch.

He pointed to the door and indicated with a twist of his hand that he was going to open it. She nodded and braced herself.

This was where they found out if she could handle her part of the assignment. The chips were down and the hand was to be played out with their lives the stakes. Could she walk into the room and master the dog within the first few moments?

Or would the dog attack her?

Sarah nodded.

Alex, grim faced, carefully opened the door.

Sarah slid past him. His eyes met hers and she saw the fierce possessiveness in them before he could clamp it off. She struggled against the almost uncontrollable urge to throw her arms around his neck and kiss him. There was no time for that. She touched his chest lightly with her hand as she brushed by. As she stepped inside, she heard the sounds of a dog's nails scratching the floor as he trotted across the room. And the low, threatening growl warning her not to intrude.

She was inside, and she pulled the door closed after her, as she'd told them she would. She had told them over and over that it was the only way she could envision being able to establish control over the Doberman under the circumstances. Raymond had eventually understood and concurred. Alex had understood. But he'd obviously disliked the idea. After all, he was the one who'd have to deal with her lacerated body if it didn't work, he'd sarcastically said.

Sarah stared at the black-and-brown animal crouching low as it approached her and wondered if perhaps Alex was going to have to face just such a scene. She stood perfectly still, standing straight and as relaxed as she could while she met the dog's narrowed gaze without any evidence of fear. Years of experience were carrying her now. She was in charge here, not the Doberman, and she wouldn't let him think otherwise. The hostile animal was bristling in front of her, his teeth bared in a growling snarl, and he was stalking her with murderous intent, deciding when to spring at her.

Sarah didn't move a muscle, but there was authority in her posture, in the slight frown on her face, in the tone of her voice when firmly she ordered, "Down."

The dog stopped. He snarled more loudly, his lips curled up to expose the threat of his sharp white fangs. He poised, gathering himself to spring at the stranger who'd invaded his domain.

"Down, Borgia!" she commanded. This time she gave him the hand signal as well, sharply. She recognized the animal now. He'd grown some, fleshed out. He'd been reluctant to accept training. But they'd been friends when he'd left her. She saw no lessening of his threatening behavior. But at least he hadn't gone for her throat, yet. "Little Borgia," she said, smiling slightly as she used the pet name she'd had for him. She saw him blink. The teeth became less threatening, the lip slid back to cover them somewhat. His ears came forward slightly, instead of being flat against his head. "Sit!" Sarah ordered calmly.

At first she didn't think he was going to obey. He lifted his nose and sniffed the air, studying her scent, staring at her with suspicious killer's eyes.

Sarah gave him the hand signal and repeated the order with the authoritative voice that was becoming familiar to him, bringing back small fragments of memory.

He sat.

Sarah grinned at him and tried to control the rush of euphoria that was gushing through her like Niagara Falls. She put her hands on her hips and nodded at him in approval. "Good boy, Borgia. You're a big improvement over your namesakes. I'll bet they'd have slit my throat without a second thought."

She walked around him, petted him, carefully at first, so as not to push him too fast, too soon. When it was obvious he knew her, had completely remembered who she was, and had accepted her right to give him commands, she knelt down in front of him and said, "I'm going to introduce you to a friend of mine," she said solemnly. "He's a good guy. I want you to be nice to him. Okay?"

The dog's brow was wrinkled and his ears tilted forward as he strained to understand her message. The emotions got through, although the words were unintelligible to him.

Sarah walked over to the door and pulled Alex inside.

"Borgia, meet Alex. Alex, meet Borgia."

Alex looked down at the dog staring suspiciously at him while sitting exactly where Sarah had told him to sit.

"He's a big improvement over the Italian branch of the family," Sarah said. She was looking around, trying to see where Gabrielle might be. "But then, like I said, people can't hold a candle to dogs."

Alex laughed. "Under the circumstances, I won't argue the point."

They both turned as a voice came from an open doorway.

"It certainly took you long enough! And why did you bring my sister?" Gabrielle Lorenzo stood there, pulling a rope from her wrist and wriggling her fingers to get back the circulation. She was wearing a cotton dress that must have come from Kee-kee's exotic collection and she was sporting a grin that would have lit up New York City. She opened her arms and met Sarah halfway across the room. "Oh, God! Am I ever glad to see you. I hope this means I'm leaving soon."

Sarah, laughing and crying, hugged Gabrielle and nodded. "Yeah. We heard you'd had as much of a vacation with Moreau as you wanted."

Alex stood by the door, hands on hips, muttering, "Cut the humor, ladies. We've got a boat to catch."

Gabrielle and Sarah, arms around each other's waists, joined him. "Who's he?" Gabrielle asked, running her eyes up and down Alex. "He looks like a cross between James Bond and a Greek god."

Alex rolled his eyes and Sarah giggled.

Gabrielle was mystified. "Did I say the wrong thing?"

Sarah shook her head. "Not exactly. That description came up recently. Alex didn't appreciate it."

Gabrielle shrugged. "Alex? Nice to meet you. I'll call you anything you like for the rest of my life. Assuming I've got a rest of my life."

Sarah gave her sister an elbow in the ribs and glared at her. "I came all the way down here to give you a piece of my mind. You're not going to die until I give it to you."

Gabrielle shook her head. "You were always a bossy little kid," she muttered.

They were at the door to the hall and Alex was peering outside, checking to make sure the way was clear.

As they started to leave, Gabrielle whispered, "What do we do with my pet rock?" She glanced at Borgia, who was still sitting where Sarah had left him.

Sarah glared at her. "You want to take him along?"

Gabrielle looked as if she were considering it. "I wouldn't mind having you sic him on a couple of men whose acquaintance I've made during my stay at this lovely resort."

Sarah shoved Gabrielle after Alex and gave her sister a threatening look. "I think you like trouble, Gaby. Shut up. And don't make any more stupid remarks."

Alex gave them both a ferocious glare and indicated he'd cut the throat of the next woman who spoke. Sarah and Gabrielle crept down the stairs behind him.

Alex could feel the adrenaline pumping through his system. Sarah's part was nearly done. She'd come through like a pro. Now he had to get them all to the docks and onto one of the boats. And he had to retrieve Wiley, who'd been left guarding their door to prevent anyone from knowing they'd left, or delay that discovery for as long as possible.

The moon broke out from behind some clouds, turning the palm leaves and brushy plants into silvery figurines, and the sand into a ghostly white desert.

He motioned for them to keep close and they retraced their path back to the main complex. They had about fifteen minutes before a guard came back on patrol with Rocco or Mitla.

If Raymond was right. And if Moreau's guards kept to the schedule.

If...if...

Chapter 13

They could hear the sounds of the night. A woman laughing at a man's petulant plea in a darkened room as they crept beneath its open window. The sound of a bird calling its mate in the trees. The sound of the breeze lifting the great palm leaves overhead.

The soft scraping of their own feet on the sandy cement path as they followed its sinuous trail back to Moreau's den.

Alex led them back as quickly and quietly as he could. When they finally reached the stairs hewn from limestone that would lead to the piers, he motioned for Gabrielle to come with him and for Sarah to stay where she was and wait for him alone. As Gabrielle moved a few feet ahead of him, Alex turned back, trapping Sarah between his body and the smooth limestone wall.

"I'll be back as soon as I can," he whispered to her, catching her by the hair, speaking the words against the soft skin of her lips. "Stay in the shadows. If anyone discovers you, say I was so violent in our room that you escaped from me and have been hiding out ever since."

Sarah nodded mutely. He was sweating and his muscles were taut, ready for a fight. His tension was contagious, she found, and she fiercely wished that she weren't being left behind. Not just for her own sake, although she didn't relish being completely alone. More than that, she wanted to help Alex if she could. He wasn't smiling as he turned to leave. She managed a thumbs-up signal of encouragement and a tired smile of self-confidence. The smile quickly faded, however, when he looked away. She watched him silently melt into the night shadows and silvery moonlight that dappled the steep, rocky incline all the way down to the dark and rippling sea. Good luck, Alex.

Good luck. Sarah closed her eyes in misery. She wished she'd told him that. She slumped back against the hard rock and tried to count the seconds passing. One minute. Three. Ten. Twelve. She heard footsteps on the path over her head and froze, trying to sink into the unyielding stone. Voices. Laughing. A little drunk. Men. A woman, giggling at something one of the men had said.

Silence. Except for the restless wash of sea on the sandy shore and breeze on the bristling palms.

She heard footsteps and before she could react in fear, Alex was back beside her, falling against the rock, breathing softly next to her cheek. "So far so good. Remember the next part?" he asked.

Sarah was relieved that Gabrielle was safely hidden near the boat, and she breathed a soft sigh of relief. Then she remembered what came next and her nerves began to tingle in fearful anticipation. She wet her lips and nodded. "Yes. I remember what comes next."

"Come on, then." Alex put his arm around her shoulders and, after a quick and reassuring squeeze, he descended the steps with her. He began humming a roughly worded sea shanty; soon he was swaying slightly on his feet. The guard, whom they found slumped against the pier's first giant piling, straightened as they approached. He had a gun on his shoulder and at sight of them, he ran his hand up the stock to the trigger. He looked at them suspiciously and said, "Hold. Who's there?"

"'Tis just I and my dog-eating wife," Alex said with a harsh laugh. He placed an intimate kiss on Sarah's neck, making her blush. "We're here for our midnight cruise," Alex announced in a slurred, demanding voice. "My wife thinks I need to cool off," he added sardonically. He peered curiously at the guard. "Are you married?"

The guard shook his head and stared at the couple, obviously trying to decide what to make of them.

"Take my advice," Alex said, his voice becoming ponderous. That only served to make the slurring even more pronounced. "Don't get married. They'll do whatever you want before you sign the contract. Then—" he snapped his fingers and gave Sarah a baleful look "—then they do what they please and you have to take it even if they make themselves look like a fool. Or worse, make you look like a fool." There was a trace of bitterness beneath his sarcastic remarks.

The guard's hand slid away from the trigger and he began to look a little sympathetic. "Your wife's a pretty woman, though," he pointed out, as though that should be compensation for some of her other, less desirable traits.

"Yes." Alex peered into her face and then, quite crudely, ran his hand down over her front, squeezing her breast, his hand fondling her thigh and sliding threateningly close to her crotch. "She is pretty."

Sarah grabbed Alex's boldly wandering hand and lifted it firmly from her. "Alex! You've had too much to drink."

He laughed and gave her a very intimate look. "Don't worry. I haven't drunk so much that I can't accommodate your bedtime needs, my dear."

Sarah blushed and struggled away from him. "You're embarrassing me," she said irately.

He managed to look the picture of innocence as he threw up his hands in dismay. "Sorry, darling." He winked at the guard and whispered to him conspiratorially, "She only likes to hear me talk about sex in bed. Women! They pretend to be offended, but turn off the lights and strip off their clothes and bang, you can talk as dirty as you like and they'll claw your back for more."

The guard guffawed and nodded his head energetically, saying "Ain't that the truth, man?" His rotund belly was literally shaking with mirth. "Go on," he managed to tell Alex, motioning for him to go ahead to the boat. He cast another appreciative look up and down Sarah's compactly curved body. "Don't make her too mad, man, or it won't be so much fun later on. You don't want her pouting in the ladies' room all night.''

"Very funny," Sarah muttered through gritted teeth. She glared at the guard and then she glared at Alex.

"I'll remember that," Alex said, stumbling over the *r*'s. He gave Sarah's behind an affectionate pat, letting his hand linger on the rounded surface until she batted his hand away in annoyance. "The captain should be waiting for us," Alex confided in the guard. He leaned more heavily on Sarah's shoulder and squinted at the boats.

"Yeah. The last one down at the end is the boat you want. It's Mr. Moreton's boat. He told Jaime Lefevre to take you out, if you showed up." The guard had lost all respect for Alex by now and was leaning against the piling, picking his teeth.

Alex grinned. "Wasn't that nice of 'im?" He placed a slow smooch on Sarah's neck, making a lot of noise for the benefit of the guard they were leaving behind. In the wake of the guard's disrespectful laughter, Alex whispered. "Phase two complete. Now there's just the little matter of getting Wiley."

Sarah hated to think about it. "Yes. I hope this works...."

Jaime Lefevre was a gnarled-looking man, lean as a drought-stricken sapling and as twisted as an ancient olive tree. There was a scar running the length of his right arm and he wore a forty-five automatic strapped to his hip. He'd heard their noisy arrival and was waiting for them on a fifty-foot boat called the *Stingray*.

Alex teetered a little on the wooden planks of the pier and grinned down at the captain of the boat he was about to hijack. "Evenin', Cap'n. I hear you're ready for us. Heard all about my wife's little bet."

"*Oui.* Everybody hear about dat. Come aboard. Dis won't take too long." The captain jerked his head and a couple of men who'd been sipping beers along the stern rail made ready to cast off.

Sarah jumped onto the boat and turned to Alex, saying, "Where's Wiley?"

Alex, one foot on the pier and one suspended in the act of jumping onto the deck of the *Stingray*, stared at her in stupefaction. "Wiley?"

Sarah tapped her foot on the ground and put her hands on her hips. "Yes. Wiley. My dog. The big black Lab that saved your bacon back there in Antonio's dining room."

Alex nodded and brought his suspended foot back to the pier. "Wiley." He sighed deeply and gripped his head with both hands, shaking it mournfully. "You want to take Wiley."

"Of course," she said with a careless flip of her hair. "Wiley goes everywhere with me."

Lefevre was looking at them suspiciously. "You intend to take a dog on ze boat?" He was incredulous.

Sarah nodded serenely. "Of course. I'm taking him on my honeymoon. Why wouldn't I take him on a midnight cruise? He loves boat rides." She looked at Lefevre with guileless brown eyes. Slowly she half lowered her lashes and smiled just the tiniest bit. "You wouldn't mind, would you?"

Lefevre couldn't remember why it didn't seem like a good idea, now that he was drowning in her innocent wide-eyed gaze. He gave a shrug. "*Mais non.* If you can talk your husband into it, who am I to object?" He gave Alex a disappointed look. "You certainly are a surprise, Mr. Sutter," Lefevre said coolly. "I would have thought you would put your foot down." He shook his head and the cool look disintegrated into a mild sneer. "Go get ze dog. We will wait." Lefevre motioned for Sarah to sit next to his chair at the helm. "And we will take good care of your wife." Lefevre laughed.

Alex stared long and hard at Sarah and the crew on the *Stingray*. "I've had enough, Sarah!" Alex growled. He made an unsteady leap onto the deck of the boat. When he got his balance, he grinned triumphantly. "To hell with the dog. Let's go, Lefevre."

Lefevre was surprised to see Alex stand up to Sarah's demand, but he assumed that once he had, that would be the end of the argument. He turned on the engines.

Sarah shot to her feet and grabbed a whistle hung around her neck. She blew on it. Five short blasts. One long. Two short. Then she repeated it. Alex grabbed her wrists. "I said I didn't want him along," he roared.

The captain and the two crewmen, who were casting off the lines, stared at the warring couple. Then they heard the guard at the end of the pier shout and their heads swiveled in his

direction just in time to see a blur of black tearing down from
the limestone staircase and onto the wooden plankings. Everyone came over to the pierside of the boat as Wiley tore noisily
across the wood. Everyone except Alex.

Sarah gave Wiley a hand signal to stay while calling loudly
for him to jump. The boat was drifting wide of the pier. Three
feet separated it from the wooden beams. The guard was
standing over Wiley, shaking his hands and pulling at his hair
in consternation. Sarah kept signaling for Wiley to stay, to pace
back and forth, to jump up, to back up. All the time she kept
shouting at him to jump onto the boat, to come to her.

It was pandemonium. The captain, the crewman and the
guard were riveted to the prancing dog who apparently lacked
the courage and confidence to leap to the boat as his mistress
was commanding him. They began yelling at him themselves.
Some yelled to stay. Others yelled to jump. Wiley looked from
one to the other and whined frantically, caught up in the general
hysteria.

Sarah felt Alex at her back and heard him bellow. "Jump,
you stupid son of bitch!" Which meant that he had hauled
Gabrielle up over the side and stowed her safely below somewhere in the cabin section. Sarah grinned. They weren't out of
shark-infested waters yet, but they were getting there.

She called out, "Come, Wiley." And this time she also signaled for him to come to her.

The crew had thrown a line back to the guard, who'd nearly
been pulled into the sea by the drag of the boat. He managed
to coil the line around a piling and stay the craft's drift. It
would be a long jump, though.

Wiley whined softly and walked around, backed up and
made a dead run at the end of the pier. He sailed through the
air, his front paws tucked up tightly under his chest, the wind
pressing his long black hair flat against his muscular body.

He landed with a soft thump on the edge of the deck, his
hind legs barely catching the rail as they cleared it.

Sarah fell to her knees and hugged him. "Good boy, Wiley,"
she exclaimed. Her heart was hammering in her chest. After a
minute, she gathered herself together and raised her face to
look at Lefevre. "I'm ready to go whenever you are, Captain," she said cheerfully.

The men stood staring at Sarah and her dog for a long, incredulous moment. Lefevre knifed the air with his hand and grunted, "Cast off." He scowled at Sarah and added, "Again!" In French he muttered his poor opinion of the fair sex and their incomprehensible ways.

They were a quarter of the way around the island when they saw lights flashing on in the rooms of the fortress where Gabrielle had been held. Moreau had discovered that Gabrielle was missing. Soon he would realize that Sarah, Alex and Wiley were gone as well. When he radioed the boat to order them back, Lefevre and his two men would have the upper hand. Alex had to get rid of them before he lost the element of surprise.

Alex motioned for Sarah to go to the stern and keep her head down.

"Say," Alex said to the crewman next to him, "what's that?" Alex was bending over the waist-high rail, pointing to something in the foaming water beside the boat.

The crewman, who'd been standing nearby, turned to look down. "What?"

Alex pointed down into the water. "There. See that light?"

The crewman squinted hard and bent over as far as he could. "Naw. What light?"

Alex took a quick look toward the helm. Lefevre and the other crewman were watching for reefs up ahead and paying no attention to him. He yanked the man up by the waist of his pants and with a burst of strength tossed him the rest of the way over the rail.

"*That* light," Alex muttered.

By the time the man surfaced, the boat had pulled far away, leaving him floundering angrily in its wake. His sputtered shouts for help were easily drowned out by the cruiser's powerful motor. Not wanting to leave anything to chance, Sarah was shrieking at the top of her lungs that she'd just spotted a sea turtle off the port bow. She waved her arms in enthusiasm and felt a whoosh of relief as the men turned to look in the direction she was indicating, which was the opposite direction from the man swimming in the sea behind them.

Lefevre and the other crewman were too busy looking for the mythical turtle to notice that anyone had fallen overboard.

Sarah furtively glanced at the waters astern. She could barely make out the sailor now. He'd abandoned yelling and was stroking toward the shore. She figured he wouldn't get to anyone on the island for another twenty minutes at the very earliest. She hoped that would be enough time. She crossed her fingers and held her breath.

Alex had joined Lefevre and the other crewman at the helm, and Sarah sternly repressed the urge to nervously chew on her lower lip. Both of Moreau's men were armed. Alex was not. She closed her eyes and prayed that he'd be good enough to handle them without getting himself hurt. It was two against one now. Of course, she and Wiley could try to help, but Alex had been explicit in his rejection of that. He wanted her in the stern with Wiley protecting her. He'd nearly laughed in her face when she suggested that she and Wiley help even up the odds for him. Then he'd grimly reminded her that he was the pro and she was to do as he said. She hadn't liked that. On the other hand, she couldn't exactly argue the point. He was the pro on this mission. Reluctantly she went along with him.

The men began laughing loudly, vastly amused by something that Alex had said. Another off-color remark, no doubt, she thought in disgust. Moreau's men had the wallowing minds of wild boars. She watched Alex continue to trade jibes with them, still pretending to stagger a little each time the boat's prow lifted against the ocean waves. Lefevre laughed and his seaman grinned, exposing several missing teeth. The seaman slapped Alex on the shoulder, laughing even more loudly when the force of his blow sent Alex staggering forward a step.

Alex leaned forward and turned on the radio. With a quick flick through the dial, he located a station blaring out the metallic rhythms of Caribbean music. He turned up the volume and began dancing, holding an imaginary woman in his arms, sliding his hands over her voluptuous figure while Lefevre howled in amusement.

Alex shook his head and braced himself against one of the seat backs with both hands. "I don't think I should have tried dancing, Lefevre. I don't feel so good..." he muttered bleakly.

"Take 'im to the side," Lefevre ordered crisply. He wasn't about to have someone get sick all over his helm. "You shouldn't 'ave come after 'aving so much to drink!" he pointed out rather grumpily. He kept his eyes straight ahead while his subordinate helped Alex.

Alex leaned heavily on the crewman's shoulder. The man, convinced that Alex was in too weakened a condition to be of any harm, relaxed his guard. When they reached the rail, Alex twisted the man's arm up behind his back and roughly pulled the gun from the man's holster before he knew what was befalling him. His openmouthed look of amazement was comical.

"You can jump in the water on your own, or I can break your arm as I toss you in," Alex growled softly. "Take your pick."

Alex shoved the man's arm up to the breaking point, and his face twisted in agony. "I'll jump," the man whispered hoarsely.

Alex kept the man's arm up against his spine until he'd gingerly swung himself over the rail and was ready to leap into the restless sea. "Adios, amigo," Alex whispered harshly as he released the man and gave him a hard shove into the swirling waters. The man's scream was lost in the cacophony of music at the helm.

The ship-to-shore radio crackled and all trace of humor left Alex. Someone was trying to contact them. Things were going to unravel soon. The crewman's gun dangled from Alex's hand, and he glanced at Sarah to make sure she was all right. He wasn't grinning, but he sent her a silent message of reassurance and strength. Then he turned toward the helm and Lefevre.

Moreau first realized something was amiss when a man burst into his private suite shouting that the woman was missing.

Moreau, who'd been entertaining one of the kitchen women, was absolutely furious at the unexpected interruption. He'd been reclining on his couch, imagining that the woman had blond-brown hair and feisty brown eyes and hoarsely calling her "Sarah." Moreau ground his teeth together in rage. Red faced in fury and frustration, Moreau sat up, leaving his flustered companion to hastily refasten her clothes and cover herself as best she could. "What woman?" Moreau snarled.

The terrified man hung back near the door, in case he needed to make a hasty retreat. Then he said in a rush, "We searched everywhere, but she's disappeared. She couldn't have been gone for more than forty-five minutes or an hour. The guard saw her then.''

The first woman who came to Moreau's mind was Sarah, since he'd been visualizing her with every pore of his body for the last thirty minutes. He didn't even consider the possibility of the vanished woman being Gabrielle. She was completely imprisoned.

"So, she had to sneak out and get lost in the brush. Good. Maybe the dogs will find her and not be so kind this time," Moreau muttered. "Get out," he added.

"But…" Moreau's man was close to tears. "It wasn't the one with the dogs." He choked.

Moreau was attacking the woman with an aggression close to violence, shoving her down, stripping her bare. The bearer of bad tidings slid out of the room.

Moreton appeared and was concerned by the agitation apparent in the young guard's face. He frowned as he inquired about its cause. "What is it?"

"The woman escaped." It was all he could manage to say, so afraid was he now of the bind he was in.

"Which woman?" Moreton asked sharply.

"The diver."

From inside, Moreau heard the devastating news and staggered out of the room on shaking legs, to yank the frightened guard around by the shoulder.

"Why didn't you say that? Search for her at once! And check our other guests," he added with the acid of suspicion lacing his every word.

Moreton was puzzled. "I tried their door half an hour ago, but the dog wouldn't let me in. He was growling inside everytime I tried the handle. I assumed they were asleep. Or else Sutter had beaten her into unconsciousness and then he'd passed out from too much to drink." That made perfect sense to him. And there'd been a lot of noise.

Moreau was refastening his pants and striding barefoot down the corridors to the room where Alex and Sarah had stayed. He knocked. When there was no answer, he kicked it in. It was empty. The breeze blew the curtain into the room and Moreau walked quickly to it to stare out into the night. He pointed to the sloping tile roof a few feet to the left of the small balcony. There was room for a dog to have jumped from between the wide-spaced, old wrought-iron grillwork to that sloping rooftop. And from there to the ground below. In the area where he would have landed, there were marks in the sand, and a broken piece of the roofing.

Moreau could make out the pier, and it took him less than a split second to realize that the *Stingray* was gone. The drug czar swore violently and slammed his hands against the iron railing in his fury. "A little midnight cruise around the island!" he hissed furiously.

Then he swung around and hit the man who'd tried to warn him, knocking him unconscious with the force of the blow. He ignored the body slumping to his feet and ran out of the room with Moreton following close at his heels. Moreau was swearing viciously every step of the way. And with every stride, he swore that each of the three escapees would pay most dearly for the humiliation that they'd dealt him this night.

He shoved one of the seamen awake with a rude kick to his ribs.

"Get on the boat!" Moreau screamed. He turned toward Moreton. "You take the *Carib*. I'll take the *Sea Eagle*. Get every one of the boats in the water. Now!"

"You will pay," Moreau swore as the crews scrambled to launch the boats.

He reached for the radio and called the *Stingray*. That had to be where they were. He would kill them all for this. He would make that stubborn diver talk. He would make that silly blonde watch while he forced Gabrielle to tell him what he wanted to know.

And he would make Alex Sutter watch both of the women die before him. When death came, they would be screaming their thanks. Moreau's cold eyes glittered and his lip curled in anticipated triumph.

No one made a fool of Antonio Moreau.

"Lefevre!" Moreau shouted into the mouthpiece. "Lefevre!"

The sound of Moreau's voice shouting over the radio and laced with hatred immediately drew Captain Jaime Lefevre's complete attention. He was lifting the radio to respond when Alex put his arm around the man's throat and yanked his right arm up in a painful wrestling hold.

Lefevre gasped and struggled. The two men were locked together, Lefevre fighting to be free and Alex fighting to bend him to his will.

Sarah watched as their muscles bunched and twisted, as they grunted from the effort to best each other. It seemed like slow motion, dragging on and on and on until Sarah was sure that they'd both collapse from the tremendous effort they were expending to destroy the other's strength to resist. Then Lefevre began to grow limp. He slumped against Alex and, after a moment to make sure he was truly unconscious, Alex let him fall to the deck in a heap.

Sarah rushed forward and held the wheel steady as Alex tied the captain. She saw him put a life jacket on the man first and asked in surprise, "Are you throwing him overboard?"

Alex shook his head. "No. But if Moreau catches us, we may be shot out of the water and all of us will be taking a swim. I may have done many things, but murdering a man by letting him drown isn't among them. I'd just as soon keep it that way."

Alex jumped up to take the helm. "Go get your sister. She's in the second cabin on the left."

Moreau's voice was still shouting through the radio at them and they were yelling to hear each other over it. Alex turned down the volume and pointed the ship north-northeast, heading into the open sea.

As Sarah disappeared below to get Gabrielle, he could see a small flotilla of boats charging around the end of Moreau's island in hot pursuit.

"Hell," he muttered. He opened the throttle all the way and the big cruiser surged forward like a racehorse. Behind him, two of the boats were slowly closing the distance between them.

Gabrielle and Sarah came up on the deck and huddled on either side of Alex.

"You can drop me off over there," Gabrielle said, pointing in the general direction of Grand Cayman, which was nowhere close enough to see.

"Another comedian," Alex murmured.

Sarah slipped her arm around his waist and rested her head against his arm. "It runs in the family."

"So where're the marines?" Gabrielle asked hopefully.

"That's a hell of a good question," Alex said tightly. "They're supposed to rendezvous with us in ten minutes about two degrees to the east of our present position. You don't happen to see any ships out there, do you?"

Chapter 14

The silver light played over the dark waves as the moon gleamed down on the sea. The clouds were scudding away. Visibility was clearing.

Alex swore.

"What's the matter?" Sarah asked.

"We'll be very easy to see," he said, jerking his head in the direction of the moon overhead. "Put on life jackets. Keep down, but stay up at the bow."

Sarah and Gabrielle didn't argue. Sarah handed Alex a vest and then helped Gabrielle rig a makeshift one for Wiley.

There was a sound of rapid gunfire from semiautomatic weapons. Pieces of the deck splintered as bullets struck a few feet from Sarah.

Alex swerved the boat and made a slow zigzag to make them a more difficult target to hit. Another burst sprayed bullets across the water and struck a broad path across the stern. The next barrage fractured deck furnishings and the glass enclosing some navigational equipment. Flying pieces of glass slashed superficial cuts across Alex's arms and chest.

Sarah leaped to his side.

"Are your eyes all right?" she asked anxiously, seeing a trickle of blood along his cheek.

He nodded grimly. "Lie across the starboard bow," he ordered her. "All three of you." He pointed a quarter mile ahead of them. "That's the connection we're trying to make."

Sarah and Gabrielle struggled to keep Wiley, whose claws were more hindrance than help on the relatively smooth surface, from being tossed overboard everytime they came down hard on an unusually high swell.

Sarah peered in the direction Alex had indicated. Rising above the water she saw the scope and emerging hatch of a submarine.

Automatic weapons strafed the deck. The boat lurched and one of the engines began to flutter disastrously.

"Hang on to Wiley," Sarah told Gabrielle.

She crawled back along the deck, keeping as low as she could. When she found Alex, she felt a wave of fear. He was draped over the wheel, fighting to keep from passing out. There was a gash on the side of his head.

She grabbed his shoulders and tried to hold him. "Alex! Alex! Can you hear me?"

He looked at her and struggled to focus his vision. "Yeah. There's nothing wrong with my hearing." His voice sounded comfortingly irritable. "I thought I told you to stay up on the bow."

"Sorry. I can't hear you. All this noise has damaged my ears." She helped him steady the wheel and leaned closer, dipping under his arm and pulling it around her.

"It's safer up front," he said angrily.

"It's not *that* safe." She glanced over her shoulder. "I think they're gaining on us."

"Yeah." He sounded very tired; he rubbed one hand over his eyes, as if trying to clear them, then shook his head. "Sarah, can you see the sub?"

"Yes."

"Do you think you can swim to it?"

"Sure. If nobody shoots me full of holes first."

He pulled her close and kissed her hard on the mouth. "I'll see what I can do about keeping the bullets away," he murmured. "Tell Gabrielle and Wiley to jump when I give the signal."

"Okay." She was scared to death. Jump into the middle of the ocean in the middle of the night while men shooting automatic weapons pursued them as they tried to swim to a submarine now about a quarter mile away? She took a hard grip on her shivering nerves and nodded. "Fine. When are you jumping in after us?" She wanted to know which direction to watch for him.

His jaw tightened. "As soon as I can. Go! We don't have much time." He figured their pursuers would be overtaking them in ten or fifteen minutes. That is if they didn't simply blow the *Stingray* out of the water first. He pushed Sarah toward the bow. "Hurry up."

Sarah explained the plan as soon as she reached Gabrielle.

"I wish I had my scuba gear," Gaby mumbled as she helped maneuver Wiley into jumping position. "All set."

Alex shouted, "Jump."

They did. Cool water closed over them and they went down deep. They were tossed and lobbed in the rhythmic motion of the sea, struggling to come up for air, to stay close, to keep a sense of up and down. The roar of the cruiser's engines diminished as Alex steered a course in a northerly direction, turning away from the sub, and away from the three figures lost in the waves.

Sarah's face broke through the surface. She gasped for air and frantically turned, searching for Gabrielle and Wiley. Gaby broke through the wave a few feet to her left. The sound of Wiley coughing and snorting and splashing like mad made it easy to locate him a few feet to her right. Sarah and Gabrielle swam over to Wiley and began treading water near him, calming him down and turning him so they could swim toward the sub.

Sarah watched the cruiser, waiting for Alex to jump off. It was getting far away. She couldn't see anything but the boat and the water. A man in the water was difficult to see at night. *Come on Alex. Jump.* The cruiser kept getting smaller and smaller in the distance.

"Gaby, do you see Alex?" Sarah asked worriedly.

The three of them rode up on a swell, then eased down as it passed on.

Gabrielle wiped water off her face and peered in the direction he'd be coming from. "No. But if he's already in the water, he can see the sub about as well as we can. We'd better get to them before they decide we aren't here. Come on, Sarah. The man said swim for it. So swim for it."

Sarah tried not to think of the miles of ocean below her, around her, filled with predatory denizens of the deep. She saw Moreau's boats pursuing the *Stingray* and suddenly she had an awful feeling that she knew what he'd done.

"No, Alex," she said in a strangled cry. "Oh, no. He's still on the boat. He's leading them away from us. He's using himself as bait. Damn you, Alex Sutter! You tricked me."

Gabrielle dragged her arm and began a steady kick. "He didn't strike me as dumb," Gaby said. She choked. "We can't talk out here. It's too wet. Come on, Sarah. Swim! He'll be with us soon. He doesn't strike me as the suicidal type. Much too ornery for that. And he can't find us in the middle of the Caribbean any more than you can find him. We're needles in the haystack. We've got to get to the sub. It's our only chance. Unless you've grown gills since I last saw you."

There was another violent burst of automatic weapon fire. The *Stingray* burst into a giant fireball. Both women were frozen with horror.

"Alex!" Sarah screamed. "Alex!"

Gabrielle looked at the great burning mass, aghast. "Sarah, we can't do anything. If he made it, he'll be at the sub... eventually."

They treaded water, aware of the cold sinking into their limbs.

Sarah, tears running down her cheeks, dragged her eyes away from the horrible sight and concentrated on swimming toward the waiting sub. He *had* to have escaped. Oh, God. *Alex.*

Sarah looked at Gabrielle. There was doubt in her sister's eyes. She wasn't at all sure that Alex had jumped free before Moreau's gunfire had ignited the fuel tanks. That must have been what caused the explosion. Sarah felt the will to go on waver. She wanted to search the seas for Alex. But she knew

Gaby was right. Rendezvousing at the sub was the only work-able plan. Maybe they could help search for Alex.

Sarah began the long swim to the waiting submarine.

They were spotted when they were a few hundred feet away from the ship. Four navy frogmen jumped into the water and swam out to meet them. Sarah hadn't realized how exhausted she was until the diver who came to her aid held her and let her piggyback a ride. Her body felt like iced lead. She was only numbly aware of the hands on her ribs and hips as she was hauled up onto the sub and helped down the narrow steps that led into its belly.

"Alex . . . He's out there somewhere . . ." she said anxiously. Her lips felt frozen and her skin was covered with goose bumps. She began shivering uncontrollably.

"Sutter?" the man next to her asked. "The man who was with you?"

"Y-yes," Sarah said. She grabbed the lapels of his white shirt and spoke straight into his bearded face. "D-don't you d-dare leave here without him. Y-you've g-got to s-search for him. He j-just c-can't b-be . . ." She found she couldn't say the awful word.

Tears started running down her face again. They were hot against her chilled skin. Someone put a blanket over her and she hugged the edges around her with stiff fingers as Wiley was handed to two sailors holding blankets to rub him down.

The bearded officer who'd listened to Sarah beg him to help find Alex had turned to talk to several other members of the crew. Someone was calling out that a signal was being picked up on the sonar equipment and it wasn't at the right depth for a whale or a ship.

"Excuse me, ma'am," the bearded officer said. "I'd better go check on this. We'll do our best to find Mr. Sutter. I'll send someone back as soon as we have any word for you." He pat-ted her reassuringly on the arm and shouldered his way through the narrow opening that led into another section of the sub.

A sailor offered her some hot coffee.

A man in slacks and a cotton turtleneck swung into the room. He glanced at Sarah, but when he saw Gabrielle, he looked ten years younger.

"Gabrielle Lorenzo?" he asked.

Gabrielle nodded between sips of her own hot drink. "That's me."

"I'm John Drake. Would you feel up to looking at some nautical charts with a couple of other men and me? We're looking for that plane you came across..."

Gabrielle nodded. "I thought I'd be hearing from somebody about that." She stood up and put down her empty cup. "Do you suppose I could squeeze in a hot shower first?"

Drake grinned at her and motioned for her to follow him. "I think I can arrange that. And a fresh set of clothes, if you don't mind navy issue?"

Gabrielle smiled back. "Anything clean and dry will be perfect." She sighed. She hugged Sarah before she left. "Hang in there, kiddo. Alex looked like he could take care of himself. Want to come get in line for a shower? It might make you feel better?"

Sarah shook her head. "Maybe later. I want to be here, if they find him." She crossed her arms stubbornly and restated. "When they find him."

"Okay," Gaby said softly. "See you later." She followed Drake out of the small cell that doubled both as a bedroom and sitting room. "John Drake. What do they call you? John? Jack? J.D.?"

Sarah listened to their voices disappear down the narrow tube that appeared to be the main thoroughfare in the sub. A manually wound alarm clock hung from the wall, ticking softly. The sound eventually drove her close to madness. In agitation, she made her way in the direction the bearded sailor had gone earlier. Sailors flattened against the sides of the walkway as she passed, smiling at her sympathetically. Apparently everyone was familiar with her plight, from the looks on their faces.

She heard the captain and his senior officers talking; she slowed her pace and listened anxiously.

"...they got the boats out at sea. When they realized they were being chased by the navy, they stopped shooting. Guess they realized they were outgunned for once. By then, one of the boats was taking on water and another was losing power. They put everyone in irons."

Sarah felt a small surge of satisfaction. At least Moreau was out of business and locked away where he deserved to be.

The naval commander who'd been conveying the report was still talking. "....haven't seen Sutter yet, but that signal the sonar's been picking up is getting closer so we're sending out some underwater teams to see what it is. They'll keep their eyes open while they're out in the water. If we don't see him soon, we can try to ease in at a slow speed, going toward the spot where his boat blew up. Maybe he's in the water and can't get to us. He might be unconscious...." The voice trailed off, leaving a significant silence.

Sarah knew what he wasn't saying. Alex might be unconscious or simply too incapacitated to swim to them. But he also could have been killed when the boat was blown to kingdom come. Sarah refused to believe that. Alex was...unconquerable. He wouldn't *dare* die on her, she thought fiercely.

The men turned as Sarah came through the small entryway. All conversation ceased, and their faces filled with uneasy sympathy. Nobody wanted to tell her that Alex had not yet been found. Or mention the reasons why he might not have reached the sub. Several of the younger officers looked at the captain. The middle-aged chief petty officer cleared his throat uncomfortably.

"We've been told that the men who were holding your sister have been captured," the captain explained. He gave her a kindly look. "Could I have one of the crew show you a shower and help you locate a change of clothing? Get you something to eat?"

Sarah shook her head and delivered a level look at the naval officer. "If you don't mind, I'd rather go back up and watch for Alex," she said simply. "I know I'm not likely to see him before you or your men spot him, but all the same, I'd like to be up there, trying."

"Certainly, Miss Dunning," he agreed. "Commander Franks will take you up. We're pretty informal here, so don't worry about the 'Commander' part. He responds well to Frankie," he added with a grin.

"Thanks, Captain," she said. She tried, not too successfully, to smile.

"This way, Miss Dunning," said the commander, leading the way back up into the cool night air. He went over to talk to some of the underwater teams dropping equipment to others already in the water.

Sarah watched them depart. With their aquatic speeder bikes, they were pretty fast, she thought. She hoped fast enough. She kept her vigil on the seaswept ship and time stretched out into infinity. There was just the ageless roll of the waves, the relentless swell of the sea, the glistening of the moonlit sky.

Nowhere did she see what she was searching for.

She had no idea how long she stood there. It felt like all night, but she knew it was probably less than two hours. It was then that she saw the orange life vest bobbing up above a wave, then hidden behind the next. She felt such a surge of hope that she nearly stopped breathing. Was there a man in it? Was it Alex? She didn't want to entertain the chance that it could be empty or contain one of Moreau's savage thieves.

There were divers coming. Some ahead of the orange vest, some on either side, some behind. She strained to see. There was a man in the vest. He was kicking his feet, but he'd hitched a ride with one of the frogmen. Someone had given him a snorkel and mask to make the ocean going easier. She told herself it had to be Alex. Yet she couldn't be sure until she saw him, up close, without the mask.

The first man in scuba gear reached the boat and pulled out his mouthpiece. "We got him," he shouted triumphantly. "Tell Cookson he owes me fifty bucks!"

Men scrambled over the ship, helping to pull their shipmates on board, reaching to aid the man in the life vest.

He came up over the side, and Sarah recognized his clothes, dripping wet and clinging to him. He was pulling off the face mask and shedding the snorkel tube as she threw her arms around his neck and looked into his tired face.

"I was beginning to think you were going to skip the sub and swim for Cayman Brac," she said unsteadily. She knew she couldn't laugh, or she'd break down completely. Feelings were crushing her with the strength of their force. She was shaking hard. "I'm so glad to see you," she whispered.

He was dripping wet, cold and still wearing his vest, which made it very hard to have a satisfactory hug. He held her so tight that she couldn't breathe. "Sorry you had to swim in on your own, Sarah," he murmured.

Had he ever been relieved when the divers had told him that the others had made it. It wasn't until he'd dived clear just before the *Stingray* exploded that he had faced the possibility that Sarah could have been lost in the night sea.

Sarah buried her face in his neck and tried not to sob so hard that everyone would notice. She just couldn't seem to stop herself, though.

"Hey," Alex murmured in her ear, caressing her sticky hair and kissing her salty ear. "It's all over. Now's the time to break out the champagne. We've got a happy ending."

"Yeah," Sarah mumbled into his cheek. "I'm happy."

Frankie was urging them down into the bowels of the ship. "We can leave," he pointed out with a grin. "What say we do, huh, folks?"

The captain was obviously pleased to see Alex as they came down the narrow stairs. "Welcome aboard, Mr. Sutter," he said, extending his hand to shake Alex's.

Alex handed his life vest to a seaman standing around as if just waiting to perform such a service. He was tired, but very glad that they were all alive. He grinned. "I have never been so glad to step on a ship in my life, Captain," Alex admitted.

The captain laughed. "I can understand your sentiment, sir. I think you two ought to be ready for a nice hot shower and a long rest." He noticed the bloodstains on Alex's clothing. "Perhaps you'd like to visit the ship's medical officer."

Alex grimaced and gingerly pulled the wet fabric away from some of the bleeding cuts on his arms and chest. "That might not be such a bad idea, Captain," Alex agreed.

"Come on," Sarah urged him. "Let's see how much glass is still stuck in you."

"You sound like a medical student discussing her first cadaver," he pointed out in outraged amusement. He ruffled her Raggedy Ann hair, looking tremendously relieved to see her. "Come on, then, Mrs. Frankenstein. You can watch." He grasped her hand and kept her close as he followed Frankie to the ship's medical service.

Sarah's heart sang. She squeezed Alex's hand and thankfully counted her blessings this night.

"While you're with them, I'll see to your rooms," Commander Franks said as he ushered them into the medical section.

Alex frowned and he swiveled in the direction of the departing Frankie. "Rooms?" he asked in surprise. He looked sharply at Sarah.

"They know we're not married," she explained, having guessed what had surprised him. "The captain calls me Miss Dunning all the time."

Alex frowned. "Oh? How did that happen? I thought we all went to considerable trouble to make sure everyone thought otherwise."

He winced as his wet shirt was carefully pulled off by a lanky sailor, exposing the crisscross pattern of cuts on Alex's chest and arms. Sarah ran her eyes over him anxiously. Most seemed superficial, unless glass was still embedded. A couple might need bandaging. All certainly required cleansing and antiseptic. After his swim in the sea, she thought they might give him some antibiotics, as well. Basically, however, he was whole and well.

She lifted her relieved gaze to his and brushed a light kiss on his firm lips. "I don't know how they found out," she replied, answering his question now that she'd seen he was not in any serious danger from his injuries. Until he'd raised the question, she hadn't even thought about it. Now that he mentioned it, she supposed it was a little unexpected. "Maybe Raymond told him..." she suggested. What difference did it make at this point anyway? She frowned at his sharp expression. He obviously didn't like unexpected things happening. His suspicions were aroused. She shook her head. "It's all over, Alex. It doesn't matter."

Alex held her gaze with his. "You didn't tell them?"

"No."

He frowned. He didn't like loose ends. Raymond wouldn't have gone to all the trouble to fake the marriage only to broadcast the truth to the navy. He wanted to talk to the captain and discover how he'd found out.

Sarah couldn't hug him because the medical officer had finally come in, bustling with good cheer, and was looking over Alex's cuts. She contented herself with trying to reassure him with words instead. "You've been in this business too long," she said softly. "This isn't reasonable skepticism. It's paranoia." She smiled at him affectionately, then an impish smile tickled her lips. "I know an antidote for that," she said mysteriously.

Alex's eyes were shuttered. "Is that so," he muttered. Reluctantly he asked, "What would that be?"

"Come to my room after you're cleaned up and I'll explain," she promised with a grin.

The forbidding expression on Alex's countenance softened into a warmer, more intimate one. His black eyes locked with hers over the head of the ministering naval officer. "It's a date," he agreed softly.

He watched her leave with an intentness that made Sarah feel light-headed. She was laughing as she found her way to the shower designated for her and Gabrielle that evening. It was over, she thought exuberantly. We're free. Free.

When Alex was cleaned up, medicated and dressed in clean clothes courtesy of the U.S. navy, he went looking for the captain. He eventually found the man in his quarters, getting ready to retire for the night.

"If you wouldn't mind, Captain," Alex said tersely, "I'd like to ask you a few questions."

The captain stopped taking off his shirt. "I can imagine you have a few," he admitted. "Sure. Sit down, Mr. Sutter. What's bothering you? I'll try to fill in any blanks that I can."

Alex sat down at the captain's desk. "Perhaps you could start with how you found out that Sarah isn't legally my wife."

The captain was surprised. "I'd have thought you'd be more interested in how many men we rounded up on that island and plucked off the boats this evening," he said in amusement.

Alex wasn't about to be deterred. "I'm interested. But there are a few threads of communication that I'd like to unravel first, with your help."

The captain shrugged. "Sure. A man named Rostik told me. Jones was being held up in a meeting with his superiors, and being pulled onto another job, so he had Rostik talk to me. You ought to know him. He said he was one of your 'witnesses.'"

Alex's jaw hardened in anger. "Rostik," he murmured acidly. He was a man with ambition, according to Jones. His zeal to flaunt his knowledge and appear to be an insider and highly informed could have proved disastrous to the mission. Raymond would hear from him on this foul-up.

"Let's hope he didn't let anything else slip to any of Moreau's goons that weren't on Raymond's pickup list," Alex muttered.

"Do you think there are still members of Moreau's band on the loose?" the captain asked.

Sutter laughed harshly. "Men like Moreau's cutthroats are as hard to destroy as the hydra. He has a sophisticated network of contacts throughout the Caribbean basin. Only the hard core of the gang was on that island. His tentacles may have been severed, but they're still flopping around, waiting to sting whoever comes too near. I can't imagine that Raymond was able to convince half a dozen different governments down here to press charges on the tentacle in their backyard and put it in jail, all at the same time. The probability is that some of them undoubtedly escaped."

The captain nodded slowly. "I see your point."

They talked for over an hour as the captain filled Sutter in on the details of the naval operation. After Alex had finished with him, he found a radioman and contacted Raymond, who was still overseeing the operation from his gray metal desk in Washington.

The first words that Alex heard when Raymond answered his phone were, "I've been waiting here for *hours* for you to call, damn it. What took you so long?"

Alex felt not a twinge of guilt. "I've been busy, Raymond," Alex said succinctly. "They called you to tell you the operation was a success?"

"Hell, yes. *They* obey orders," he complained. "I told them to keep the phone open as soon as anything started happening and to keep me informed every step of the way. I thought I told you something along those lines."

"Are you going to complain, Raymond? Or are you going to listen?"

Raymond's exhausted groan was easily audible. "Sorry, Alex. I've been worried about you and Sarah. And about our girl who knows where the plane went down. Drake's already pointed a couple of ships toward the wreckage, by the way. They're staking it out, playing guard tonight. The plates will probably be retrieved as soon as it's daylight tomorrow."

Alex lifted an eyebrow. "I'm sure a lot of people are very happy to hear that."

"You wouldn't believe the ecstasy," Raymond exclaimed. "Mine included. As soon as we hand everybody back their toys, I will finally be able to get out of this damned office and go play with my kids again."

"Raymond, are you sure they got everybody? Moreau? Moreton? Some of his other key bad boys on the other islands down here?"

"I won't know for sure until I see the photos. They should be faxing them up pretty soon."

Alex disliked having to wait. He and Sarah were getting off the sub at daybreak and returning to civilian life. He wanted to know if he was going to have to look over his shoulder for retribution from gang members who might have slipped away in the confusion.

"Let me know as soon as you've positively IDed everyone."

"Sure, Alex." There was a slight pause. "Do you think someone got away?"

"I won't know until you tell me, Raymond," Alex said dryly. "I wasn't in a very good position to see who they picked up."

Raymond laughed. "They told me you were all okay. Even Sarah's dog. Geez. I still can't believe she talked us into taking him along. Was that straight? You are okay, aren't you?"

"Yeah. Just a few marks. But they'll fade." He looked at the fresh bandage on his arm where the Doberman had bitten him and he grinned. "It was lucky for me that Wiley came along. And you were right about Sarah, too. We needed her there." He fell silent, frowning as he realized that soon she wouldn't be in his life anymore. There was going to be an emptiness then. Hell.

"So our little amateur came through like a pro, huh?" Raymond asked with a laugh. "I'm glad to hear it. I've gotten a lotta gray hair worrying about her."

"I know what you mean." Alex frowned more fiercely. "Speaking of professionalism, Raymond, would you mind telling me why that blowhard Rostik was shooting off his mouth, telling the navy that our marriage was just part of the game?"

Raymond swore. "Geez, I'm sorry, Alex. That shouldn't have happened." He was startled, and very angry.

"Damn right, it shouldn't have. Until we're sure that all these bastards are in jail, I won't know what kinds of risk I'm running walking around some of the islands down here. In case you've forgotten, Raymond, I make my living traveling around the Caribbean. I don't intend to retire simply because my bank balance has swelled thanks to this little mission." He was also worried about possible retributions to Sarah, although that ought to be very unlikely, since she was living up in Maryland. Moreau had never been known to try to conduct any assaults or killings on the mainland soil of the U.S. He'd confined himself to the vast possibilities closer at hand.

"I'm really sorry, Alex. I'm sorry as I can be. I'll see to it that Rostik is out of the operations end, out of a job, if necessary. I'll try to track down anyone else he may have spilled the beans to, and check around with our people on the street in the islands to see who's heard. We can put out some disinformation to reconfirm the original story and make Rostik look like an unreliable source." Jones sucked in his breath. "I'll try to make it right, Alex."

There wasn't much more Jones could do and Alex knew it. "Do what you can, Raymond," he said curtly. He just hoped that that was Rostik's only slip. "Talk to you tomorrow. Or whenever you've got some news."

"Right, Alex. Say, good work, man." Jones's elation could be felt through the radio.

"Thanks, Raymond."

Sutter rang off and went in search of Sarah. Screwups like this were one of the reasons he'd stopped working with the agency. Raymond was as good as gold. So were a few of the others, whom he knew from their deeds and their trackless ways, not from ever having met them. All you needed was one small slip by some careless or arrogant individual and everything could fall apart in your hands at the worst possible moment. Usually the last possible moment.

It was such a slip that had led Moreau and his band to that village, years ago, to hunt for Alex. All those villagers massacred because of a careless word spoken over lunch in an open-air café by someone who wanted to brag a little about some intelligence tidbit he'd erroneously concluded wasn't very important. It still made him feel sick with rage. And there was still no one to turn his rage on.

He reached Sarah's corridor and stopped in front of her door. He knocked softly enough not to wake her if she were already asleep, but loud enough to alert her that he was there if she weren't. He had no intention of waiting to be let in, however, after living so intimately with her. He opened the door and walked into her quarters, shutting the door after him with a soft and very final-sounding click.

Chapter 15

She was lying in a berth hung from the wall, one arm flung across her chest. As he knelt beside her, her eyes opened and she lifted sleepy fingers to touch his hand close to hers on the bed.

"All patched up?" she murmured sleepily. She was so tired, she could barely wake herself up. Her body felt leaden. Her mind, like raw cotton.

"Yeah. All patched up," he replied softly. "Tomorrow morning we get off the ship near Cayman Brac. It may be a couple of days, though, before you can catch a plane home." He caught her fingers gently in his. She'd be safer under his wing until they knew what had happened. Afterward, well, she'd be safer at her own place. Safer in general, and safer from him. "You're welcome to stay with me," he whispered softly.

Sarah smiled at him sleepily. "Thanks. Wiley, too?" she teased.

Sutter grinned slightly. "Wiley, too. I owe him a steak for standing up to Rocco. How does he like them?"

"Any way he can get them," Sarah said with a tired yawn. "We won't be in your way?" She blinked at him and her eyes were a little unfocused. In the shadows, and half asleep, she couldn't see his face well, or guess what was in his thoughts. "We wouldn't want to get underfoot . . . or . . . outstay our welcome."

His mouth formed a straight, tight line and he lifted her up in his arms. It hurt where the cuts tore open again, but he didn't give a damn. He slid onto her bed and let her sprawl across him like a sleepy kitten. God, she felt good against him. He hadn't admitted how much he'd wanted just to hold her in his arms again.

"You couldn't outstay your welcome, Sarah," he murmured as he wrapped his arms around her warm, relaxed body. She curled comfortably on top of him, mumbling incoherent sounds of pleasure.

He pressed a lingering kiss on her mouth. "You sound like I feel," he whispered huskily.

"Mmm." Even half asleep, Sarah felt the familiar sizzle and she slanted her mouth against his and kissed him back, as thoroughly as she could when she could hardly move a muscle. When she finally pulled a little away, her eyes closed as sleep became undeniable, she murmured hazily, "You've got the body electric, Alex. How do you do that, that electricity thing that you do? Hmm?"

He grinned as she fell asleep on him. He couldn't have described it better himself. It pleased him that she felt it in such a similar way. But then, a lot about her pleased him. Touched him deeply. Awakened feelings that had never been touched inside him before. Stirred others that he'd buried as a child, as a youth.

"It takes two," he whispered into the night. "Electricity goes nowhere unless you've got a complete circuit." He ran his hand over her in a tender, lingering caress. How could he feel as if he'd known her all his life? For all of eternity?

He didn't know. But that described the feeling perfectly.

"Sarah..." he murmured as he gradually fell asleep. *I could love you, Sarah Dunning.* . . . The thought drifted through his semiconscious mind; he was too relaxed to fight it off or deny it. He was too exhausted to disregard it, or call it lust or mere proximity. The knowledge made him shudder and murmur, "No."

"Sarah..." It was a sigh of distress, and there was raw anguish laced through it, as he finally fell into the abyss of a profoundly needed sleep.

Gabrielle burst in on them bright and early, sending Alex nearly onto the floor, and Sarah along with him. When he realized who it was, he groaned and resettled Sarah on the bed, sitting on the edge himself while glaring at their unexpected visitor.

Gabrielle stopped dead and her mouth hung open in astonishment. "I didn't know you were sleeping together," she blurted out in amazement.

Alex felt his cheeks darken and he was furious. He'd never been embarrassed by something like this before. Why now? He didn't know why exactly, but Sarah was different. When he was sleeping with her, he felt mated to her, welded to her. As if he belonged at her side, and she belonged at his. Gabrielle was making it sound cheap and casual. A friendly slaking of lustful impulses.

He clenched his teeth. "What in the hell do you want? Is the ship sinking?" he growled irritably.

Gabrielle recovered her aplomb and chuckled at the disgruntled look on Alex's face.

"Sorry. Did I say the wrong thing?" He looked even more ferocious, and it was all she could do not to laugh. She'd recognize that look anywhere. So would any woman. "You're a lucky girl, Sarah," Gabrielle murmured enviously.

"You took ten years off my life by charging in here to say that?" Alex demanded darkly.

Gabrielle laughed. "No. Of course not. John is taking me with him over to the underwater search and rescue operation so I can watch them bring stuff up." Sadness chased away her laughter, leaving her hollow eyed as she remembered the tragic circumstances of her original involvement in the sea hunt. "They said that since my friend Milos died because of it, and because he and I were divemasters, that the least they could do was to let me have the satisfaction of seeing the wreck salvaged by the good guys." She brushed away tears. "I'll be watching for Milos, I guess you could say. The divers all lobbied for it. Professional courtesy, I guess you could call it."

"*Esprit de corps*," Alex murmured, nodding his head in understanding. He sighed. He couldn't stay infuriated with a reason like that. "I take it you're leaving right away?"

"In five minutes," Gabrielle confirmed.

Sarah had curled up onto her knees beside Alex and was rubbing her eyes and yawning. "Are they going to bring you back to Grand Cayman?" Sarah asked.

"Yeah." Gabrielle glanced at Alex. "If you give me your number, I'll give you a call when I get home." She hesitated and glanced at Sarah. "I assume you'll be staying with Alex for a while?"

Alex jotted down his number on the scrap of paper she handed to him and answered for Sarah without even glancing her way. "Yes. She will." He ignored the surprised look on Sarah's face.

"Thanks," Gabrielle said. She looked at him curiously. "You don't give this out much, do you?"

"No. Very rarely."

Sarah complained, "He didn't even give *me* his phone number!"

"You didn't need to call me," he pointed out with infuriating calm. "We've been traveling together, remember?"

"How could I forget?"

Gabrielle wiggled her fingers and stepped out of their room. "See you two later, then." She blew Sarah a sisterly kiss and disappeared.

Sarah wrapped her arms around Alex's neck and planted a kiss on his cheek. Before he could trap her and roll her down for a more leisurely test of her kissing ability, Sarah was laughing and scrambling off the narrow sleeping berth and standing up just beyond his reach. She stretched and asked, "I wonder what they did with Wiley?"

Alex, who'd been watching her breasts rise and fall as she stretched, dragged his mind to what she was saying. "I think he had about half a dozen sailors vying for the honor of playing host after they cleaned him up. They were trying to rig some sort of sleeping pad for him, and a kingsize litter box for him to use to answer nature's call.''

Sarah doubled over laughing. "Did they get him to use it?" she gasped.

Alex shrugged and gave her a broad grin. "I have no idea. He's on deck H, I think. Unless he got bored and started taking his new friends for a walk."

They fell silent and looked at each other, and after a while there was an ache between them that Sarah felt in her heart.

"How long do Wiley and I get to visit with you?" she asked quietly.

He didn't answer at first. He seemed to be turning over the possibilities in his mind. From the sober expression on his face, she assumed none of the possibilities were tremendously pleasing to him.

"Perhaps a couple of weeks would do it," he said musingly.

"Would do it?" Sarah repeated, mystified. "Do what?"

His eyes were dark and he looked as if he were having that argument with himself again that she'd noted several times before. "A couple of weeks might be enough time for us to get over our problem."

"And . . . what problem is that?" Sarah asked, although she was fairly sure she knew what he meant. Perversely, she wanted to force him to say it.

"Getting over our . . . mutual attraction."

He said it softly, and his dark eyes were unrevealing.

Was it that he didn't want her to see the feelings? Or that whatever feelings had been there were gone now and there was simply nothing to see? Sarah felt an awful ache gnaw at her heart. Had she been wrong about him, then? Had he just been caught up in the drama and some of the excitement spilled over onto her? No. She couldn't have been that wrong. Surely not.

She drummed up her resolve. She told herself not to take his brush-off at face value. She told herself he was just not used to the feelings and that was why he was acting this way.

Bravely she faced him. Quite clearly, and gently, she said, "I think you underestimate it. People don't get over something like this in a couple of weeks, Alex."

He was very tempted to tell her that he agreed. He crushed the impulse, however. Chaotic, primitive emotions like this were the most unreliable things in the universe. His whole life was a testament to that. Sarah, in his opinion, had been protected from that brutal fact, first by her family, later by her isolated living conditions.

He smiled at her, but the smile was tinged with a cynicism that made it harsh and forbidding. "People get over things like this all the time," he argued. "For some it takes a few minutes. For others a few weeks." He shrugged. He'd conceded the elasticity of time that could be involved. "A few continue the insanity for months or even a few years. But in the end, it dies a natural death, Sarah. Nothing lasts forever."

Sarah felt the prick of hot tears behind her eyes. Fiercely she refused to let them well up for him to see. "You don't really believe that, do you?" she asked in an intense whisper. "I can't believe that you do. I remember..." Her cheeks grew warm as she saw his vulnerable expression, the one he'd worn as he'd made love to her, as he'd devoured her as though he couldn't get enough, as he'd sighed her name in near reverence.

Alex frowned. He felt his resolve waver a little. Damn her. He was losing a battle of wills with a slip of a woman with one-tenth his experience in slippery negotiations and nowhere near his aptitude for manipulation. And he was losing his edge because he was tempted to believe what she was saying. Because deep inside, part of him wanted to believe it.

"Oh, hell," he muttered. He rubbed the bridge of his nose and tried to shut out the wisp of temptation that was waving to him so enticingly.

Before Alex could say anything else, Commander Franks dropped in on them, carrying a thick stack of papers. He was wearing a serious expression. This wasn't going to be a light social call. It was business.

"Good morning, Miss Dunning, Mr. Sutter. Sorry to interrupt you," the officer apologized crisply. He thrust the sheaf of papers at Alex without waiting for them to reply. "These came in a half an hour ago. The captain said you'd want to look at them ASAP." He left.

Alex quickly thumbed through the stack. "Damn it." He smacked the papers against his palm angrily. He was furious. And he was worried. He looked at Sarah as a deadly light appeared in his angry eyes. "How in the hell could they have let that happen?"

Alex paced across the small room like a caged tiger. His eyes glittered. His hands flexed as if he would have dearly loved to strangle someone, and he swore explicitly.

Sarah flinched. "What is it?" Sarah asked, very concerned.

"Moreau escaped." Alex's reply was terse.

"Oh, no!" She couldn't believe it. Suddenly the threat was back. "No."

"Oh, yes." A lifetime of bitterness filled Alex's words.

Sarah stared at him. "How could they let him slip through their fingers?" she asked in dismay. "Good Lord, there was no place for him to go!"

Alex laughed cynically. "I'm sure Raymond is breaking their backs asking that very question. There are two common explanations when something like this happens. Nine times out of ten, one of them is responsible."

"They are . . . ?" she prodded.

"Careless stupidity. Or someone was paid off." His face was a mask of granite. If it was the latter, they'd have real trouble. That would mean someone inside was leaking information to the drug syndicate that Moreau had controlled.

Sarah was shaking her head in utter disbelief. "Maybe I should have left Wiley out at sea. I'll bet Moreau wouldn't have slipped away from him!" It had been a multinational effort, they had told her, so she had no idea which nation's navy had captured Moreau, and then, accidentally or intentionally, let him go.

Alex grabbed Sarah's arm. "We're getting back to my place on Brac as soon as this tub gets close enough for George to pick us up. Then I'm going to have a long conversation with Raymond while you and Wiley stay out of everyone's sight."

The first thing that Sarah did after George Ebanks dropped them off at Alex's house on Cayman Brac was to phone home and see how the dog handler was making out with Groton and Sweet Pea.

"Groton and I get along pretty well," the handler said with a laugh. "But I'm just a garden variety trespasser as far as Sweet Pea's concerned. He growls everytime I pass in his food. It's a good thing he's got a big run and a connection to his own shelter next to the house, because I don't think he'd leave me in one piece if I tried to take him for a walk, or let him run loose for a while."

Sarah was relieved to hear his report. And it was easy to visualize Sweet Pea's visceral distrust. Just like him, she thought affectionately. "It sounds like you're doing a great job with them," she told him. She felt sorry for her big rottweiler. He was just trying to do what she'd trained him for, and he was being kept in a lockup as a result.

"When are you coming back?" the canine expert asked hopefully. "I know a couple of dogs who'll be happy to see you," he joked. Then he laughed. "And a couple of local cops, too. That sheriff and his deputy come by almost every day. At first I thought they believed I'd done you in and hidden your body. They kept nosing around, looking for fresh mounds of dirt on the place."

Sarah rolled her eyes and laughed. "Oh, no!"

"Yep. And then there's your brother..."

"What's *he* done?" she asked with a great deal of trepidation. Christopher had never learned to put a leash on his initial impulses. And his initial impulses were almost invariably rather hotheaded.

The dog handler was chuckling. "He called last night. When he heard my voice announcing that you were out of town and I was dog-sitting, there was the longest, coldest, sharpest silence I have ever had the misfortune to hear. He said, 'Oh, yeah?'" Cal made a sound of amused resignation. "I think he's on a plane down here to personally check me out and make sure you aren't tied up in the back room."

Sarah groaned again. "I'm sorry. I'll try to catch him in Ontario before he leaves."

"If you miss him, I know right where you're gonna be able to find him in about twelve hours," he pointed out in amusement.

"You're sure taking this well, Cal," Sarah said with genuine admiration. She knew how trying all those people could be. "Thanks."

"No sweat. Professional courtesy," he said with a laugh. "Next time, you can baby-sit my bunch. Brace yourself for a long line of military types traipsing by your quarters hoping to get you to teach their pet to do a trick. I can see the crowd now...every dog face will have his pet chihuahua, rented for the hour, just to make a little time. And they'll all want to discuss it over dinner!"

"Don't call me, I'll call you," she warned him. "And if Christopher walks through the door, your opening words to him can be to call this phone number. Have you got a pencil?"

"Yeah. Shoot."

She gave him Alex's number and finished up the conversation. She hoped she'd get through to Christopher before he did something typically stupid, like a little crude dental work on Cal's front teeth with his right fist.

"Sometimes my family drives me nuts," Sarah said mournfully.

"I wouldn't be surprised if they say the same about you," Alex observed in amusement as he joined her.

He had changed into some casual clothes while she was talking to the army canine specialist. He looked sinfully handsome, she thought. She started dialing her brother's number. The interested look in Alex's face as he studied the sleek curves of her legs didn't make it any easier to remember the sequence. She misdialed once and turned her back on him to get it right the second time. When she turned around to face Alex, she found he'd been enjoying a leisurely perusal of her back.

When her brother didn't answer, her face fell. Despondently she hung up the phone.

Alex lifted his brow questioningly. "Something wrong with the dogs?" he asked, concerned.

"Oh, no. They're fine." She put her hands up helplessly. "It's my brother. Cal thinks he's going to save me from a fate worse than death."

Alex was surprised. "He's coming here?"

Sarah laughed. "Not yet. He thinks Cal's locked me away. But I gave him your number to flash at Christopher before he takes the first swing."

Alex nodded and pushed out his lower lip thoughtfully. "I see. Then he'll be flying down *here* to take a swing at me, I suppose."

Sarah laughed. "No. He wouldn't . . ." Her voice trailed off and her face fell. She turned stricken eyes on Alex. "Well, he might," she conceded.

Alex shrugged. "It's no more than I deserve," he said magnanimously. There was a teasing light in his eyes. When he saw how obviously distressed Sarah was becoming at the possibility of physical conflict between him and Christopher, he came to her and wrapped his arms around her, drawing her close. "Hell, it'll be a pleasure. I won't even punch him back, if that'll make you feel any better."

Sarah sighed unhappily. "Did you see the Stanley Cup Playoffs last year?" she asked gingerly.

"Um-hmm." Alex was running his hands through her hair and sliding his mouth across her cheek. He couldn't have cared less about sport statistics.

"Do you remember the brawl in the first round of games? The one where one player was ejected after knocking out three other guys even though they were padded up?"

He found her backside and leisurely explored the soft curves that he'd grown so attached to recently. "Yeah," he replied reluctantly. Then it occurred to him why she was telling the story. He stopped caressing her and looked into her large, cinnamon brown eyes. "*That* was your brother, Christopher?" he asked.

Mutely, Sarah nodded. She touched his jaw teasingly. "I hope this isn't glass. . . ."

Alex groaned and closed his eyes. "I must be getting used to your half-baked comedy," he admitted. "I almost laughed at that one."

The phone rang and Alex answered it. When he hung up, he turned to Sarah and asked, "Would you like to take a little drive to the other side of the island? There's a jewelry designer whom I need to see. She says she's got a new piece for me to take a look at."

"Sure. Jewelry? That's the business you're in when you're not in *this* business?" she asked.

"That's *the* business I'm in. Period," Alex said with exaggerated firmness. "My one and only business."

Sarah nodded her head but her face said she didn't believe it for a minute. Then she looked down at the diamond wedding band on her hand and her face sobered. She began to twist the ring loose. "I guess I'd better give this back." She glanced at him with sudden insight. "The ring came from your jewelry store, didn't it?"

Alex captured her hand and prevented her from removing the band. "Don't."

Sarah looked at the ring shining brilliantly between their tangled fingers, and shook her head. "But...I'm not...we're not..." She felt him tighten his grip and she looked up at him anxiously. "I feel like a fraud."

He lifted her hand to his lips and kissed her knuckles. "I want you to keep it," he said softly. "A personal gift, from me to you. Raymond didn't have anything to do with it."

Sarah looked away. "That makes me feel..."

"How?" he asked warily. He watched her eyes cloud unhappily.

She knew he wouldn't like it. "Like I'm being paid for services rendered."

He pulled her close, and this time he wasn't gentle. There was anger burning in his black eyes and tension in every muscle in his body. "No," he said tersely. "That's not how it is. Damn it, you must know that."

She lifted her chin and faced him squarely. "I'll wear it while I'm here, if you like, but when I leave..." She swallowed. "When I leave, I'll give it back to you..." Her voice trailed off to a faint whisper.

Alex didn't like it and his reaction was stamped on his face. He pulled her head with both hands and captured her mouth with his, fusing them together with a searing blend of fire and need. When he reluctantly parted his lips from hers, he muttered, "I give. You give. And we're each the richer for it. We both came out ahead in this madness. I could never pay you enough for the magic that springs up between us, Sarah. That can't be bought. And you damn well know it."

He was frowning, but there was a confused expression hidden beneath the frown. As if he knew he couldn't leave it at this.

Sarah put her arms around his neck and they swayed together in each other's arms for a long, silent minute. What was she going to do without this proud, reclusive, cynical man? She could feel his heart beating against hers, and all she wanted out of life was to go on feeling that joyous sensation for all her days. If two weeks were all that the stubborn man would offer them, well, she'd take it. And she'd spend the rest of her life treasuring the sweet memory.

She lifted her face to look at him. Slowly she smiled. "Why don't we wait till I leave to talk about the ring, Alex?" she suggested.

He wasn't crazy about it, but he could live with it, he supposed. Just another example of Sarah in her naiveté being able to wrap him around her little finger, he thought. He found he was becoming accustomed to it. He didn't really mind it anymore. Hell, he liked it. Wouldn't Blake and Grant be laughing at how hard he'd fallen? Just as they'd said.

He pressed a quick, hard kiss on her lips and located the car keys in his pants pocket. "All right. It's a deal. Now, let me introduce you to Anna Jenet, one of the finest jewelry creators in the islands."

Sarah would have gone with him to watch machines stamp out cornflakes. "Does she have a family?" Sarah asked as she trotted along behind Alex.

Alex grimaced. "Yeah." A daughter, among others, he recalled. Well, maybe she had found a new beau, he thought hopefully.

Sarah found going with Alex very enlightening. The first visit to Anna Jenet was followed by several others over the course of her stay on Cayman Brac. Anna clearly loved Alex, and admired him greatly. So did her daughter, who draped herself over Alex every chance she got, much to Alex's discomfort. Sarah teased him unmercifully every time they went to look at a new piece in Anna's shop. And Alex made certain that she was properly punished for her impish and disrespectful assaults on his dignity as soon as they got back to his house.

Of course, making love wasn't exactly a way to discourage the behavior, but Alex wasn't thinking rationally enough to worry about that, and Sarah enjoyed her punishments too much to quit teasing him.

George Ebanks visited every other day, bringing what news he had of comings and goings on the islands. Moreau had not been seen, but Alex didn't think that would continue forever. Sooner or later, he'd hunt them down for revenge. It was just the way he was.

Every day Alex watched more carefully, looking for some sign of Moreau's approach—a new boat in the harbor, an unscheduled docking by a cruise ship, a group of divers staying in an especially secluded spot—and his nerves grew tighter as each day passed and Moreau's whereabouts were still unknown.

Sarah liked lying on the clean, white beach and snorkeling in the warm, shallow water best of all. She was surprised that Alex was willing to spend so much time with her. He kept looking around, and she knew he was watching for approaching strangers who might mean them ill, but much of the time, he just relaxed and enjoyed himself with her.

"Did you see the trumpet fish?" Sarah called out exuberantly as they floated side by side in the shallows near some flat limestone rocks.

Alex looked at her through his mask and nodded. He pointed down through five feet of water to their right. A small head poked out of the rock and spit a tiny pebble at the mouth of its home, then elusively it disappeared back inside.

"A tidy little housebuilder," Sarah exclaimed.

They were wearing fins and kicking in slow, leisurely strokes, gliding through the water calmly. The fish were used to them and didn't dart into the rocks anymore. Bright yellow and vivid purple blue tangs skated regally by. A lone sergeant major whipped past, flashing his dark and light stripes as he dodged in and out of the scores of blue-green wrasse swimming through the crystal sea.

They went to shore and dropped their gear on a clean, flat limestone slab. It had been a beautiful day.

Sarah lay in the shallows, sunbathing, soaking up the last few hours of pleasure before she had to leave. She'd only mentioned it once, offhandedly, as she'd packed this morning. She had a business to get back to, she'd reminded him. She couldn't stay in paradise forever, however much she wished she could. He wasn't offering her forever, but she hadn't reminded him of that. It had been left unsaid. Alex had been frowning. He knew. She had to go on with her life.

Alex had made it clear he thought she should stay. He was concerned about Moreau; Alex wanted her under his own roof until the man's whereabouts were pinpointed. He wanted to protect her. That had been a reasonable excuse for two weeks. But then she'd begun to fall silent when he mentioned it. Finally she'd started shaking her head. *I can't be kept in your protective custody forever.* It had been meant as a friendly joke to ease the growing tension between them. It hadn't eased anything. They'd argued about it. Fiercely. But Sarah had stood her ground. She couldn't stay indefinitely, however tempted she was. And when Alex had turned on the persuasive charm and exerted every effort to make her change her mind, it had taken every last shred of her failing will for Sarah to hold out against him. But hold out she had.

She supposed that she would have succumbed to Alex's efforts to convince her if she'd had a slightly bigger dash of her siblings' devil-may-care personalities. For a swift, aching moment, she'd wished she did. Christopher had never worried about whether something was wise to do. And Gabrielle certainly hadn't been noted for that kind of restraint, either. But Sarah had been the sensible one of the three. She'd always been thoughtfully cautious about what she did. She didn't take risks in relationships of any kind. Until Alex, she'd never even taken the risk to have a truly intimate relationship with a man. Her smile was bittersweet as she thought of what he'd given her. Alex had been worth the risk. She would never regret the brief, precious time that fate had given her with him. Having known Alex was worth the pain.

Sarah felt the smooth ebb and flow of the tide washing over her. Like the hours that were passing, never to come again. Sorrow filled her heart. There was only a little time left. Then Alex would be just a part of her past, instead of the only-too-real lover floating languidly at her side. She let her hand float closer to him. To touch him one more time...

Alex was sprawled out comfortably in the water next to her, thoroughly relaxed, as he usually was with Sarah close at hand. Unless she was being infuriating, of course. A small canary-yellow fish tickled his foot and he grinned slightly. Sarah was like the little fish, he thought. She fit into the environment as easily as the rainbow-colored parrotfish that filled the sunny reefs.

She was as relentlessly inquisitive, and as unexpectedly delightful, too. His house, which he'd previously felt had suited him perfectly, had become vividly warm with Sarah wandering through it. He'd seen the vibrant sunsets freshly through her enthusiastic eyes over dinner on his patio. Had the colors always been so rich? He'd laughed at her determined shows of force over chess and poker. Games. He'd been so used to playing other kinds, he'd forgotten how much fun it could be just to play for entertainment. To laugh in triumph or in honest amusement.

Had he laughed here before? Really, genuinely laughed? If he had, he couldn't remember it anymore. Sarah brought an optimistic zest to the place that was contagious. The beach house was a home with her in it. When his control had slipped once, he had almost imagined children laughing at their feet. He was able to press that ridiculous image away, but when she left, he knew it wasn't going to be the same without her. It probably wouldn't ever go back to how it had been before she'd breezed into his life like a September hurricane. It would be cold and empty without Sarah. He would get over it eventually, of course. It might take longer than he'd thought at first, but he'd get over it. But he didn't want to have to start getting over Sarah Dunning just yet.

He fiercely wanted her to stay; two weeks together had had the opposite effect on him than he'd planned. The longer he was with her, the more they made love, the greater was his hunger for more. He'd tried everything he could think of to talk her into staying longer. Everything short of admitting why he really wanted her to. But he'd lost his magic touch of persuasion where Sarah Dunning was concerned. It seemed she was the one person on this planet who was immune to his charmed tongue. That had left him gnashing his teeth in frustration and raking his hair in annoyance. Damn her stubbornness anyway.

In more rational moments, he actually did understand her need to regather her life around her, to get back to her work, her business. He knew she was right to do it. He wasn't offering her anything that would make a sensible person throw that security away. He knew that. And every time he was tempted to offer her something truly compelling, he took a long, fast swim in the cove, or threw on his shorts and ran for a mile or two. He didn't come back to her until the increasingly powerful urge to claim her on a long-term basis eased up and he could ignore it again.

But damn it, he didn't want her to leave yet. Not yet. Just a little longer. Then maybe he could let her go. Without feeling as if he was destroying himself by letting her out of his life. It was too soon for her to leave. Too soon.

He rolled closer to her and began to pull at her bikini top suggestively with his fingertips. It was a brilliant tropical red that seductively cupped her breasts. He could see the outline of her nipples pressed against it. The bottoms were a shimmering scarlet slash seen through the glassy waters. Her legs were clean and smooth floating out in the water. He wanted to touch her all over. He could have devoured her with his body, so much did he want her. He forced himself to stop looking at the beautiful shape of her and turned his attention to her face. A shadow passed away and sunlight curved her lips.

"Why are you smiling?" he asked softly. He wondered about the sadness that had preceded it, grateful that whatever it was had passed.

Sarah opened her eyes. To her surprise, they began filling with tears. "I was thinking of how happy I've been the past two weeks here with you." She blinked and tried to control the welling emotions. "Sorry. I think I'm springing a leak. Too much of a good thing, I guess."

He frowned. "Tears aren't usually the hallmarks of happiness," he pointed out huskily. He gently captured her lips and kissed her with thorough and very devastating tenderness. He explored the inside of her yielding mouth and a familiar ache coiled in his chest. Pain and pleasure twisted together inside his heart. "I never meant to make you cry, Sarah," he murmured against her lips.

The ties of her top floated loose beneath the skillful onslaught of his experienced fingers. When she was free, he slid his hand possessively over each breast in turn. Gently he stroked her soft flesh amidst the water's warm caresses. He loved to touch her, and it was clear in the way he handled her.

Sarah felt the familiar searing pleasure spear through her and she arched against him helplessly. Silently she helped him remove the ties of the cinnamon-red bikini bottoms, and she moaned as he explored her naked body with his hands, finding all the places that ached for his attention, applying just the right pressure at just the right time. He followed her body's silent requests, more than willing to give her what she wanted, knowing when she wanted it almost at the same moment she did.

His caresses brought more pleasure each time he touched her. The powerful attraction between them had just deepened and become more gripping every time they made love. Sarah knew it would happen again, this time, leaving her forever branded as his. Part of her ached for it to happen; part of her mourned that it should be so when he wasn't willing to keep her at his side. He was strong yet gentle, fiery yet restrained, an eager yet patient lover. He was everything she needed, everything she wanted. Everything she would ever dream of in a man. She felt him jerk loose his trunks and felt the fabric brush her bare hip as it was tossed aside. They were as nature had intended, man and woman. Mates.

Alex pulled loose the narrow scarf that bound her head in a band of blazing reds, oranges and yellows. He wanted her completely unclothed in his arms. As naked and open to him as it was possible for her to be. With nothing to remind him of the rest of the world, and the things that were taking her away.

He knew why she had cried. She didn't want to leave, either. He hated it, but he couldn't let himself stop her. Letting her go was the last gift he could give her. After he gave her himself, one last time. He would try to soothe the ache in both of them by making love with her.

She slid her hands along his hard, flat belly, down to the swell of his hard, eager flesh and she felt a heady rush of excitement as he sucked in his breath at the contact.

Such sweet, addicting torture. To feel his hungry need of her. To feel it in the increasingly hard, demanding touch of his mouth and hands. To feel it in the throbbing rhythms of his hips. To hear it in the hissing gasps that became his breathing, and the soft groans as she found his pleasure points. His nerves were on fire and he writhed against her, pulling her up and onto his hard male flesh. Her silken heat encased him and he filled her, pushing high and hard, until she moaned against his mouth.

They couldn't hold out against the sands of time that were running against them. The thrusts that he would have made slow and lasting became harsh and frantic. Sarah met him with her own desperation, faster, faster, faster. Crying out. No. No. Yes. Yes. Harder. Grinding pleasure that wrenched the core and erupted outward with molten volcanic force. Shaking hard, clinging harder, moaning into each other's mouths. Their dying cries were lost in the kiss that neither could bear to break. Shaking, convulsing. A mournful, *No*.

Until at long last, they knew the end had come.

Sarah caressed his back slowly, savoring their warm, wet bed in the sea shallows. "I have to go, Alex," she whispered brokenly as tears spilled over. "I love you. But I have to go."

When his face contorted in pain, she laid her lips tenderly on his, trying to soothe the raw wounds both of them were carrying. "Don't say anything, please," she murmured. "When I tell you that I love you, there are no strings attached. You've given me wonderful memories that I will treasure all my life. I hope you'll remember me like that, too."

She didn't want him to say something he wasn't completely ready to acknowledge. She knew he loved her. She also knew he didn't love her enough. He was letting her go. Even though it was with great reluctance. His actions spoke louder than any words of love could have. She didn't want to hear it, if he didn't mean it in the sense of forever.

He closed his eyes and composed his expression after a fierce inner struggle. He pulled her face into his shoulder and cradled her in his arms, crushing her to him for a moment before replying. In an emotion-choked whisper he said, "I'll remember. You're engraved in my soul, Sarah."

They lay in the shallows for a long while. Then Sarah staggered to her feet. Alex wrapped a towel around her, and another around himself, and they slung their snorkeling gear over their shoulders. Hand in hand, they silently walked back to his beach house to change clothes.

It was time to take Sarah to the airport.

Chapter 16

"You look like hell."

Alex looked up from his drink at the bar and straight into Grant Macklin's face. "Thanks," Alex said dryly. He lifted his glass. "Care to join me? Maybe I'll look better after you've had a few."

Grant swung his leg over the stool and ordered a rock and rye. It was a classy place but small enough to have an atmosphere of quiet intimacy. Where people could talk quietly about things that really mattered.

Alex looked at him curiously. "Blake said you were in San Francisco on a buying trip. Find anything interesting?"

Grant took a long sip. "Naw. But I think next time they'll take me seriously and bring out the good stuff. They thought I was as ignorant as the last East Coast buyer they'd seen. These things take time." He lowered his brows. "You know all about that, though."

Alex shoved his empty glass toward the bartender. He'd already had two. He didn't normally drink much, but, what the hell, he felt lousy. He motioned for a third and turned back toward Grant. "When did you get back into town?"

"This morning, on the red-eye." Grant pursed his lips thoughtfully, as if trying to decide how to put his questions. "Blake asked me if you were all right. I said I sure didn't think so, but since you weren't inviting either of us into your confidence, I was as much in the dark as he was."

Alex drew down his brows. He took his fresh drink and twirled it gently in front of him on the gleaming mahogany wood.

Grant shrugged as if he sympathized with Alex. "I wouldn't pry, but Blake's worried about you, so I thought I'd ask. Is there anything wrong?"

Alex laughed, and he realized there was no trace of humor in the painful, mocking sound. He swallowed half the drink straight and sighed. "No. You see before you a man who got exactly what he wanted," he said bitterly. "Only once he got it, he found he didn't want it after all."

Grant was perplexed. "I see." He hadn't talked to Alex about his trip, but he remembered hearing about some of the details beforehand. He thought maybe a little disarming, neutral conversation might help lubricate his partner's stubborn tongue. "How did the night-vision 'sunglasses' work out?" he asked with professional curiosity.

"Great."

"And the sonar signal device on the belt?"

"Like a charm."

"Hmm." Grant nodded and put both elbows on the bar. He noticed that Alex was holding something in the palm of his hand—the diamond wedding band he'd taken. He was looking at it as if it contained a lost dream amidst its sparkles. Perhaps . . . "And how did you like being a honeymooner? Think you might consider trying it for real someday, now that you know what you'd be getting into?"

Alex's expression was as fearsome as an arctic winter. "No."

Grant didn't believe it. But it was written all over Alex's face. He could see it, because he knew Alex very well. They had no secrets. They'd walked through too many of the same kind of hells. Grant peered closer. "Hell, Alex. Is that girl— What was her name?"

"Sarah Dunning," Alex muttered through clenched teeth.

"My God." Grant was stunned.

Alex glared at him. "What's with you?" he demanded angrily.

"If I didn't know you better, Alex, I'd say you fell in love with her," Grant said, dumbfounded. "That's it, isn't it?"

Alex bristled and warned Grant off the subject with a bleak scowl.

Macklin sighed. There wasn't much that he and Blake could do to help Alex get over that kind of problem. Alex would have to work it out with Sarah himself. He gave Alex a sympathetic look. "Have you told her?" he asked quietly, ignoring the danger of talking to a wounded lion who wanted to be left to lick his wounds in private.

Alex gave him a look that would have forever silenced a lesser man. "There's *nothing* to tell," he said tightly. He lowered his eyes. "Besides, it's better for her if we just drop it now."

"Are you sure about that?" Grant was doubtful. He hadn't met the woman for whom Alex couldn't have held quite a chunk of appeal. It was hard to imagine this Sarah not having some little softness in her heart for him somewhere. What had gotten in the way? he wondered.

Alex lifted an eyebrow in self-deprecating amusement. "I'll be a colorful memory to tell her grandchildren about," Alex said cynically. Although she was certainly going to have to do some heavy editing in what she told them, he thought. Well, let her blush as she told them, he thought hard-heartedly. He hoped she got as hot thinking about it as he did. Still. Damn.

Grant dearly wished that he could meet the woman who'd finally felled his handsome, arrogant friend. For Alex's sake, he also hoped she cared more than Alex thought she did, and that she'd fight for him. Which apparently Alex was unwilling to do. Odd.

"If there's anything I can do . . ." Grant offered.

"Like I said, I've already done everything that needed doing." Alex said tersely.

He downed his drink. He felt like a hatchet murderer. He kept seeing the tears glistening on Sarah's lashes when they'd gotten off the plane in Baltimore. She'd been determined not to let them fall and it had made his throat ache to watch her pretend they weren't waiting to tumble. She'd held out her hand and said goodbye in that soft, firm, hopelessly optimistic voice of hers. And she'd looked him straight in the eye when she'd said, *I'll always remember, Alex. Take care of yourself. Okay?*

Alex didn't want to stay. He'd just keep drinking, and that certainly wouldn't help. Nothing helped. It had been three miserable weeks since they'd parted and the ache in his gut showed no signs of diminishing.

"I think I'll call it a night." Alex slid off the stool and put some cash on the bar for both of them.

He thought maybe he'd call Sarah, just to see if she was all right. Just a few words. *Hello. Are you okay? No suspicious characters hanging around? No unexpected consequences from our making love?* If she were pregnant, she still wouldn't listen to him. But he'd make her listen, in that case. He knew it was unlikely she'd gotten pregnant. He'd been careful about that. Especially under the circumstances, he hadn't wanted to add that to her plate. Calling her was not a good idea. He knew it. It would just make it that much harder for both of them. For him, certainly. But at least he'd know she was all right.

He wanted a lot more than that. Why was he driving himself nuts? *Because I love her.* He tried everything he knew to kill the love, to drive it away, but it simply refused to go. The love had taken root and relentlessly entangled itself with every fiber of him, every cell, every breath he took. He loved her with a deep, hungering tenderness that he still found hard to accept. She was a part of him, and always would be. He couldn't kid himself that this was going to fade in a few years. He laughed in pain at the memory of what he'd once told her. Get over it in a matter of days? Weeks?

He would always love her. He knew that now. Which meant he was going to be feeling this awful emptiness, this aching hurt, for the rest of his life.

As they walked through the etched-glass doors of the bar, Grant patted him on the shoulder in a show of masculine moral support. "Hang in there, Alex." He resurrected his grin and added, "Since you were buying the drinks, how about if I supply the transportation? Come on. My chariot's around the block. I'll take you home."

After Grant dropped him off, Alex stood in front of the wide casement windows of his living room overlooking Rock Creek Park. He'd been losing the debate with himself for hours, but he didn't throw in the towel and admit it until nearly eight o'clock that night.

"Damn it, Sarah. This isn't going to work," he muttered darkly.

His bag was always packed, the legacy of a lifetime of living on the run. Tonight it came in handy. He picked it up and grabbed his car keys. He'd had enough. If Sarah was willing to discuss it, he was willing to offer her whatever she wanted. Then he was going to make love to her until they both passed out. And then he was going to tell her everything.

He was too far from Washington an hour later to be able to receive Raymond's call on his mobile phone. At Alex's apartment, the answering machine went on. "Alex, this is Raymond. Moreau's slipped into the country. Call me as soon as you get this. You know the number. This is urgent."

The receiver clicked. The dial tone wailed mournfully.

Sarah had been to the only movie in town. She was going out every night if she could manage it. It was the only way she could keep from going completely crazy. The silence of her lonely house was more than she could bear. The sheriff had been happy to treat her at the ice-cream parlor when he'd seen her there Monday. An owner of a thriving heating and plumbing business had insisted on picking up her tab at the local fast-food place. People were lifting their eyes in surprise left and right. She'd gone from being a reclusive workaholic to a mainstay of the local entertainment and restaurant service industry. But every little bit helped.

And all because she was trying to forget how much she was hurting. How much she missed Alex Sutter.

She had a headache, undoubtedly from eating too many chocolate candies at the movie. She deserved it, she told herself puritanically. It was easy to leave and go straight home. She'd take some aspirin and go to bed. At least she was sleeping better now.

She wondered how Alex was doing. A lot better than she, no doubt, she thought dismally. She didn't even know if he'd stayed in Washington. She'd seen how much he traveled, and by now he could have been gone on two or three different buying trips already. That is, if he'd really stayed with the jewelry business. He wouldn't need to.

There was all that money that Raymond had given him, sitting in his bank in George Town, waiting to take him wherever he wanted, with whomever he wished to go. Or not go with, such as herself.

She turned the steering wheel and pulled down the dirt drive. In the bushes, she saw Sweet Pea stealthily examining her. She honked hello and watched the big rottweiler lope into full view, wagging his tail enthusiastically. Sweet Pea recognized her car, of course.

She parked and patted the big male dog on the head affectionately. "You keep your eyes open, Sweetie," she murmured. "I'm going to call it quits. See you in the morning."

Half an hour later, having showered, donned a thigh-length nightshirt and soft cotton slippers, she was turning off the lights in preparation for going to bed. The phone rang. She went to answer it.

She checked her watch. Nearly ten-thirty. Rather late for a phone call. It was either a prankster or an emergency. She'd given up hoping it could be Alex. For days, every time the phone had rung, she'd raced to it, sure it would be him just wanting to talk to her, perhaps asking if they could see each other again, in spite of the unresolved differences that rose like a wall between them. How she'd hoped he might have a change of heart and call. "Hello?"

"Sarah? It's Raymond. I want you to get your dogs around you and lock your doors until I can get some people over there to keep an eye on you." He'd never sounded so crisply alert and ice-water professional.

Sarah's blood chilled and she was instantly alert. "What is it? Is Alex . . . ?"

"I haven't been able to reach Alex yet. He's not at home. Moreau's been spotted on a videotape of passengers clearing customs in Miami yesterday morning."

"But I thought you said he'd never come in the continental U.S.?" Sarah was appalled. Then she was afraid as she fully realized what Raymond was talking about. Alex had believed they would be targets.

"Apparently he hoped we'd think that way and be looking for him every place but here. And while he's here, he may want to seek revenge." Raymond sounded sorry to have to tell her that.

"Revenge against us," she murmured through frozen lips. "You've got to get to Alex."

"Don't worry about Alex. At least he's got years of practice at keeping the eyes in the back of his head open. It's you who's the most vulnerable. I'll try to get some people there in a few hours. Lock up and bring in the dogs. Call up your local sheriff, too. They could help."

He hung up. Sarah depressed the phone and would have dialed the sheriff then, but she heard the sound of a car coming down the lane. Not already, she thought in horror. Her heart began to pound.

"Don't panic," she told herself firmly as adrenaline surged in her veins, producing a light-headed rush. She turned off the last inside light and cautiously peered out through a window, trying not to be seen. The light pouring out across her property was broad and strong. The car was easy to recognize. By the time the driver stepped out, she had no trouble seeing who it was. As he opened his back door, she ran to him with her arms wide open.

"Oh, Alex!" she cried as she flung herself into his arms.

He was holding the piece of luggage he'd just lifted off the back seat and had only one arm to hold her to him, but it was more than enough. She was up against his chest and he was kissing her. Kissing her just the way she would have wanted him to. For a split second, her heart rejoiced. He'd come back. Oh, God, he'd come back.

Alex would have prolonged the kiss, but he quickly realized that she was struggling desperately to get away from him. Confused by her mixed signals, he frowned at her and released his hold.

Sarah grabbed his hand and pulled him toward her front door while she whistled for Sweet Pea. "Come inside, Alex. Quickly."

"Sarah, I want to talk to you," he said grimly as she shoved him through the front door and closed it behind them. What was going on?

"Yes. Right after we get Sweet Pea in here," she whistled again. It wasn't like Sweet Pea to take this long. She glanced worriedly outside and told him, "Raymond just called. Moreau's in the U.S. Raymond's sending some people to help protect me. He couldn't reach you. He said something about your answering machine."

She was whirled around. Alex held her shoulders firmly. He looked grim. "How long ago did he call?" Alex asked curtly.

"Oh, five minutes." She opened the door again a little and whistled. Then she called Sweet Pea's name. "Where is that dog?" she muttered.

Alex picked up the phone. He started to dial Raymond's number. Before he finished, it went dead.

"Sarah, is the house completely locked? Doors? Windows? Any possible opening into the structure?"

"Yes," she said. Something in his face told her they were in real trouble. She swallowed and gripped her nerve—hard.

"Do you have any weapons?" he asked as he drew the drapes in the kitchen and living room.

She felt cold with fear, but she focused on thinking about defending them. "A target pistol. A couple of hunting knives. Butcher knife. An old archery set—no, that's in the shed. We'd have to go out for that." She met his carefully shielded stare. "You think he's out there already?" she asked, not wanting to believe it could be possible. Especially so soon.

Alex nodded. "Your phone's been cut." He checked the windows in her bathroom and bedroom. All locked. Wiley had awakened from a long nap and was following them around. He sensed the tension and the hair on his back began to bristle defensively. "Keep Wiley with you," Alex said curtly. He looked out in front. "Sweet Pea never came," he noted softly.

Sarah had an awful feeling. "Oh, no. Not Sweet Pea. He couldn't have gotten Sweet Pea. That dog was stealth itself.

How could he have gotten close enough to stop him?" She desperately hoped Alex could think of a reason why the rottweiler would be all right.

Alex was visualizing the effectiveness of a weapon with a silencer and night-vision scope on it. Top of the line. The drug runners got them before the army did. Moreau could have shot the dog with no trouble at all. He found that he couldn't tell her that. He went to Sarah and cupped her face in his hands. "All we have to do is survive until Raymond gets his boys down here," he told her as calmly as he could considering he could murder Moreau with his bare hands for threatening Sarah. "Is there a basement to this old house?"

Sarah nodded. "I keep supplies down there. It looks like a warehouse."

"Is there an outside entrance?"

"No."

"Good. Where's Groton?"

"Outside." She put her hand over her mouth. "The dog runs. Two of them have openings into the house. One is Groton's."

"Show me," he said curtly.

They let a suspicious and hackled Groton into the house and sealed his run entrance. In two minutes the other opening was sealed and locked, too. Outside, Groton and Wiley must have been able to hear Moreau's steps. They watched the wall, ears cocked forward, growling a low rumble.

Sarah grabbed the target pistol and ammunition from the hall closet and followed Alex down into the cellar. She showed him where the light bulb on the ceiling hung. He yanked the string until it broke, turning off the light with it. Then he put her behind a thick wall of boxed supplies. He hoped it was thick enough to slow down any bullets passing through it. He knew it wouldn't stop anything high-powered.

"Stay here," he whispered, crouching in front of her. "Keep the dogs quiet and between you and anyone who comes down the stairs." He loaded the gun and handed her one of the knives. "Don't think about it. If you have to, use it." He pulled her into his arms and raked his hand through her hair. "No matter what you hear, I want you and the dogs to keep your heads down and lie still, flat against the floor." Even whispering, the note of command steeled the words. "Promise me?"

She nodded. As he released her, she held his hand. "You didn't know this was happening. Why were you coming to see me?"

"Because . . ." He heard the soft scrape of an upstairs door being forced open. He kissed her hard on the mouth. "I'll explain later." And he melted into the cellar darkness with the target pistol in his hand.

The waiting seemed interminable. Sarah could hear someone moving around upstairs. The footfalls were very quiet, very cautious. It was someone who knew he was trespassing and was taking care to stalk his victim with care. She tried to quiet the dogs with a firm, calm stroke of her hand on their heads. She leaned close to them and said in a whisper, "Stay." They would, until she ordered otherwise. Unless she were attacked. In that event, they'd move as quickly and as lethally as they possibly could.

The cement was cold against her. The thin cotton nightshirt wasn't much help. Unlike the Caymans, it wasn't all that warm in Maryland in spring. Especially in her basement. She began to shiver a little and strained to keep from letting her teeth chatter. She wished she knew where Alex had positioned himself. She wanted to be able to guess when Moreau was getting too close.

There was another sound of a door opening. It was the door at the top of the cellar stairs. It had to be Moreau, she thought. Then she heard the top step creak softly as he began to descend.

Her heart beat so hard and painfully, she was sure Moreau could hear it. She concentrated on imagining that she was invisible. That Alex was invisible. That the dogs were invisible. That Moreau would see nothing when he came down into the darkness.

The darkness. What if Moreau had a flashlight? Or night vision like Alex had had? She stopped thinking and concentrated every cell on listening. She could follow his progress, almost sense his thinking. He'd paused, then moved again. He had his back against the wall and was looking over the room.

He might have his gun trained in her direction, she thought, if his back were against the stairwell wall. And no doubt his finger was on the trigger.

Sarah closed her eyes and prayed and listened. The dogs didn't move a muscle. Somewhere there was a sound, like something small falling. A deadly stinging sound was followed by a dreadful ricocheting and then the crashing of several steel cases and metal shelves.

Moreau laughed. "You are all alone now, Sarah. Your friend is lying under that metal bookcase. Send out your dog quietly, and why don't you and I talk."

He didn't know she had another dog, she thought. She didn't let herself believe what he'd said about Alex. She hadn't heard the pistol fire, and she was certain that Alex wouldn't have revealed his position unless he'd been able to squeeze off at least one shot.

The silence stretched until her nerves were wire thin. She heard the soft sound of Moreau's footsteps. He was moving closer to her. Suddenly there were more shots, as if he were spraying a small area. Dog-food boxes squirted open and dry cubes geysered out, cans popped onto the floor and rolled violently across the open spaces.

Another test, Sarah thought. Then she heard the small bore sound of her target pistol. Three shots in rapid succession, interrupted by Moreau's screamed profanity and his opening fire. There was pandemonium as the contents of her shelves were blown into the air.

She heard someone grunt in pain. It had to be Alex. Desperately Sarah crawled on her belly to the edge of her protective wall, even as it was shot through above her, showering her with a rough dusting of debris. She saw Moreau on the steps, blood running down his chest. He'd been hit near the heart, and was beginning to stagger. If the target pistol had been a more powerful weapon, he'd have been dead. In the darkness, with Moreau moving, Sarah was amazed that Alex had hit him so accurately. If he'd seen Moreau well enough to make a shot like that, Moreau would have been able to see Alex. Her stomach twisted sickeningly. She remembered the sound she'd thought must have been Alex as he'd been struck by something. She couldn't see him, and she was beginning to shake badly, straining to make out a fallen male form. *No, Alex. Be all right. You have to be all right.*

Out of the corner of her eye, she saw a motion and it drew her attention. She turned to see Moreau lift his weapon and aim it toward the far corner. He must think that Alex was there, she realized in horror. Sarah had already gauged that Groton and Wiley might be able to reach Moreau from this distance before he could kill them, especially since he wasn't looking their way.

She pointed toward the man on the stairs and ordered, "Get him!" Groton and Wiley tore out into the room and leaped onto the steps just as Moreau began to fire. Seeing the blur of motion coming at him, he turned the rifle toward the dogs as they lunged at him with fangs bared in fury.

A bullet stopped Groton cold. Moreau swung his arm in front of his face to keep Wiley off his throat and the big Lab bit down hard, nearly cracking the bones. Moreau began pounding at Wiley with the rifle barrel, but the dog hung on, clawing and growling and biting again and again.

Sarah scrambled out of her hiding place and ran toward the corner, searching for Alex. He was pulling himself up from under a pile of crushed boxes and metal shelving. As he staggered to his feet, she heard Wiley cry. She turned to see her loyal friend crumple limply at Moreau's feet. He viciously kicked the dog away from him, knocking the animal's body off the stairs and onto the hard cement floor.

Alex pushed free of the debris at his knees and began to run toward Moreau. He stopped dead in his tracks as the drug czar snatched a small silver revolver from a shoulder holster and aimed it straight at Sarah, grinning like a viper.

"Checkmate," Moreau whispered harshly, eyes glittering with a deadly cold. "Drop your gun." Moreau pressed his bleeding chest with his free hand. His hatred grew more intense.

Alex was as still as granite. He was holding the target pistol waist high, pointing at the floor. He calculated that Moreau could kill Sarah before he could aim and shoot. He couldn't move without signing her death warrant. On the other hand, as soon as he dropped the gun, they'd both be dead in a matter of minutes. Perhaps he could draw Moreau's ire and force him to shoot at him first, giving Sarah the extremely slim chance of fighting for her life with him. If she would go for the gun in Moreau's hand after he fired, she might be able to do it. Moreau must be weakened from loss of blood. But how could he get Moreau's undivided attention? Perhaps he could appeal to Moreau's sense of greed. Money had always been a driving force....

"We can be worth more to you alive than dead," Alex suggested in a hard voice.

Moreau's eyes flamed. Sarah feared he would shoot Alex for having the audacity to try to negotiate. She took a step toward Alex, instinctively trying to protect him.

Moreau roared, "Take another step, *puta*, and you're dead!"

She stood absolutely still. She was six feet away from Alex, whose attention was fixed unwaveringly on the man on the stairs.

"Does a million dollars interest you in listening a little while longer?" Alex asked softly.

Moreau's eyes flickered. Money had always been his true love, his only weakness. "*You* have a million dollars?" He sneered doubtfully.

Alex smiled grimly. "Do you think I'd be stupid enough to steal something from the infamous Antonio Moreau for anything less?"

Moreau's expression became arrogant. His ego swelled. "Ah. They paid that much?" He was obviously pleased.

Alex could have spit in the man's face in disgust. Moreau's gargantuan ego was his Achilles' heel. *Just keep stroking it into complacency. We need to buy ourselves time. Lots of time.* "You've made your point, Moreau. I'm impressed. You can go anywhere you want, do anything you please, to avenge yourself."

"Yes," Moreau snarled arrogantly. He waved the small pistol slightly to underscore his power. He patted his wounded breast in fury. "I owe you two shots near the heart, though, Sutter."

Sutter nodded. "True enough. But before you take them, why not see what I have to offer in trade for my life?" He left Sarah's name out of it. He wanted Moreau focusing entirely on him. He wanted him to forget Sarah was even present.

Moreau looked faintly amused. "You aren't going to buy the woman's life, too?"

Alex's eyes turned the color of the arctic sea at night. Moreau was too shrewd to forget such a useful bargaining chip. If he tried to bluff that he didn't care about Sarah, he wouldn't have been surprised if Moreau decided to shoot her out of hand. "If you hurt her, I'll kill you before you can pull the trigger a second time," he said in a low, threatening voice.

Sarah's skin crawled to hear the pure violence in Alex's voice. God, where were Raymond's people, she wondered desperately. *Hurry, hurry.*

Moreau was tempted. "How will you give me this money since we are here in the middle of a country that doesn't relish my visit and won't be pleased to see me leave with you in my company?" He sneeringly added, "And I don't believe you would go willingly, or quietly."

Alex nodded. "We can work out a plan, Moreau. Between the two of us, we've moved everything conceivable through every port in the Caribbean. I'm sure the three of us and a million in cash won't be much of a problem."

Sarah held her breath. Alex's ploy was working. Moreau was considering the deal. Obviously he thought he could get the money and kill them somewhere else. Then he'd have the pleasure of both. He was opening his mouth to agree, when they heard people coming into the upstairs. A man's voice called out, "Sutter?" At the same time, a voice she recognized—it was the sheriff's—was yelling, "Sarah Dunning? Where in the hell are you?"

Moreau snarled and moved the pistol. Instead of pointing at Sarah, he was aiming straight at Alex.

Sarah moved without thinking, as soon as she saw the pistol shift. "No!" she screamed angrily as she threw herself at Alex.

Two shots went off.

Moreau clutched his heart and sank to the floor, dead, his silver pistol still clenched in his hand.

Alex crushed Sarah to his chest, staggering under her assault to stay on his feet. The target pistol was still in his hand as he put his arm around her for added support.

"I don't ever want to live through a split second like that again," Alex breathed, closing his eyes. He opened them to look into Sarah's startled expression. She looked peculiar, and she was beginning to feel heavy in his arms. "Are you all right?" he asked sharply.

Sarah felt a hot, burning sting in her back. Heat was rushing through her; it occurred to her what it must be. "Not completely," she said weakly. She lifted her hand to his face as it went a little out of focus. She tried to think of what she wanted to say, but her mind was muddling and it was easier not to try.

Men were beating on the wall outside the open entrance. "Whoever's down there, throw out your weapon" came the harsh, authoritative order.

"It's all right," Sutter yelled as he anxiously ran his hands over Sarah's back. "Moreau's dead or close to it. It's just Sarah and me down here." Then he felt the warm, sticky blood on Sarah's back and his voice caught in his throat. "Someone call an ambulance! Sarah's been shot."

He swung her up into his arms and climbed over the wreckage as men clattered down the steps.

"Sarah," he said in a hoarse voice. "Sarah, don't leave me."

Chapter 17

The world became jumbled and contorted for Sarah. She heard Alex's voice demanding that she hang on. Something was pressing hard against her back and she was lifted and moved and hands were on her, carrying her. She heard the siren and the paramedics talking in technical terms while they worked on her. And someone was holding her hand. Alex. Every once in a while, she heard his voice near her ear, telling her to hang on, she'd be feeling better soon.

Bright lights. More cold air as she was moved from one hard surface to another. She opened her eyes and saw lots of people in green. Someone was asking questions about her, the names of her next of kin, a responsible party. She heard Alex's voice reply something. He sounded grim.

"Alex..." she whispered. It was hard to hear now. She thought she heard him say, *I'm here, Sarah,* but she was feeling very groggy and they were wheeling her away like a baby on a cart and she was losing the threads of everything happening around her. Then the darkness swallowed her completely.

Sarah heard the crisp sound of hospital sheets being lifted. Someone was checking her back and had raised the sheet off her. She was lying on her stomach with something pinching her arm. She opened her eyes and tried to get them to focus. Her mouth was dry. "Can I have something to drink?" she asked in a cracked voice. She looked at the place where her arm felt pinched. An IV tube was sticking out of it.

The recovery room nurse leaned over to make it easier for Sarah to see her face. "Welcome back," she said, smiling warmly. "Can you tell me your name?"

Sarah blinked. "Sarah Dunning."

"Can you tell me how you're feeling, Sarah?"

Sarah's memory was foggy but she remembered what had happened. She managed a tired grimace. "Like somebody shot me in the back," she mumbled. "Is Alex all right?"

"If he's the good-looking guy with dark hair and black eyes and a habit of sticking to you like glue, he's outside the recovery room door waiting to hear me tell him you're going to be just fine."

Sarah felt breath slide out of her body in relief. Everything had been so chaotic at the end, she wasn't sure she'd have known what had happened. Later, when they wheeled her to her room, he was there. He didn't stay long. He merely bent and kissed her lips and said, "Good night. I'll see you tomorrow."

Sarah was sitting as comfortably as she could with her bed tilted up and her breakfast tray swung over her knees when Alex walked into her room the following morning. He looked exhausted, she thought. Like a man who'd been through a long walk in hell and still hadn't quite recovered. He smiled at her and stood next to her bed while she finished sipping her juice.

"How are you feeling?" he asked.

Sarah grimaced. "A little sore."

"You were very lucky," he said gently. He walked over to her window and, after pulling back the curtain, he looked blindly outside at the clear spring day. "That bullet could have killed you if it had gone an inch farther to the left. It could have paralyzed you, left you without the use of an organ." He put his hand on his forehead as if he would rub the endless, awful possibilities out of his mind. "I'd have rather taken that bullet myself, Sarah." His voice cracked and became a whisper.

Sarah pushed the wheeled tray table away from her bed and held out her hand to him. "Do you have to stand so far away?" she asked weakly.

He reluctantly came to her bedside and took her hand in both of his. "No," he said huskily. "I'll stand as close as you want." He lifted her hand to his lips and kissed it tenderly.

Sarah thought his eyes looked suspiciously bright and her heart ached with love for him. "Are you okay?" she managed to ask after a long, anguished moment. "In the cellar, I thought I heard you groan...and you were half-buried beneath so much rubble..."

He shrugged. "A bruised rib," he admitted dismissingly. "A few minor cuts, scratches and black-and-blue marks."

Sarah smiled in relief. She loved the feel of their hands laced together the way they were now. She could feel the warm strength of his palm and fingers pressed tightly to hers. She swallowed and forced the question out of her mouth that had been plaguing her since she'd awakened. "My dogs? Are they...okay?" she asked. She was afraid to hear.

Alex pulled a chair next to her bed and leaned close to her, offering what comfort he could. "Moreau killed Sweet Pea and Groton. They both died from rifle shots. It was very quick. I don't think they were in pain for very long, if that's of any small comfort to you," he said softly. He watched her eyes fill with tears of pain; gently he squeezed her shoulder in support. "Wiley's alive and recovering from broken ribs and a concussion. Your vet says he'll get the royal treatment." Alex grinned awkwardly. "Your sheriff and deputy have offered to take care of your place for you, notify anyone who tries to get in touch that you'll be indisposed for a few weeks. They're also arguing over which of them Wiley would be willing to have as a dog-sitter if he's ready to leave the vet's before you're ready to leave here."

Tears slid down Sarah's cheeks. "That's very nice of them all," she said unsteadily. She gave Alex a stricken look. "I loved them so much," she cried.

He held her in his arms, very gently, while she sobbed on his shoulder. "They were good friends," he said softly. They'd laid down their lives for her. It was a long time before he felt her stop shaking, and the sobs became sporadic sniffles.

Gently he disengaged from her. He kissed her cheek. She looked stricken that he was leaving. He smiled a little and explained. "I'm going to get your box of tissues."

He'd walked around the bed and handed it to her when the door to her room was opened and a well-knit man with a jock's swagger strode inside. He took one look at Sarah and grinned from ear to ear. "Dammit, I knew you were too ornery a little kid for a bullet to stop."

Sarah stopped in midsniffle, holding her tissue in the air. She grinned like a little girl. "Christopher!"

He bent over her bed and kissed her fraternally on the cheek. When he straightened he asked gruffly, "How're you feeling?"

"Fine." Sarah was beginning to tire of hearing this same question. She frowned. "How did you get down here so fast?"

He glowered. "I got tired of hearing your sad voice on the phone and I was on my way to fly down and give you a piece of my mind. Gabrielle told me all about your shacking up with that Caribbean Romeo and then eating your heart out ever since."

Sarah blushed and gave him a warning look. "Christopher!"

Christopher kept skating along. "When I got to your place this morning, it looked like someone had filmed a war movie on it. I called Gabrielle and she said that jerk you've got the hots for called them after midnight to tell 'em you'd been shot trying to save his damn life."

Sarah shot a look at Alex. He was standing a few feet away listening grimly. "Christopher!" she hissed angrily. "Will you—"

Christopher talked a little louder, drowning her out. "Mom, Dad and Gabrielle are going to try and catch a plane tonight. They oughta be here tomorrow sometime, if they can make connections without having to hang around L.A. or Chicago for too long. Until then, I'm here to make sure that *nothing else happens to you.*"

Sarah tried to sit up as straight and tall as she could. It was hard to intimidate her big, muscular brother when she was half lying down and dressed in a hospital gown. "You're as bossy as ever, Christopher. And your mouth is leaping ahead of your brains as usual!" she exclaimed irritably.

The squabbling siblings glared at each other.

"Hey, this is just like old times, Sarah!" Christopher laughed arrogantly. He crossed his arms in front of his chest, relaxing a little. If his sister could yell at him, she obviously was going to be all right. He glanced critically at Alex. Giving a sharp nod in Alex's direction, he asked ungraciously, "Who's he?"

Sarah's eyes grew very round and she opened her mouth but didn't speak. She glanced anxiously at Alex and motioned with her head that he should go out into the hall. "He was just leaving," she said in a nervous, light voice.

Christopher looked unimpressed. When Alex didn't move, but remained standing there as if he had every right to, Christopher began to look annoyed. "I didn't ask where he was going, Sarah. I asked who he is."

Sarah stubbornly crossed her own arms in front of her chest. It pulled the wound, and she stifled a yelp and relaxed her arms a little.

Alex guessed why Sarah wasn't identifying him. He recalled their discussion about her brother when they were in Cayman Brac. He figured a few more bruises would hardly be noticed at this point. He'd been in enough pain for the past twelve hours to inure him to more for half a lifetime. He held out his hand and said firmly, "I'm Alex Sutter."

Christopher's mouth dropped open and his arms fell to his sides with fists formed. "The son of a bitch that's been..." His graphic comment was never completed. Instead of talking, Christopher switched to a more visual form of communication. He hauled back his arm and punched Alex in the jaw.

Alex fell back a foot and his head snapped to one side from the viciousness of Christopher's assault.

Sarah slid out of bed and shrieked, "Christopher Dunning, you cut that out!"

The two men growled, "Sarah, get back into that bed!"

Sarah glared at them both and, holding onto the table to balance, went on rubbery legs to Alex. He put his arms out and held her, careful to avoid the bandages on her back, while she touched his jaw tentatively. "He didn't break it, did he?" She shot her brother a murderous look.

Alex laughed and experimentally worked the jaw back and forth. It hurt like hell. "No. But I can imagine he could if I gave him a second chance."

Christopher was giving his sister a disgusted look. "Don't you have the brains to call it quits when a man makes it clear he doesn't want you?"

Sarah fell silent and looked at the floor. She really couldn't argue with her brother on that. And she knew he was behaving like Attila the Hun because he loved her and couldn't stand to see a man whom she wanted not want her back.

"You're wrong," Alex said, speaking to her brother.

"About what?" Christopher demanded, hard and unimpressed.

"I do want her."

Alex met Christopher's gaze steadily.

Sarah sensed the silent communication passing between the two men. Men. They must be born with some extra gene that permitted same-sex telepathy, she thought in disgust. "What's all this man-to-man eye contact mean?" she demanded. Her knees began to feel wobbly and she let Alex carry more of her weight.

He glanced down at her worriedly. "You need to get back into bed," he growled, helping her to do just that. He looked at Christopher. "I have a few things I want to say to Sarah. Maybe afterward, you and I can have a cup of coffee?"

Christopher's demeanor had relaxed. He nodded slowly. "Okay. You're on." He glanced at his sister. "Don't take him if you don't want him." And with that succinct advice, he marched out of the room, saying he'd seen a nurse who looked familiar and he wanted to track her down. He'd drop in later, after Alex and she had had their talk.

Sarah found a comfortable position and the nurse came in to take her temperature, give her some medication and check her bandages for bleeding. Alex left briefly to call his partners and let them know how she was doing while the nurse took care of Sarah.

The nurse left just as Raymond Jones cautiously poked his head inside. "Sarah? Mind if I come in?" he asked diffidently.

"Of course not, Raymond." She smiled at the paunchy little intelligence operations expert. "If it weren't for your getting your troops to my house, I might not be here for you to visit."

Raymond looked pained. "If you hadn't gotten involved with our operation, you might not have been attacked in the first place," he pointed out uncomfortably.

Sarah shrugged. "We made the right decisions, Raymond. Don't try to be a Monday morning quarterback."

He grinned sheepishly. "Okay. How—"

Sarah could hear it coming. She interrupted his question and finished it for him. "Am I feeling?" She laughed. "Just about how you imagine I do," she teased him. "Thanks for stopping by and asking, though. It makes me feel a little better."

Raymond blushed with pleasure. He straightened his face and cleared his throat. "Uh, I saw Alex on the phone as I came down the hall. I take it he's been here to see you already?"

Sarah wondered why Raymond looked so uncomfortable talking about Alex. "Yes. And last night."

"My men told me how upset he was when they were bringing you in for surgery," Raymond said, lowering his voice, as if he didn't wish to be overheard. "Would you mind if I asked you a . . . personal question, Sarah?" he asked, treading cautiously.

"No." Sarah couldn't imagine Raymond asking something so personal as to be embarrassing to her. "What is it?"

He leaned forward slightly. "Are you and Alex . . . still seeing each other?" He phrased it very delicately.

Sarah caught his meaning. She felt her cheeks reddening in spite of herself. "I don't know. We became . . . very involved during that trip to free Gabrielle." She hesitated and saw him slowly nod his head. He'd heard all about that obviously. Probably from reports by other people who'd seen them together. She doubted that Alex would have mentioned it. "Alex and I went our separate ways after we got back." She couldn't help the discomfort at saying it. She knew it must have showed in her face. She'd felt as if her heart were being twisted in two. "But he was coming to see me last night, so I don't know exactly how to answer your questions. I guess we are still seeing each other. But perhaps not for long." She didn't want to raise her hopes only to have them destroyed again. She was glad that Alex was here now. She was just going to enjoy that and try not to worry about the future.

Raymond sighed. "I don't suppose he ever told you why he took that assignment with you?"

Sarah looked perplexed. "I thought it was because you paid him a lot of money." It still bothered her that that had been the deciding factor. Not as much as it had at first, because now she knew that he had a heart, that he wasn't just a mercenary. But, still . . .

Raymond smiled sadly. "He's never told me anything about his past. He rarely tells anybody anything unless they need to know it. I thought that habit might have kept him silent on the matter of why he went." Raymond patted her hand. "I want you to know this, because I like Alex Sutter and he's one of the finest men I've ever known and I don't want his pride and feelings about his past to stand in the way of your happiness."

Sarah listened in mystified expectance. "Go on."

Raymond nodded, obviously pleased that she wanted very much to know. He explained about the massacre and Alex's sense of guilt and obligation to those who'd been slaughtered while protecting his identity from Moreau. "And then I found out that he knew the boy who was helping fly that plane." He held up his hands. "Until he saw that, he turned down the money without hesitation." Raymond grinned. "He also had a pretty poor opinion of the agent I would have sent in his place if he'd continued to decline. He thought you'd never get out in one piece." He patted her hand affectionately. "I think he knew he'd been hooked even then, but he was too arrogant to admit it."

Sarah smiled unconvincingly. "I'm not so sure about the last part. He seems convinced that whatever it is we feel, we'll get over eventually."

Raymond stood, but he was laughing. "Rakes like Alex are always the last to know when they've bitten the dust. But all their friends see it without any trouble at all. Well, I just wanted to tell you all that, because I was afraid he wouldn't and I thought you deserved to know."

Sarah smiled at him warmly. Raymond had a soft heart. "Thanks, Raymond. You know, you're a real romantic at heart." She blew him a kiss.

Raymond chuckled as he ambled to the door where he met Alex coming in.

Alex lifted his eyebrows questioningly. "Did I miss a good joke?" he asked, seeing Raymond's good humor.

Raymond patted him on the shoulder and shook his head. "No." He waved at Sarah. "Glad you're okay, Sarah. Let me know if you need any help getting your place back in order."

"Thanks, Raymond." She watched the door close behind him, his offer jogging her memory of the kind of disaster she'd sustained. She sighed and closed her eyes. "I guess I'm going to have to do some carpentry when I get back," she muttered. She thought of her two dear four-footed friends and a lump formed in her throat again. They couldn't be rebuilt. She'd just have to endure until the pain became a dull, bittersweet memory.

Alex stood by the window. "Do you feel up to hearing a story? One that's . . . not very pretty?" His face became taut. One hand was clenched at his side.

Sarah wondered what was torturing him. She sensed it wasn't simply what they'd been through the previous night. She pushed away her grief and asked him quietly, "What's the matter, Alex?"

His head was unbowed but he looked as if he were a man who'd been whipped and was both furious and guilty for having suffered. "Do you remember telling me the story of my life as you fantasized it?" he asked.

"Yes."

"I'd like to tell you my version of that story." He looked at her, waiting for her to indicate whether she wanted to hear it or not.

From his grim expression, she could see that the telling would not be an easy thing, nor would be the listening. If she wanted him to continue, there would be consequences she couldn't yet know. She was touched and honored that he was finally willing to share it with her. "Please. Tell me," she told him softly.

He nodded curtly and began. "I grew up on boats and ships. My father, as you guessed, was from the Caymans. He was a ship captain and worked around the Caribbean mostly. That was how he met my mother. He'd been stopping in St. Croix to visit his brother, who owned a nightclub. His brother was older and obsessed with his business, so my father spent the evenings entertaining his sister-in-law at the bar. She was young, a pretty woman from the Virgin Islands. Her parents were artists who'd gone there to escape the predictability of life on the continental U.S. She was hungry to have children, but her husband felt he was too old for them. He didn't want to be bothered with diapers and college educations."

Alex turned to look straight at Sarah. The cynical harsh light in his eyes was for himself and his father and his family that had been so disappointing. "But my father was more than willing to help her out. He bedded her every fortnight, when his ship was in, until she got pregnant." His jaw muscles flexed in anger.

Sarah felt shock and sorrow but she didn't know if Alex would appreciate her showing them. This was obviously very hard for him to tell. She swallowed and searched for words that would convey what she thought and not embitter him further. "I see. She became pregnant with you."

"Yes."

"Did your uncle realize what they'd done?"

Alex ran his hand over the back of his neck. "Not at first. He was angry at my arrival. He raised me as his child until I was five. Then one night, the man I had always thought was my uncle got into a fight with the man I always thought was my father. When they were through, the man I'd called father lay at the bottom of the stairwell, dead with a broken neck. The man I'd called uncle was charged with manslaughter. My mother, when she finished weeping, told me we'd live with my uncle when the court matters were settled.''

Sarah ached for him. "Did you do that?" she asked neutrally.

He nodded. "Until I was twelve. And I'd seen the way it was between them for years by then, of course. She'd refused to marry him, because her husband's will would have cut her off and she preferred money to a stable, honest family relationship. So she basically lived in sin, sleeping with the man she'd committed adultery with. The man who was my father, but whom I couldn't call father.'' The bitterness was like a knife in every word.

"How did you find out the truth?" she asked softly.

He lowered his eyes briefly, then raised them honestly to hers. "I found a letter my biological father had written to her during the first year they were together after the death of her husband. It made it quite clear." He shook his head. "It warped everything I've ever done since. I never saw women the same way after that. I never wanted to be a part of anybody or anything. All that I'd believed in had been destroyed by passions that these people didn't seem to be able to control. So I made sure that I never got close to losing control. I never got close to people at all, in any emotional sense."

He sat next to her and leaned back in the chair. "It worked fine like that for years. If you don't get involved in other people's lives, they don't mind not knowing anything about yours. It only becomes a problem when you want to link your life with another's." He paused and turned to look at her. The emotion in his dark eyes took Sarah's breath away. "You deserve to know exactly what kind of man you'd be getting involved with if you got involved with me, Sarah," he said grimly. "I've lived a life on the knife edge of illegal. I got into Raymond's line of work because I knew all the tricks. I've come as close to being a criminal without technically being a criminal as it's possible to get." He obviously wasn't particularly proud of that.

He stopped talking and reached out to her. Gently he caressed her cheek with the back of his knuckles. "It never particularly bothered me before. I've never liked it. I've always been ashamed of the people who brought me into this world. I didn't cry for them when they left it."

There was something he wasn't saying and it hung in the air between them like an ache that would not ease.

Sarah caught his hand and kissed it. Her wide brown eyes were full of love as she asked softly, "Why are you telling me this, Alex?"

He took a deep breath and the look in his eyes was that of a man who could almost taste fear for the first time in his long, lonely, hardened life. "Because I love you. Because I want you. Because I don't want to ask you to marry me unless you know who I am, what I am." He leaned forward and kissed her trembling lips. "I love you. How much you'll never know . . ." He rested his face against her hair and took a long shuddering breath, remembering how close he'd come to losing her.

Sarah caressed his face and smiled. Tears glistened on her eyelashes. "Do you still have that wedding ring?" she asked.

He pulled away and looked at her. "Yes."

"Well, it looks like all my relatives are going to be here for the next three or four days. If you could find it, and if it wouldn't rush you too much, and if you don't mind their crazy ways, maybe—"

He didn't let her finish. He laced their fingers together and against her lips murmured, "Marry me."

Through the warm, melting kiss that ensued, Sarah sighed, "Yes."

The nurse was bringing in a huge vase of champagne-and-peach-colored roses. She was muttering. "The card is very confusing, Miss Dunning. On one corner it says to Sarah Dunning, but on the other corner it says to Sutter's Wife, and it's signed Blake and Grant whom you'll be getting to know soon. Now isn't that . . ." She saw Alex half-sprawled across the bed, and the patient kissing him in a robustly healthy fashion. She backed out of the room, laughing. "Well, they can straighten all this out later, I'm sure."

* * * * *

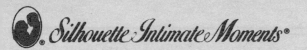
Silhouette Intimate Moments®

COMING
NEXT MONTH

#329 BETRAYED—Beverly Sommers

Journalist Bolivia Smith, assigned to investigate strange goings-on in the
jungle outside Miami, is taken prisoner by a mysterious war-gamer
named Tooley. Determined to get the exclusive story, Bolivia is willing to
risk her life—but is she also willing to jeopardize their love?

#330 NEVER SAY GOODBYE—
Suzanne Carey

What begins as a marriage of convenience for the American Katya Dane
and KGB agent Nikolai Dvorov becomes a union of love. Four years
later, after a forced separation, they are reunited amidst a brewing
controversy to find their passion as powerful as ever. Will loyalty to their
countries again divide them, or will love prevail—now that they have
a son?

#331 EMMA'S WAR—Lucy Hamilton

Lady Emma Campbell is assigned to work with cynical State
Department agent Tyler Davis, to help a Romanian diplomat defect.
Caught in a web of suspicion and deceit, they must fight not only for the
diplomat's freedom, but to save themselves—and their growing love.

#332 DANGER IN PARADISE—
Barbara Faith

Troubleshooter Matt McKay was almost certain that beautiful Ariel
Winston would lead him straight to her stepfather and the missing
millions. But others were after the money, too, and soon their Mexican
paradise became a jungle of danger...and desire.

AVAILABLE THIS MONTH:

SILHOUETTE DESIRE

Another bride for a Branigan brother!

"Why did you stop at three Branigan books?"
S. Newcomb from Fishkill, New York, asks.

We didn't! We brought you Jody's story, Desire #523,
BRANIGAN'S TOUCH in October 1989.

"Did Leslie Davis Guccione write any more books
about those Irish Branigan brothers?"
B. Willford from Gladwin, Michigan, wants to know.

And the answer is yes! This month you'll get a chance to
read Matt's story, Desire #553—

PRIVATE PRACTICE
by Leslie Davis Guccione

**You won't want to miss it because
he's the last Branigan brother!**

AVAILABLE NOW

Silhouette Special Edition®

proudly presents

Taming Natasha
by
NORA ROBERTS

In March, award-winning author Nora Roberts weaves her special
brand of magic in TAMING NATASHA (SSE #583). Natasha
Stanislaski was a pussycat with Spence Kimball's little girl, but to
Spence himself she was as ornery as a caged tiger. Would some
cautious loving sheath her claws and free her heart from
captivity?

TAMING NATASHA, by Nora Roberts, has been selected to receive
a special laurel—the Award of Excellence. Look for the
distinctive emblem on the cover. It lets you know there's
something truly special inside.

AVAILABLE NOW—

the books you've been waiting for by one of America's top romance authors!

DIANA PALMER

DUETS

Ten years ago Diana Palmer published her very first romances. Powerful and dramatic, these gripping tales of love are everything you have come to expect from Diana Palmer.

This month some of these titles are available again in **DIANA PALMER DUETS**—a special three-book collection. Each book has two wonderful stories plus an introduction by the author. You won't want to miss them!

Book 1
SWEET ENEMY
LOVE ON TRIAL

Book 2
STORM OVER THE LAKE
TO LOVE AND CHERISH

Book 3
IF WINTER COMES
NOW AND FOREVER

Available now at your favorite retail outlet.

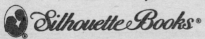